This Isn't
a Game

Books by David Moss

This Isn't a Game

This Isn't
a Game

David Moss

Poisoned Pen Press

Poisoned Pen Press
6962 E. First Ave., Ste. 103
Scottsdale, AZ 85251
www.poisonedpenpress.com
info@poisonedpenpress.com

Printed in the United States of America

To Nancy and Art

Thursday

VegasVegasCasino.com posted the movie director's murder trial on its entertainment page alongside odds on *The Bachelorette* and *The Voice*.

Will Kristen chose Jake or Richard? Will Ian or Tina land the record deal? Did Andrew murder Audrey?

Too many customers were betting "Yes, Andrew did," so Jackson Oliver, the VegasVegas owner, asked his linemaker to adjust the odds to attract acquittal money.

"No time for your sideshow bets," Kenny said.

Which was his derisive term for celebrity trials, political elections, reality TV shows, and all the other novelty propositions that defiled the purity of sports wagering.

"Maybe your next prop you can ask if Jake and Tina are having a boy or girl? Or what color wedding invitations they're going with? Fuchsia, 5 to 9. Mint green, even odds."

Jackson resisted the urge to antagonize Kenny by pointing out her name was Kristen, not Tina, and actually the smart money had her choosing Richard over Jake.

"BigFatJackpot.com made more off the Michael Jackson trial than the World Series. Twenty-eight percent of their bettors on the Phil Spector murder trial were new customers who stuck around to play casino games. Andrew Marvel's a big-time Hollywood director, and we've got unlimited space on our site. Why shouldn't we get in on the action?"

"My uncle finds out I'm setting odds on celebrity trials, he'll never talk to me again."

"Save you the hassle of remembering inmate visitation hours."

This didn't offend Kenny. If anything he'd repeat it to his uncle, who'd actually been out of prison for over a year.

"Maybe I should thank you for posting your murder trial. I already moved the numbers twice, and wasting time on this thing is giving me a killer headache, which is making me forget about my ulcer, which has been driving me nuts. So, thank you."

Like most online casinos, VegasVegas was located in San Jose, Costa Rica. The long, rectangular betting room was formerly a restaurant. A blue seascape with colorful fish still covered the walls. More than one of the bet-takers had likened the writhing sailfish with the hook in its mouth to the bettors on the other end of the computer and phone lines.

Kenny had on his Yankees cap, circa 1961. He might live in Costa Rica now, but he'd never give up his New York Yankees citizenship. Dark hair curled out the bottom of his cap. His pale skin was untouched by the Costa Rican sun. The circles under his eyes, pushing outward like ripples on a pond, gave the illusion he only slept a few hours a night when in reality he never slept at all.

Baseball and soccer games with muted volume played on a row of TV monitors bracketed to the wall. The streaming broadcast of day one of the trial was on the monitor farthest from Kenny's workstation. It looked like the prosecutor was about to deliver his opening statement, so Jackson unmuted the volume.

The prosecutor hunched his shoulders and lowered his head like an angry bull. If he had a tail, it would be twitching. "Audrey Marvel returned to her home in Greensboro, Vermont, from an antique fair in Chelsea. She was excited to call a friend and send pictures of a vase she found. She never made that call. The call she made was to 911. But loss of blood from eight knife wounds made her too weak to say anything when the dispatcher answered. The police arrived seventeen minutes later and found Audrey dead on the living room floor, phone beside her hand.

They found a knife and Andrew Marvel's clothes, with traces of Audrey's blood, at the bottom of the lake behind the house. They found Andrew Marvel's footprints near Audrey's body. What they didn't find was Andrew Marvel."

Kenny didn't want to show interest in a novelty prop, but he couldn't help himself. "I don't know about murder, but the guy's guilty of being a stupid fuck. Like the cops won't check the lake."

"If someone framed him, the lake's perfect," Jackson said. "Make it look like he tried getting rid of the clothes, but pick a place the cops will check."

The prosecutor jerked his head at Andrew and pawed at the floor. "...Andrew rode up to the house on his bike the next morning and told the police a story. If he tried to sell this story to his Hollywood studio friends, they'd laugh him out of the room. His lawyer is going to try to sell the story to you, ladies and gentlemen. He's going to tell you Andrew was having a drink on the porch waiting for Audrey to get home from the antique fair. When he went inside to use the bathroom, a mystery person drugged his drink. After a few more sips, Andrew passed out and came to the next morning in an abandoned barn on Barr Hill, a mile and a half away, his bike leaning against the wall. He rode home and found the police waiting for him.

"When he told the police this story, they gave him a urine test and guess what they found? He was drugged with a sleeping pill called chloral hydrate. Andrew Marvel had a bottle of it in his toilet kit. His doctor had prescribed it for insomnia four months prior to the murder.

"It didn't take the police long to piece together the true story. Audrey Marvel returned home from Chelsea. She and Andrew had a fight, and he murdered her. He used his kayak to dump the knife and clothes in the lake. But he didn't have an alibi. So he invented a story about a mystery person who drugged his drink and framed him for the murder. He rode his bike to the abandoned barn and took his chloral hydrate so it would show up the next day when they tested him.

"Andrew Marvel's legal team had fourteen months to locate this mystery killer, but they couldn't do it. Of course they couldn't. Ladies and gentleman, the killer of Audrey Marvel is no mystery. He's sitting right in front of you. Her husband, Andrew."

The camera cut to the forty-three-year-old Andrew Marvel, his hands folded on the table, his head tilted like he was watching an actor audition for the part of prosecutor who wanted to put him away for life.

"*Shattered Worlds* was a pretty damn good movie," Kenny said.

"I liked *Frontier Zero* best."

"What's a Hollywood director doing in a little town in Vermont anyway?"

"Most of the houses on Lake Caspian are owned by summer residents. It's an exclusive place. Greta Garbo used to have a house there. William Rehnquist, too, not on the lake, but nearby."

"That guy killed it in *Jackie Brown*."

"He wasn't in *Jackie Brown*. He was a Supreme Court justice."

"My bad."

Kenny got a text that lit up his eyes like a kid handed an autographed baseball. "Can you believe it? Fucking Van Gogh left Stinton's. He's the new linemaker at ParadiseCoastCasino."

Vincent Belasario, nicknamed Van Gogh for his linemaking artistry, was a fixture at Stinton's sports book and an icon among linemakers like Kenny. It pretty much summed up the status of online gambling that the arrival of a guy with two racketeering convictions under his belt had boosted the industry's legitimacy.

Of the twenty-two VegasVegas bet-takers who worked different shifts, two thirds were locals, with about a fifty/fifty split of students and adults. The rest were Westerners, either expats or travelers on an extended pit stop from the Lonely Planet caravan. Over ninety percent of the bets came in on the Internet. Kenny or his assistant Jorge monitored incoming bets, adjusting the line whenever they started taking in too much money on one side or the other. Periodically, one of the bet-takers would call out to Jackson or Kenny, asking if a customer could exceed the betting limit.

Maria sat at her terminal importing bets. She worked part time to help pay her tuition at the Universidad de Costa Rica, where she was studying literature and probably inspiring it, too.

Jackson picked up the book off her desk. *The Idiot.* "You know Dostoyevsky was a huge gambler."

"Yeah, I do know that, Jackson. It almost ruined him."

Wait...was her tone saying he indirectly shared some of the responsibility for Dostoyevsky's gambling habit?

"It's a good thing he lost. He might have written *How to Win at Blackjack* instead of all those classics."

"Ha ha." She tossed her hair back and smoothed the outer tip of her right eyebrow with her finger.

She toggled to another page. "Twenty-eight 'guilty' bets came in during the prosecutor's statement. Total of seventeen hundred dollars."

"Hopefully the defense attorney earns his money and gets us some 'acquittal' bets."

The latest odds were at the top of the screen.

No murder trial equals no action

Will be found guilty 2 to 5

Will be acquitted 7 to 4

Trial will result in mistrial 11 to 1

Charges will be dropped 100 to 1

Kenny's contempt for novelty props was understandable. When linemakers favored North Carolina over Middle of Nowhere State by twenty-four points, people thought they had to be pulling an arbitrary number from the whiskey fumes of some back room. But after the final whistle, they were almost always within one or two points if they didn't nail it exactly. With sports, you knew everything, from the scoring average of the star to the free throw percentage of the back-up point guard in the last minute of a tied game.

But you could never take a peek at the ethical makeup of a juror or project the group dynamics of twelve strangers thrust together in a cramped room and forced to stare at each other's expanding sweat stains until they reached a unanimous decision.

Or as Kenny put it, "I'm a basketball encyclopedia, but we don't know jack shit about dumb fucks who can't get out of jury duty."

To guard against too much exposure, which was the maximum amount of money a casino could lose on a given proposition, VegasVegas had a five hundred-dollar betting limit on novelty props. The objective here was to balance the "guilty" and "acquittal" betting so VegasVegas took in more than it paid out, regardless of the verdict.

A photo from Andrew Marvel's IMDB profile was pasted beside the odds. With his dark tortoise Hugo Bosses and lips pursed into the near-smile of ironic insight, Marvel looked like he made independent, boundary-pushing character films far outside the mainstream. In reality, he was known for movies where asteroids and other oversized objects blew up, usually in slow motion.

Jackson recalled watching the "making of" portion of *Frontier Zero*. He'd expected a brash loudmouth, but Andrew Marvel was quiet and precise, almost shy. He spoke in a soft voice you had to strain to hear. He had so little to say that most of the sound bytes came from the assistant director and special effects crew.

Was this the face of an unlikely killer? Was there any such thing as an unlikely killer?

Maria's phone rang, and she used the eyebrow-smoothing hand to shove Jackson away. "Actually, Sir, the run line is a combination of the money line and point spread. So you're betting one-twenty to win one hundred, but you're also getting 1.5 runs. So if the Brewers lose by a run, you still win your bet. Does that make sense?"

Probably not, but the "sir" on the other end of the line wouldn't acknowledge betting-related ignorance to a woman.

He'd end up doubling whatever he intended to bet, in the hopes of earning back the status he'd lost through imperfect knowledge of the run line.

One seat over from Maria was Jeremy, formerly Jake, who'd left his home in Albuquerque in a big hurry one day ahead of something—a warrant-bearing marshal, angry spouse, deteriorating sense of self-worth, Jackson wasn't sure and he didn't ask.

It was time for the opening statement of the ambulance chaser Andrew Marvel hired to the shock of the world, or least to the TV legal-commentator part of the world. The lawyer stood in front of the jury box, his suit uncreased, his hair frozen in neat layers.

"I was listening to Mr. Damron's statement, and I kept waiting for him to get to Andrew Marvel's reason for killing Audrey. But he never did. Maybe he felt he'd already gone on too long. Maybe he's saving the reason for later in the trial. Or maybe he realizes Andrew Marvel never had a reason for killing the woman he loved.

"Here's a statistic that will tear your heart out. I know it does mine. 34.6 percent of female murder victims are killed by husbands or boyfriends. The police know this statistic. So do prosecutors like Mr. Damron. Going after the husband improves their conviction rate. Does that sound cynical? I'm sorry. But I'm angry. This man suffered the loss of his wife and now he's being unjustly accused of killing her."

"How's he doing?" Jackson said.

Maria checked incoming bets. "Two for acquittal. Fifty bucks and twenty-five."

"This lawyer sucks."

Kenny called out from his work station, "Where the fuck's Johnny Cochran when you need him? 'If the motive isn't worth shit, you have to acquit.'"

"I know the facts are against him," Jackson said, "but don't our bettors have any faith in the incompetence of juries?"

The defense attorney gestured at the prosecutor. "Mr. Damron said I had fourteen months to track down the person who murdered Audrey and framed Andrew. Mr. Damron had those same fourteen months to interview all Audrey's friends, all Andrew's friends. Were there problems in the marriage? Dark hidden secrets? Fights? Squabbles? No, no, and no. Andrew and Audrey Marvel had a happy marriage. The kind of marriage we all want to have.

"The prosecution isn't obligated to prove a motive. And that's a fortunate thing for them. Because there is no motive. Mr. Damron is quick to ridicule Andrew's story. But if someone wanted to murder Audrey Marvel and he didn't want to be found out, doesn't it make perfect sense to frame the person the police always suspect first? How hard is it to take some of Andrew's clothes from the bedroom and soak them in Audrey's blood? How hard is it to dump the clothes in the lake? How hard is it to walk into the Marvels' bathroom and take some of Andrew's chloral hydrate? The Marvels didn't lock their doors. Nobody in Greensboro does.

"Ladies and gentlemen, if there's one thing I've learned in this sad business, it's this: people kill for a reason. They don't kill for no reason. *They kill for a reason.* And the man sitting in front of you didn't have a reason to kill the woman he loved."

Jackson muted it again.

Maria said bettors placed another two hundred dollars' worth of "acquittal" bets. "I'm surprised, that's all," she said. "The lawyer's right. He's the husband, but he still needs a reason."

"*Shattered Worlds* was like ten years ago," Kenny said. "He hasn't done shit since. Maybe that pisses him off and he took it out on her."

Jeremy pulled his headphones off his ears. "He could have a reason nobody sees."

Jeremy seemed a bit too familiar with undetectable homicidal impulses. It squelched the conversation.

A little black cat trotted up to Jackson. "*¿Tienes hambre, Tomás?*"

Sometimes he said "Are you hungry?" instead. He liked the idea of a bilingual cat. Tomás was a stray who'd wandered in a few months after they opened and lived there ever since, though judging by his appetite, he would have preferred the all-you-can-eat buffets of the Vegas casinos.

Kenny cursed an incoming text. "Got to pull the Reds game off the board. Carne's a scratch. How the fuck do you strain your back getting in the shower? I've been taking showers over thirty years and every one's been injury-free."

Jackson fed Tomás in his office and watched a gray tour bus stop in the middle of Calle 3 outside the Teatro Nacional. The door in front swung open and a slow line of people with that weird American combination of obesity and wanderlust filed out and stood in a circle beside the bus, blinking in the heat. The American package tour crowds loved the Teatro Nacional. They'd go in with their sandals and straw hats, camcorder strap sunburns and worldviews lifted straight from the lyrics of a Jimmy Buffet song. They considered countries like Costa Rica just another of America's many theme parks, the only difference being there were natives instead of costumed characters and they needed their passport to get in instead of a coupon from a soft drink cup.

Maria called out from the betting room. "Well, this is interesting. One of our customers lives in Greensboro, Vermont. His name is Cass Gallaway, and he wants to know if he can bet more than the limit on the trial. He's on hold."

"How much?" Jackson said.

"A thousand."

"On guilty?"

"No."

"Take it. We need all the 'acquittal' money we can get."

"Not that, either. Dropped charges. 100 to 1."

Jackson had heard of charges dropped in the middle of a murder trial when an eyewitness testified the police instructed him to lie. And no doubt charges were dropped in other trials when important witnesses died. But the Marvel trial didn't rely on witness testimony. The DA would never drop charges.

"A 'dropped charges' bet balances out the 'guilty' bets, too," he said.

He didn't want to lose money on their first celebrity trial and have to listen to Kenny say, "I told you so."

Maria shifted into conspiracy-theory mode. "A local. What if he knows something?"

"That the cops and DA don't?"

"Maybe a new witness came forward who saw the real killer dump the clothes in the lake."

"They'd recess the trial."

Kenny snapped his fingers. "I know who the real killer is. It's the same guy who murdered Ron and Nicole. He's older now, but he keeps in shape. That's how come he could carry the passed-out director to his car."

Maria wouldn't let go. "Maybe the witness hasn't come forward yet, but our bettor knows he's about to."

"Do you really believe that?" Jackson said.

"No. But now that I hear myself say it, kinda maybe."

"The DA's had investigators crawling over that town for over a year. He wouldn't let a murder witness fall through the cracks."

"I grew up in a small town. People know secrets. The bettor could be dating a secretary in the lawyer's office. Or his niece cleaned the Marvels' house. Or he was sitting on a bar stool beside someone who saw something that didn't make the news."

"Or he was sitting on a bar stool and got hammered and he has no clue what he's doing."

Kenny squinted like he was deep in thought. "So before I flunked out of junior high, I took this subject called math. One of the things I learned, a thousand at 100 to 1 equals a hundred grand."

"You've got to turn down the bet," Maria said.

But Jackson wasn't in the business of turning down free money from fools. "The murder was fourteen months ago. Nothing stays hidden that long. We should tell Cass Gallaway we're having a two-for-one special on dumb ass bets. Dropped charges and the Sixers to win the NBA championship."

"Take the bet?" Maria said.

"Take the bet."

Saturday

Jackson made his money off human weakness but who didn't? Humans had so many weaknesses you couldn't help it. Car companies made money off vanity. Brokerage houses, greed. Fast food places made money off gluttony, the ones with drive-thrus off sloth. The seven deadly sins were a salesman's dream. Late night infomercials didn't appeal to mankind's virtues. They didn't hawk altruism enhancers or videos promising a ten-fold increase in your integrity in less than a month or your money back. The guy who used to live in a studio apartment the size of a bathtub wasn't able to start a worldwide empire thanks to his patented system of treating others as he'd like to be treated himself.

Online gambling was a multi-billion-dollar industry and San Jose was its world capital. Somewhere between two and three hundred Internet casinos, owned mostly by Americans and Brits, were scattered around the city in shiny office buildings, converted stores, suburban houses, even the basement of the Catedral San Raphael, making true the priest's warning that sin was always lurking within. You had everything from two guys and a piece of software to the industry Goliaths like Bodog and BetOnSports, with four hundred employees, hundreds of millions in annual revenues, day care centers, and an Olympic-sized swimming pool.

San Jose lured the casinos with technical infrastructure essential for any Internet business and close proximity to offshore banks essential for any business declared illegal by the U.S.

government. Of course infrastructure and banks were both meaningless without a friendly government, which was short-hand for keeping the license fees and bribe requests reasonable. If a smiling Costa Rican bureaucrat needed twenty thousand to tide him over until next month, his brother wouldn't show up at the door five minutes later with his hand out. For now anyway. Sooner or later they'd want a bigger cut and the online casinos would hop over to the next country in the Caribbean basin.

VegasVegas was one of the smaller places. Jackson chose the name as an obvious spoof. He hadn't expected to find himself patiently explaining, "You see, Vegas casinos mimic cities from other parts of the world, so we're returning the favor and naming ourselves after them."

Who cared? It was a ridiculous name, and nobody went to online casinos for spoofs and satire.

The Justice Department had gotten serious about fighting offshore casinos. A lot of money was changing hands and Lady Liberty didn't want to be the one standing at the craps table in the low-cut evening gown watching everyone else rake it in. The Internet Gambling Act prohibited the use of credit card payments or electronic fund transfers for any Internet wager on sporting events.

So use wire communications to accept bets and you're a criminal. Reduce expenses by dumping toxins into rivers and depriving minimum wage employees access to health care and you get interviewed on CNBC.

This made for a nice sound byte at El Gato Hambre, but Jackson had no interest in becoming a fugitive from justice. Maybe he'd get out of the business and return to the U.S. Live on a suburban street named after a tree. Know what day is garbage day. Develop regular topics of banter with the dry cleaner.

Maybe not.

Most of the industry guys gathered at El Gato Hambre at night to drink and seduce, some with money and charm, others with money in lieu of charm. Jackson preferred the quiet of his apartment. Tonight, the rain made it smell like a wet sidewalk.

The wind had shifted and was blowing so hard the rain seemed to be falling sideways instead of down. He lowered the living room window to keep rain from soaking the sofa but left the kitchen window open. He didn't want to close the storm out completely. Even through the rain, he could make out a faint calypso beat coming from one of the apartments below.

He could be sharing the storm with Maria. But that wouldn't be cool. Or Tomás. But Tomás preferred the betting room and the night shift bet-takers liked having him around. So Jackson enjoyed the storm with a glass of Chilean cabernet while he worked on new ads for VegasVegas.

Count the places in Antigua, Barbados, and Panama along with the couple hundred in Costa Rica and you had a lot of casinos vying for the same customers. Before you could sign anyone up, you had to let them know you existed. Some casinos came up with unorthodox methods. GoldenPalace.com tattooed its name on the back of boxers. Then they branched out to streakers. Recently they won the bidding to have a newly discovered species of titi monkey named the GoldenPalace.com monkey. Maybe that sparked a surge of betting from zoologists and primatologists, maybe not. What their marketing director did know was that articles written about the GoldenPalace.com monkey in mainstream publications got them more new customers than their previous two advertising campaigns combined.

VegasVegas didn't have enough money to rename primates. Jackson stuck to mobile banner ads. Standard online casino ads featured pictures of oiled women in ripped tee shirts with the promise of unfathomably big jackpots. He preferred the death and decrepitude approach.

> You're going to lose all your money when you die.
> We have more fun ways of losing it.
> VegasVegasCasino.com

> Maximize your 401K contributions
> So you can afford a deluxe nursing home.
> You can't take it with you.

VegasVegasCasino.com

Build up your nest egg
So your kids get a big inheritance.
You can't take it with you.
VegasVegasCasino.com

Jackson checked betting on the trial, which was recessed for the weekend. The new odds had brought in more "acquittal" bets, but VegasVegas still had too much money on "guilty."

That one "dropped charges" bet nagged at the small section of Jackson's brain that housed his paranoia. It turned out the bettor, Cass Gallaway, opened his account two months after Andrew's arrest and used it to play poker a few times. Wasn't that something a person with inside information might do? Establish a presence. Play a little poker. Make it look like you didn't open the account solely to bet on the trial.

Jackson told himself what he told Maria. A local guy couldn't know something that eluded a police force and prosecutor for over a year.

No doubt Cass Gallaway heard all kinds of rumors and gossip at his local bar. He also heard about UFO landings and presidents without birth certificates. This trial wasn't taking place in Judge Judy's courtroom. The DA knew the world would be watching. Any rumor Cass heard, he heard. And sent a team of professionals to investigate.

The rainstorm was over. Jackson pulled the window open and stood breathing the warm, sluggish air. Final, swollen raindrops flicked the metal windowsill. Lives re-claimed the night. A TV blasting from one apartment, a family squabble in another. From somewhere downstairs, the smell of frying chorizo. A baby crying, staccato bursts of laughter, a chair scraping over the floor. Down below in the courtyard, couples came out in the wake of the storm, some young and awkward, fumbling in shadows, others sitting on benches or walking slow and bent toward the only thing that could ever come between them.

Standing there listening, watching, alone in his apartment, Jackson felt a stronger sense of companionship than he did when he stood face to face with people. Was this fucked up? It was.

The phone vibrated on the table. Kenny, no doubt calling from El Gato Hambre.

"Hello?"

"Hello?"

"Kenny?"

"Yeah?"

"You called me."

"Oh, yeah."

"What's up?"

"Hold on, I can't hear you. Let's move."

"My moving won't affect anything. You have to move."

"Oh, yeah. Okay."

Howling voices and the loud baritone of TV sports announcers echoed in the background.

Kenny spoke with a midnight slur. "You coming down?"

"Nah, I'll stay in."

"This pitcher of beer's better company anyway."

A few seconds after Kenny hung up, Maria called.

"Did you see?"

"What?"

"The Vermont DA scheduled a press conference for Monday morning."

Monday

The DA's grimace was a cross between getting kicked in the groin and walking in on his wife and two other men. More than once he lowered his head and said, "We wish this video had been made available at the outset."

In a separate press conference, Andrew Marvel's ambulance-chaser described how he was working at home Saturday morning when his doorbell rang. He opened the door and found a padded envelope containing a DVD. After watching it, he immediately called the district attorney and Judge Newman.

The ABC affiliate in Burlington received its copy of the DVD later in the day.

In the video, Andrew Marvel lay on a motel bed, asleep or unconscious, wearing nothing but underwear. The mirror above the dresser reflected the TV screen in front of the bed.

The backwards numbers and letters spelled out, "Revere Motel. Welcome. Press 9 to select movies." Beneath that, "6/24, 10:13:06 PM, 10:13:07 PM, 10:13:08 PM…"

The camera panned up to the window, keeping Andrew and the TV reflection in frame. On the other side of the street, the Lilly's Tavern sign said, "Tonight only, the Seahorses."

By the time ABC aired the video, investigators had identified the location as room 208 of the Revere Motel in Manchester, New Hampshire, approximately three hours from Greensboro.

The 911 call was made from the Marvel house at 10:07 p.m. The police found Audrey dead at 10:24.

The State of Vermont dropped all charges against Andrew Marvel.

Someone had ripped Jackson off. He didn't hold it against them. He held it against himself. But before VegasVegas paid out a hundred thousand he had to find answers to a few questions:

Was Andrew Marvel the mastermind or the prop in a bizarre betting scheme? Was Cass Gallaway a murderer, accomplice, unwitting bettor for someone who didn't want his name on the account, or guy with a strange and lucky hunch?

Was this Jackson's comeuppance? If so, for what—callousness or stupidity?

He took a flight from San Jose to Houston and now sat at a United gate waiting for his flight to Burlington, Vermont.

CNN had the press conferences on loop.

"Digital experts examined the video thoroughly. They've given me their assurance it hasn't been manipulated in any way. We wish this video had been made public at the outset. Withholding it for this length of time, aside from the pain it caused Mr. Marvel to endure, has made the apprehension of the actual killer that much more difficult."

A business traveler next to Jackson mimicked the DA. "'Aside from what it caused Mr. Marvel to endure.' Say what you're really thinking. 'Mr. Marvel made us look like jackasses. He made us think he did it so we arrested him, not the killer he hired.'"

"You think he framed himself?" Jackson said.

"If someone else framed him, why give him an alibi?"

The DA was wrapping up. "I'm confident our fine and dedicated police force will soon develop new leads."

"Messed up." The business traveler shook his head.

Jackson would have said "fucked up," but why quibble?

Tuesday

The town fathers who gave Greensboro its name knew what they were doing. Green hills flattened into green fields, which rose into more green hills. Where the green ended, green began. Light green patches of grass within thick clumps of dark green elms. Rolling waves of green, green horizons, green borders between green farms.

Jackson recognized the L-shaped farmhouse from the Morning Loon Inn website and turned into the dirt parking area. A porch with tables and chairs overlooked a clay tennis court between Town Highway 1 and Caspian Lake. A row of six white cottages with brick chimneys stood on the hill behind the inn.

A drug-like feeling of coziness hit him as soon as he walked through the door. The inn smelled of leather-bound books and firewood embers, with a touch of lemon. It soothed his muscles. Cooled his skin. Shrank his awareness of eventual mortality down to almost nothing.

He creaked over the uneven wooden floor to the front desk, where two wooden loons sat on either side of the desk clerk.

"Tracy?"

"Yes?"

Tracy had a light sprinkling of freckles over her roundish face and eyes unburdened by secrets. It was a face that belonged at a dinner table where applesauce was being served, not a face that smiled knowingly when someone offered a bribe to make someone else's reservation go away. Which made it a face that deceived, because not only had she accepted Jackson's bribe when he called, she'd managed to ratchet it up from two hundred to four.

"Hank Carruthers. I reserved a cottage."

"Welcome, Mr. Carruthers."

He looked at the open guest book while she slipped his envelope into her purse. In the comments section, a Mr. and Mrs. Gregory, had written, "What a wonderful, spirit-renewing weekend we'll always remember."

"Can a spirit really be renewed in one weekend?"

"Here it can. That's why we charge so much."

A well-dressed couple emerged from a hallway and waved at her.

She waved back. "That scarf looks great on you, Mrs. Jenks."

"Why thank you, Tracy."

Tracy held her smile in place as they made their way to the front door.

Most likely, nobody would do a search on Jackson, but he didn't see a downside to starting out with as much anonymity as possible, which is why he'd made the reservation under the name of a fourth grade gym teacher.

"I lost my credit card." He took out his money clip. "Actually, I'm being too charitable to my fellow man. Someone stole it. I'll pay in advance."

A calico cat hopped on the counter and rubbed against Jackson's hand as he counted out money for six days.

"No, Beetle."

"¿*Tienes hambre*, Beetle?"

There wasn't a hint of comprehension in either pair of gray eyes, Beetle's or Tracy's.

"I've sort of adopted a bilingual cat. Tomás understands Spanish and English, to a point. If you eliminate food-related words…"

He stopped himself. He was doing a stellar job concealing his identity. She now knew he spoke Spanish. So what? How would she make the jump from that to Costa Rica to offshore casino to "the guy Cass Gallaway ripped off is staying in one of our cottages?"

She glanced down at his green duffel bag. "Here on vacation?"

"Beautiful Vermont, cozy country inn, all by yourself, what a loser. Is that what you mean?"

Her cheeks reddened. "My God. No. I can't believe…No."

There was an unselfconscious coarseness to her laugh that made him think of disheveled bed sheets and an empty Makers Mark bottle on the nightstand.

"I'm part of the swarm of locusts invading your town."

"Reporter?"

"Photographer."

"The dirt roads around the lake houses are private. They'll arrest you for trespassing. The lakeshore path is public access. You can use that."

"What about in the lake?"

"That's where half you guys are hanging out, behind the Marvel dock. The lake people aren't thrilled."

"Andrew hasn't come out of his house?"

"He hasn't come here, and we're the only restaurant in town."

Tracy pulled a map from a drawer and moved her purple-nailed finger along one of the roads from Lake Caspian to Town Highway 1. "Private dirt road. Leads to his house. This here's Cozy Lane." She was tracing a longer road parallel to the lake.

She tapped a spot on the lake. "Boat reporters. No boats permitted in the lake before eight or after six. They passed that law last year."

"Only enforced against media and gawkers?"

"You know it." Her finger crossed the main road. "This farm is where the rest of you are hanging out, across from his driveway."

She handed him his key. "Number six. Cottage on the far right."

"Two more questions: What time do you start serving dinner, and did Andrew hire someone to kill Audrey?"

"Five o'clock sharp, and you're the news guy. You tell me."

"Another hundred if you keep your ears open."

"I'm kind of busy. Double shifts to pay for night school and what not. Wish I had time to keep my ears open."

"Two hundred if the information's good," he said.

"That buys one open ear."

"One's good enough for now."

Jackson picked up his bag, and she laughed. "All by yourself, what a loser. I can't believe you said that."

"I thought you were thinking it."

"No, you didn't."

"Why not?"

"You know why not."

Okay, he had his attractions and female confirmations were always welcome. Funny how the offering and acceptance of a bribe got people past the initial stages of polite awkwardness and excessive formality.

"Enjoy your stay, Mr. Carruthers."

A grass pathway bordered by walls of ferns passed under a lilac-covered wooden arch up the hill to the cottages, each with a table and two Adirondack chairs out front. On the other side of the cottages was a forest of pines, fairy tale thick.

Jackson pulled open the two double-hung windows facing the adjacent farm. Shifting winds blended the scent of pines with manure.

On the bed were two needlepoint pillows, one a cow, the other a loon. The dresser and bed frame were deep-grained walnut. A brass coalscuttle beside the fireplace was filled with firewood. A wooden loon sat on the dresser and a painting of two swimming loons hung on the wall.

Jackson took out his toilet kit, but left the clothes in the bag instead of putting them in the drawers. Someone he'd traveled with in India once told him this character-defining act revealed his fear of commitment. He told her, no, it was really laziness, that she was overlooking the obvious shortcoming in her eagerness to find bigger ones. It didn't take her long to find some of those, too. She wasn't a painful memory or a happy one either, but he could never neglect to unpack a suitcase without remembering her.

After showering off a day of travel, Jackson mapped the address from Cass Gallaway's account information. Cass had waited about three seconds after the DA announced the dropped charges to call customer service and request his winnings. The Justice Department crackdown forced online casinos to come up with new ways for U.S. customers to fund accounts and withdraw money. Person-to-person wire transfers through Western Union or Money Gram to a VegasVegas agent in Malaga, Spain, worked fine for small transactions, but they needed an alternative for amounts more than a couple thousand.

Jackson's British friend, Bernard, had started a company in Costa Rica called Lost Roads Adventure Travel that should have been called Lost Revenue Adventure Travel. They made a deal. Jackson gave Bernard money to keep the company afloat and in return Bernard let Jackson use Lost Roads Adventure Travel to wire money back and forth between VegasVegas bettors in the U.S. If a customer wanted to fund an account with his credit card, he could chose an amount that corresponded to one of the trips, like the Trek of Hidden Costa Rica for $1,499, and that's what showed up on the statement.

When Cass called, Maria told him Lost Roads Adventure Travel would wire his winnings to his bank account in ten separate transactions. Cass called back the next day to say he hadn't gotten anything and if he didn't see the first installment in his account by noon Eastern time, he'd have no choice but to complain to the Offshore Gaming Association. This noon deadline passed when Jackson was driving his rental car from the Burlington airport to Greensboro. If Cass hadn't made his complaints yet, he soon would.

The Offshore Gaming Association was an industry oversight board without legal authority, but their blacklist had ruined more than one casino. Customers were uneasy about betting online to begin with. If a casino showed up on a black list for non-payment, people would rather do business with a Nigerian prince who promised a share of his inheritance if they simply gave him their bank account number.

VegasVegas would never get blacklisted for not paying if Cass had something to do with the murder, or was betting for someone who did. That made the bet fraudulent, like fixing a game. Of course the Offshore Gaming Association wasn't going to wait for Jackson to get his detective license and conduct an investigation. He figured he had two, possibly three, days to dig around.

>>>

He passed through the inn on the way to his Corolla. Tracy was talking to someone with goldish hair tied in a blue-and-white bandanna. The woman wore a blue mesh crew shirt and faded denim pants with cuffs rolled up above her calves. A crescent moon sliver of stomach kept Jackson from noticing her black flip-flops until last. The husband, green sweater tied around his shoulders, short plaid pants, crew team in college, was probably carrying luggage in from the car.

Now that Jackson had a better look, he saw she didn't have a ring, but this was definitely the guy who'd be unloading luggage outside the country inns of her future.

Tracy looked up. "Need anything, Mr. Carruthers?"

"No, thank you."

The future investment banker's wife brushed loose strands of hair off her forehead, tucking them back under her bandanna, and Jackson felt like saying, "Yes, I see you. You know I do."

She turned away from him, studying the guestbook, politely waiting for the interruption to conclude, like he was no more interesting to her than the green-scarfed Mrs. Jenks and her pot-bellied husband. At least she saved him the bother of trying to think of something clever to say on the way out.

Town Highway 1 took him past the farm on the left and private roads leading to the lake houses on the right. A black dog of uncertain parentage sprinted along the grass at the edge of the farm, barking and trying to keep pace. When Jackson got too far ahead, this Sisyphus of dogs jogged back to the edge of the farm to await the next passing car. A cluster of eight or so photographers sat in lawn chairs behind the fence near two cows, all of them facing a private dirt road with the names Buddington, Read, Marvel painted on pieces of wood attached to a stake.

The road sloped into the main part of town. He passed the white church and white library and turned left when he reached Willey's General Store, also white.

The post office had a pay phone out front. Jackson parked and dialed the home number on Cass' account.

One, two, three rings then, "Yeah, hello?"

"Tim, how's it going?"

"Tim?"

"It's not you?"

"Sorry you got the wrong number." Polite, without a trace of the fury Jackson expected from a criminal wronged in even the most trivial way.

"Sorry for disturbing you," Jackson said.

"Not a problem. Have a good day."

"You too."

The Bend Road wound past thick groves of maples before passing rectangular, windowless homes with faded siding, disassembled machinery in the front yards, and adhesive American flags above the doors.

Cass' trailer looked as small and isolated as it did in the satellite photo on Google maps. A two-toned Suburban, three if you counted rust, was parked on packed dirt in front. A metal shed butted up against a chain-link fence behind the trailer.

When Jackson spoke to Maria on the drive from the airport, she'd said she asked around and learned Cass had placed "dropped charges" bets at eight other casinos and probably places where she didn't know people. This trailer didn't look like the residence of someone with that kind of spare money sitting around.

Jackson scanned the area for a concealed place to wait. He was used to streets filled with parked and double-parked cars, but The Bend Road was an empty strip of pavement bordered by grass and brush. If he wanted to blend in, he'd have to park in a field and replace his tires with bricks. This was a snooty thought for someone who prided himself in being a man of the people, but he was tired and frustrated about encountering kinks in the plan before it even got started.

A shaded patch of weeds in front of an abandoned lot made a decent lookout spot. An elm blocked his view of the trailer door, but he could see the Suburban.

He selected the Muse station on Pandora and settled in to wait. The first ten minutes weren't so bad, though it was probably a good stakeout principle to remain unaware of ten-minute increments.

He didn't expect anything more than a little data-gathering. Where did Cass go, who did he talk to? Hopefully, the answers weren't "nowhere" and "himself." Some of the other casinos might be wiring Cass part of his winnings today. If Jackson got lucky, Cass would pick up the money at a Western Union or Money Gram and deliver it to the person he was betting for.

There was an alternative to this roundabout approach. He could knock on the trailer door, tell Cass maybe the police would be interested in hearing about the man who bet on dropped charges two days before someone delivered the video alibi to Andrew Marvel's lawyer.

But Cass might not have anything to do with the murder, so for now Jackson would stick with the roundabout approach.

An hour and a half into his wait he started a game of Words with Friends with a randomly selected cheater named Hanabuddha, who played words nobody outside the offices of Merriam-Webster knew existed. Every time Jackson looked down at his own letters, he imagined the Suburban reversing out the driveway, so he kept putting down the first word he saw and Hanabuddha kicked his butt. He made a mental note to challenge Hanabuddha to a rematch when he got home, but no doubt Hanabuddha would recall his sub-300-point score and sneeringly reject him.

Maria was calling.

"Relieve my boredom," he said.

"Where are you?"

"In a car outside Cass' trailer. Someone named Hanabuddha thinks I'm the worst Words for Friends player in the world."

"I checked Cass' log-on history. Earliest time, a few minutes after ten in the morning, latest time, a few minutes before seven. Get this. Greensboro Free Library. Hours, ten to seven."

"That's why I pay you the big bucks."

"You don't."

"I should."

"Analytics shows only one IP address from Greensboro."

"Why bother using a public computer? We have all his information. Maybe he doesn't own a computer. Or maybe…"

"The person he's betting for," she said, nonplussed, making sure he wouldn't credit himself with a revelation.

"Use Cass to set up the account, do all the betting yourself. Don't have to worry about someone linking you to a public computer. When Cass called to complain, did you note the caller ID?

"Unknown. Maybe a pay phone, if they still have them there."

"Oh yeah, they still have them. They probably still have butter churners and stage coaches, too."

"I talked to some more people," she said. "Cass also bet dropped charges at Womper, SportZone, King's Head, and Zonk. That makes twelve."

"He bet more than the limit?"

"Tried. Nobody let him."

"Don't rub it in."

"Kenny told me to."

It was only a few minutes after he hung up with Maria that Jackson heard the trailer door rattle closed. He drove toward town and slowed as the Suburban nosed out of its driveway, blinker flashing, and turned onto The Bend Road.

The Suburban parked outside Willey's General Store. The guy who hopped out was skinny and pale. He was wearing torn faded jeans with a chain stretching from a belt loop into the back pocket, and a pair of beat-up Wolverines. His still-wet dark hair was combed over his forehead. His wispy mustache looked like a smudge of dirt.

While Cass was in Willey's, Jackson stood in front of a bulletin board beside the door, reading notices handwritten on sheets of paper and blue file cards. Frank offered to "haul wood or odd jobs." Why did hauling wood deserve its own category and not fit under the more general heading of odd jobs? Unless by "odd" Frank meant strange or bizarre. Frank probably wouldn't appreciate having his ad parsed this way. A Thursday knitting workshop welcomed newcomers. One person took civic-mindedness to freakish new heights, writing, "Was your model airplane ruined by my dog on Friday at the baseball field? Please call or e-mail. I would like to send you a new one."

Cass was missing out on free advertising space. "Betting on a celebrity murder trial but too close to it to use your own name? Let me place your bets for you."

Cass came out with an orange Gatorade. Jackson leaned close to Frank's file card, squinting and moving his index finger along the text, feigning concentration.

The Suburban door opened and closed but the engine didn't start. Jackson turned to see Cass crossing the street without his Gatorade.

He called Maria. "Cass just went in the library."

A few minutes went by.

"You still there?" he said.

"He just logged on…Now he's off. No message."

Cass took the three stairs outside the library in a jump. He raised his fist in the air and brought it down hard against his thigh, jerking his head back at the impact, and limped to the Suburban. Jackson couldn't help smiling at the slapstick exit.

Instead of returning home, Cass pulled into the post office lot and used the pay phone. He didn't talk long before hopping back in the Suburban, passing through town, and veering up Breezy Avenue. Jackson followed, slowing as he passed Willey's to let a woman with iron-gray hair in a green Subaru hatchback cut in front of him.

Breezy Avenue became Center Road, a two-lane, tree-shaded road without traffic, which Jackson was beginning to realize was the default road condition in Vermont. How long would he have the green Subaru as a buffer? He couldn't expect an iron-gray-haired woman with a "Reduce Reuse Recycle" bumper sticker to keep pace with a freaked-out criminal. But Cass stuck to the speed limit. The curving road gave Jackson a clear view of him holding his phone to his ear. Obviously he didn't want the number he called from the pay phone stored on his phone log. Another piece of data pointing to an anonymity-craving bettor.

Jackson expected certain behaviors from drivers of Subaru hatchbacks with "Reduce Reuse Recycle" bumper stickers, which didn't include gunning the engine and blasting the horn when the person in front of them slowed momentarily.

Cass stuck his hand out the window and waved, a genuinely apologetic wave in Jackson's view, but the iron-gray woman took it as a taunt. She pounded her horn and accelerated right up to his bumper.

Cass was holding the phone to his ear again. The woman gave her horn one final sustained blast and dropped back, maybe thinking he was calling the cops on her.

When Jackson's phone rang, he thought for one irrational second it was Cass. But the caller ID said Ed Trumane. Looked like one of Cass' calls went to the Offshore Gaming Association.

"How you doing, Ed?" Jackson said.

"Just got a call from a customer of yours…"

"Cass Gallaway."

"He's not happy, and I can't say I blame him. It's a lot of money."

"Only half a day late."

"We've never had complaints against you guys before."

"You never will again."

"You're paying the bet?"

"Of course."

"When?"

"Soon."

"Soon?"

"Can you give me a week?"

"Our reputation's on the line, too."

"Five days?"

"Three."

"I appreciate that, Ed."

"Got to run, buddy. The building inspector's here." (i.e., "Someone just laid out another line of coke on the stripper's belly and if I don't get off the phone I'll miss my turn.")

This was the guy with the power to convict Jackson of unforgivable violations of the online casino moral code.

Tuesday, 1:43 p.m.

Jackson was on the clock. Three days until his casino got black-listed.

The line of cars passed a sign saying "Hardwick…three miles." The woman blasted her horn twice as she screeched a left, leaving Jackson alone behind the Suburban. They braked down a steep hill past a cemetery the size of a house lot, surrounded by a white wooden fence. Cass parked beside it. Jackson parked further up the hill and watched him limp across the street, open the gate, and close it carefully behind him.

Dead people aside, nobody else was in the cemetery. For a meeting place, it was a strange one. Cass wasn't carrying anything that could contain money, so he'd only come to talk. But then what was the point of the call from the pay phone?

Cass nodded at one of the headstones, bumped his fist against another, stopped in front of a third to offer a phantom toast and throw back a phantom shot. A few rows past those three, he sat in front of a stubby headstone, wrapping his arms around his knees, and started talking. From Jackson's vantage point, the monologue looked matter-of-fact, a "how was your day" kind of talk. But a few minutes into it, Cass leaned forward and spoke with more urgency. He slammed his palm against his forehead. Made his hand into a gun pointing at his temple, threw his head back at the phantom bullet's impact.

This guy Cass was messing up all Jackson's expectations. Why couldn't he be a by-the-numbers criminal, motivated by simple greed and a desire to avoid punishment? Instead he does a Benny Hill routine outside the library, is politely apologetic to a tailgater, drives to a cemetery where he does a shot with one headstone and confesses his sins to another.

At the bottom of the hill, a thick-bodied man in a dark wind-breaker turned the corner and trudged up the sidewalk toward the cemetery gate. He moved slowly, head bent forward, wearing a Red Sox cap. Cass couldn't see him yet and anyway he was too engrossed in his one-sided conversation with the headstone.

Jackson imagined Kenny's expression if he heard the bettor was a Red Sox fan, an offense far more unforgivable to him than ripping off VegasVegas for a hundred thousand.

The man looked up, turning his head, taking in parked cars on both sides of the street, including Jackson's. He didn't stare, didn't look at all suspicious, but that would change if Jackson remained in the car. Two options, then. Walk down the hill in the direction of town and follow the man after his meeting with Cass. Or go into the cemetery and pay his respects to the dead.

He chose option two. The man was still a good fifty feet down the hill. Jackson kept his back to Cass as he paced along the first row. He picked out a cracked runt of a headstone that looked like a piece of concrete from a jack-hammered sidewalk.

The faint scuff of rubber soles on pavement got louder. The Red Sox hat came into view and stopped. Jackson crouched for a better view. The man was standing still, watching Cass, who didn't seem to notice or had been instructed not to notice. When the Red Sox hat turned toward Jackson, he shifted closer to the headstone.

The man started walking again. Ten more feet and he'd reach the gate. He kept walking, past the gate, toward the houses at the top of the hill.

The engraving on the headstone said, "In loving memory of Eugene A. Patty. May 9, 1957–November 3, 1990."

"Just a guy walking up a hill," Jackson said to the late Eugene. "Stopped to watch Cass talking to that headstone."

Eugene A. Patty died at thirty-three. Jackson's age. Did
anyone have loving memories of him, so loving they'd inscribe it
on a headstone? He could come up with people who had super-
ficially enjoyable memories and drunken partial memories, but
loving? He still had plenty of time to find someone, provided
he didn't perish before his time like Eugene. And anyway, not
to be the cynic, but there was a good chance Eugene's people
lied for appearance's sake or unthinkingly selected the line from
a list of most popular headstone eulogies.

Cass finally ran out of things to say to the one headstone, did
another phantom shot with the other, and left.

They drove down the hill and turned into Hardwick. The
Hardwick Town House & Depot, formerly a church, had a blue
tarp covering the roof where the steeple used to be. A stack of
tires stood outside the entrance to the Hardwick Apartments.
Des Grossbellier's Funeral Home was the only building on the
street with a fresh coat of white paint and a mowed lawn.

At the stop sign outside the red-bricked police station, they
turned left onto Route 15, which bisected an unused train track
and an abandoned granite-processing plant.

A few miles past the "Welcome to Morrisville" sign, Cass
flicked on his left turn signal and made the turn. Jackson kept
his eyes locked on the road ahead, counting out twenty seconds
before pulling a U-turn and making a right onto what he now
saw was Stagecoach Road.

Cass had parked in front of a house with a for sale sign, but
he walked past it to the neighboring house. Jackson nosed over
and watched Cass cross the lawn to a soccer ball and dribble
it in circles. He jerked to his right, as if juking an imaginary
defender, smacked the ball between two trees, raised both arms
in the air and fell to his knees in mock celebration of the goal.

The dark-wooded house had a hummingbird weathervane on
top. Cass rang the doorbell and banged on the knocker. Nobody
answered. He stepped back to look at the upstairs window, then
tried the knocker again.

Maria was calling.

Jackson slumped in the seat. "Can I call you back?"

"Someone just logged on."

"Shit. I followed Cass. I'm half an hour from Greensboro."

"He just sent an e-mail. 'Ed Trumane from The Offshore Gaming Association says you have three days to pay.'"

"Get in a conversation. Keep him engaged. I'm on my way back."

"He logged off."

Tuesday, 2:52 p.m.

On the veranda of the Greensboro Free Library, someone was bent over a portable metal bookshelf with a taped-on sheet of paper that said, Take One, Leave One. His clown patches of curly brown hair looked like they'd been velcroed to the sides of his head. He walked past Jackson holding two paperbacks in one of his thick freckled hands. His squinting brown eyes weren't clown eyes.

"Hey," Jackson said.

The guy stopped, turned.

"Did you leave one?"

Tilting his clown head, "What?"

"The sign says to take one and leave one. You took two and left none. This is an honor system. It only works if people play fair."

Three long strides and the guy was picking up the bookshelf, carrying it out to the parking area, and dropping it in the cab of a black F-150. "Now I took the whole fucking shelf and left none."

The truck door slammed. It was a long way from used book thievery to murder, and if the guy came to check on Cass' VegasVegas account, he had no reason to stick around an extra half hour. Still, Jackson now had at least one potential bettor.

He photographed the license plates of the three cars in the lot and two bikes chained to the rack and went inside. The librarian sat at a desk facing the door. Good. She saw the comings and goings of the visitors. She smiled and said hello. Also good.

She'd remember people she exchanged pleasantries with. Jackson smiled a return hello. As long as it wasn't a big re-shelving day, he might be in luck.

A glass-paneled room contained a row of six computers, two in use. A teenaged girl was on Facebook and a retired man was hunting and pecking a message into what looked like Earthlink webmail as his wife watched. Earthlink still existed? On a headstone in the Hardwick Cemetery, maybe, but on someone's browser? Jackson wanted to keep an open mind about the identity of the bettor, but he ruled out these three.

No point giving time an opportunity to chip away at the librarian's memory. How could he find out who was here in the last hour? What if he found something valuable and it became his mission as a Good Samaritan to return it to its rightful owner?

He prided himself on being a possession-shunning minimalist and now it was coming back to bite him. He had nothing to pass off as a lost item. No watch, no ring. He took out his money clip, removed the bills. But the librarian might think he pocketed the owner's cash, which was irrational because then why would he return the money clip? He couldn't rely on her rationality, so he put two twenties back in the clip.

He sat between the teenaged girl and the retired couple. Most public library computers were programmed to delete history, cache, and cookies after the user closed her browser. Maybe that branch of library science hadn't reached Greensboro. He opened Explorer, the only browser on the desktop, and pulled down the history menu. Nothing. When he started typing "Vegas…" autocomplete didn't spell out any urls. Just to be sure, he typed the first few letters of Facebook. Again, nothing.

Wheeling his chair back, he said, "Hey, what's this?" and reached under the table to come up holding his money clip.

"Look what someone lost."

The girl glanced over and returned to her status updating.

"I think they have a Lost and Found up front," the retired woman said.

"When I came in, a tall curly-haired guy was leaving."

"Blake? He was back at the book shelves."

Her husband said, "He might have been on the computers before we got here."

The woman nodded. "We only just arrived."

Jackson and the woman looked at the girl, who said, "Me too."

So no ruling out Blake.

"I'll ask the librarian."

"Thank you," the woman said, as if she represented all humanity.

The nameplate on the librarian's desk said Betty Turtle and she had the unblinking eyes to prove it.

"Look what I found under the computer table."

She put on her glasses and wheeled her chair closer. He placed the money clip in her outstretched hand.

"Thank you very much, sir. I'll put it in Lost and Found."

"Great." But Jackson's smile gave way to a troubled squint. "What if they don't check?"

She stroked the silver clip with her finger, "Look at it. Of course they'll check."

"It's money. They'll check places they bought things. They won't think of the library."

"We could put a sign outside Willey's."

"Willey's is one store. They might have spent money any-where. It was right out in the open. It had to be someone who just left. If you tell me the names of the people here in the last hour, I could call and ask if they lost a money clip."

Now that he was saying it out loud, it bordered on creepy.

"You're a very conscientious young man." But her eyes weren't buying what her voice was selling.

"I bet this clip means a lot to someone. I'd feel great if I could return it to them."

"Very conscientious," she said again. "When the person who lost it picks it up, I'll make sure to tell him your name. People here are appreciative."

"I'm not looking for a reward."

"You deserve one."

She was using a black marker to compose the sign as they spoke. He watched her write, "Silver and black money clip."

He'd already blown six hundred on Tracy to get him the cabin and keep one ear open. All things being equal he'd rather not give a hundred-dollar money clip to the first liar who claimed it. Not that he was in a position to pass judgment on liars, considering his elaborate deception brought the sign into existence in the first place. But he only lied to retrieve money stolen from him. Money some might say he stole from gamblers. Which made his theft far bigger than a paltry hundred dollars. So the person falsely claiming the money clip had the moral high ground after all.

"Maybe we should say 'money clip' and have them describe it."

She stared at him through lenses that doubled the size of her eyes. He could see every blood vessel and they were all judging him harshly. "That would be saying we don't trust them."

"We're doing them a service by removing the temptation."

His joke hit a brick wall of indignation, so he tried a different tack. "People who live here are honest, but this is a tourist town. Someone's driving through, they see the sign, they think, I wouldn't mind a silver and black money clip."

She made a chewing motion with her mouth as she thought that over.

"I hadn't considered an out-of-towner," she finally said.

He'd let himself get distracted by the sign. He needed the names.

"We're talking honestly. You saw right through me. I want a reward."

"Of course you do. You deserve one."

"What I'm thinking, if you mention my name, maybe the owner thinks dropping it in Lost and Found is no big deal. But if he thinks I took time away from my vacation to personally contact him, maybe he's not perceptive as you, he doesn't pick up on the fact I did it for a reward, and he's more likely to jack up the amount of money he gives me."

Her magnified eyes glistened. "You're right, he will. You want a list of people who were here?"

"Just the last hour or so. Like I said, it was out in the open. Someone must have just lost it."

She took a sheet of paper from her desk. "You deserve your reward."

Tuesday, 3:26 p.m.

Jackson glided through a gateway of rocks. Two loons floated in the green water like they were waiting for the postcard photographer. It felt good to shock his airplane-weary muscles back to life. The tips of his paddles barely rippled water as he headed toward the lake's center.

On the map Tracy showed him, Lake Caspian was shaped like a skull with a caved-in forehead. The public boat launch was at the southern end, the skull's chin, about two miles along the eastern shore. The Marvel house was about halfway to the launch.

Two other kayakers were paddling side by side ahead of him. A solitary paddleboat hugged the shoreline. Another pair of loons looked like they were sitting on clouds reflected in the still water.

As he moved further from shore, the water began to get choppier, but not enough to upgrade it from placid. Lake Caspian could never be anything but placid. Placid and peaceful. Not the kind of lake where a killer deposits bloody clothes and a knife. People around here had to feel like the shocked neighbors of the mild-mannered psychopath.

"We never saw it coming. The lake always seemed so peaceful to us."

He angled toward the media flotilla behind the Marvel dock. The stone chimney of the house peeked out from beneath clouds of elm leaves. The photographers clustered together like their compatriots in the field, minus the two grazing cows. Six sat in paddleboats, two per boat. Two others shared a canoe. One sat in a kayak, maybe thinking he could pursue Andrew if he went for a ride.

They turned in unison to face Jackson as he got closer.

"You live around here?" asked a guy with a floppy hat in one of the paddleboats.

The gut of the guy sitting next to Floppy Hat served as a big, hairy tripod for two cameras. Only one photographer wore a life preserver.

"Didn't they teach you guys water safety in journalism school?"

"You live around here?" Floppy Hat said again.

To head off one of the bored photographers taking his picture, Jackson said, "Just a visitor," and paddled toward the tall white figure standing on the opposite shore.

Before coming down to the lake, he'd asked Tracy about the Marvels' friends. She said they sometimes had dinner with Warren Gunderson, whose house was directly across the lake from theirs, with an Apollo statue in the backyard.

Jackson drifted to a stop near the dock. Apollo looked like he was offering a towel to bathers coming out of the water. Thick maples were spaced evenly behind him like Corinthian columns. The deer on the weathervane looked like she was leaping over the roof.

Jackson floated in the sun trying to process the latest data. Aside from the teenaged girl and the Earthlink couple, only four people had been on the computers after lunch—Cass Gallaway, a buffalo farmer named Blake Trotman, a bad carpenter named Wally Caiden, and a pretty out-of-towner who Betty the librarian thought was a reporter staying at the Morning Loon. When Jackson described the future investment banker's wife, Betty gave him a lens-magnified wink and said, "That's her."

Blake and Wally were locals. They'd have ample opportunity to learn Andrew's routines and break into the house for the chloral hydrate. It seemed unlikely one of them would choreograph a murder/frame-job for the sole purpose of placing bets, but he might have wanted Audrey dead, framed the most likely suspect, then freed him to make money on the side. This meant he didn't fear discovery after the charges were dropped, which in turn meant he didn't have an obvious motive for killing Audrey.

Warren Gunderson might know what kind of relationship, if any, the Marvels had with Blake and Wally. Jackson could wait for Warren to come down to the lake and try striking up a conversation. Problem was, Jackson had already done a car stakeout. He didn't have the patience to follow it up with a kayak stakeout.

All this assumed Andrew was an innocent victim. People who didn't know about the betting, like the business traveler in the airport, could only see one person who benefited from the alibi—Andrew. He hired someone to kill Audrey, frame him, and free him after enough time passed for evidence left by the killer to fade.

But time couldn't erase the money trail. When Andrew paid the killer, the police would pounce.

Unless he didn't pay the killer.

Husband hires killer, police trace payment, husband gets caught. But not if there's no money to trace. You're a Hollywood director. You've seen casinos post celebrity trials in the past and reasonably assume they'd post yours. You hire someone to kill your wife and leave evidence implicating you. Meanwhile, you're three hours away filming your alibi. After the trial starts, the killer bets his own money on dropped charges at 100 to 1, then he delivers the alibi to your lawyer. Charges dropped. Killer collects his winnings. You've paid him without any money changing hands.

There it was, so obvious Jackson deserved to lose the hundred thousand as a penalty for his stupidity. He twisted the paddle deep into the water and turned. He'd tell the police how it happened and who might have logged onto Cass' account from the library. The Offshore Gaming Association wouldn't blacklist him for not paying a contract killer.

A black lab came sprinting and barking across the lawn, followed by a teenaged girl in a long-sleeved white sun shirt and red sunglasses.

"Sorry," she said when she reached the dock.

"He's a good watchdog."

"Buddy? Ha! He's a terrible watchdog. He must have mistaken you for a loon."

Warren Gunderson's daughter? Maybe she'd know Blake and Wally. First a little trust-building chitchat to show he wasn't a reporter.

"I was admiring the weathervane. The deer looks like she's leaping over the roof."

"Yeah?"

She took his picture with her iPhone. "That deer was appraised at twenty-three thousand, but you already know that."

She took another picture. "Now you're out of luck. Guess you'll have to hold up a liquor store instead."

He couldn't tell if the combative voice was staged or real. "If I planned to steal it, wouldn't I ask about something else, like the groomed hedges or Apollo?"

"I know that, and you know I know. So you took the opposite approach, to get me off my guard."

He thought he saw a forced-down smile. "You're playing around."

"I'm keeping the pictures."

She sat on one of the sun loungers. Buddy wagged his tail in approval of the detente.

Jackson paddled close enough to let Buddy lick his hand. "People steal weathervanes?"

"It's a big problem."

"Then what, they launder the money at the tractor dealership?"

"Funny guy. Some backwoods hick sold one at an auction for half a million last year."

"I stand corrected."

"I didn't know any of this stuff either, 'til Audrey told my uncle to check his deer." She took off her sunglasses and gave him a stare. "Yeah, that Audrey."

"Sad." Jackson shook his head.

"She was cool." Then after a couple seconds respectful homage to the dead, "She kept hassling Uncle Warren 'til he got out a ladder and made sure it wasn't stolen."

"I don't understand. If it's up there, it wasn't stolen."

She jumped up and took another picture. "Playing dumb? Thieves don't leave a big empty space so everyone knows it's gone. They replace 'em with replicas. Some are so good only an expert can tell the difference."

"Why'd Audrey think the deer was stolen?"

"She didn't."

"I don't follow."

"She thought someone in town was part of a ring."

Jackson's poker face must have betrayed him here because she said, "Don't fall out of your kayak. It's not what you think. Well, it might be, I don't know, after what happened."

"Did she say who she suspected?"

"Do I know you?"

"Don't be like that."

"Okay, I won't. Uncle Warren asked. He's like, 'It's my damn weathervane, Audrey, tell me who I should look out for.' But she refused. She said it's only a suspicion and she didn't want to unfairly accuse someone."

"What made her suspect?"

"One of her favorite things was to go around the state taking pictures of antique weathervanes. Somewhere, I think Brattleboro, she saw this person doing exactly what you were doing— staking out a barn with a weathervane. She said he looked like he was studying it for the best way to climb up."

"That's not much." He pictured Cass outside the Morrisville house, ringing the doorbell, banging on the knocker, stepping back, looking up at the hummingbird weathervane.

"That's why she wouldn't say anything 'til she had proof. She was always checking local police reports. Uncle Warren got a kick out of it. Every time he saw her, he'd say, 'Did my daily weathervane inspection this morning, Audrey.'"

"He never told the police?"

"Sure he did, after she was murdered. But then it looked like Andrew did it. What's your name, anyway?"

"Hank Carruthers. Don't worry, I'm not a reporter. I'm a visitor. I'm staying at the Morning Loon. What's your name?"

"Kerry. We eat there all the time. Probably will tonight, I'm sure. I'm going back up now. Have fun in Greensboro and all that."

"Bye."

The visit to the police station would have to wait. He paddled toward the public boat launch. He could use a good, hard, thought-emptying sprint. A kayak was speeding toward him from behind. The paddler adjusted his line so he was now directly parallel to Jackson, thirty feet to his right. He had gray cropped hair and huge, tanned shoulders. Early fifties, judging by the way his skin sagged off the hard muscles. The kind of early fifties that liked nothing better than to humiliate someone twenty years his junior in a physical challenge. He was paddling fiercely, lunging forward with his shoulders as if he were trying to dig a hole in the water. He wanted to race.

If Jackson maintained his pace, it didn't look like the guy could narrow the gap. No point humiliating him. On the other hand, fuck that. Jackson shifted into his fastest gear. The splashing behind him vanished. By the time he finished his sprint to the public boat launch, the guy was barely visible, but it looked like he was holding his hand in the air in a "fuck you" configuration.

Tuesday, 4:32 p.m.

VegasVegas wasn't the fulfillment of a dream. Jackson never stood up in Mrs. Galford's third grade class after Eric who wanted to be a fireman and Sandra who wanted to be a nurse, and said, "I want to own an offshore casino in Costa Rica that showed the fastest growth in July according to a recent survey by gambling411.com."

People liked gambling metaphors. Jackson's own unscientific view was they came in second only to war. "He's holding all the aces." "You've got to play the cards you were dealt." "All the chips are on the table." If he were to add one to the list, it would be, "You do what you do in life for the same reason you bet on black instead of red." Because you had to take some action, even if there was no good reason and you'd probably end up cursing yourself for it later.

He'd been visiting his parents after graduating from college when he heard his mother's friend say, "I'm sure Jackson's happily ensconced in a job by now."

Before that, he didn't know what he wanted. Afterward he did. He wanted to do everything in his power to avoid being happily ensconced.

He traveled around the fringes of the world. As long as he steered clear of industrialized Western democracies, he didn't care where he went.

He arrived in Gaborone, Botswana, on a Sunday when the banks were closed and the only place to change dollars into pulas

was the Boa casino. He ended up getting a job dealing blackjack. After moving from country to country, casino to casino,
he spent six years at different Internet marketing firms in L.A.,
losing one job only to get a better one, self-destructing his way
upwards, before he joined Kenny and a techie named Bo and
opened VegasVegas.

Because banks were closed in Gaborone that Sunday, he was
now sitting in an elm-shaded Adirondack chair outside a rural
Vermont cottage reading a *Burlington Free Press* feature about
weathervane theft:

Benny Fielding's prized rooster Sid never
woke him at dawn, but he'd always tell Benny
which way the wind was blowing. Sid was the
name Benny gave the copper and zinc rooster
weathervane perched on top of his farmhouse
in Glover.

Last week, Benny noticed a strong wind
spinning his weathervane in circles. Thinking it might have become dislodged from the
cupola, he climbed onto the roof to investigate. It turned out it wasn't his weathervane
at all. A thief had removed it and replaced
it with a realistic-looking replica.

"It had me fooled, completely," Benny said.
"It looked identical to Sid. I never would
have checked if I didn't see it spinning out
of control that morning. I don't know how
long it was up there."

Sid is one of the growing numbers of
antique weathervanes stolen from buildings
throughout the state. They've become highly
sought-after pieces of American folk art,
commonly selling for $10,000 and up. A loco-
motive weathervane that sat atop the Woon-
socket, R.I. train station sold at a recent
auction for $1.2 million.

How thieves manage to remove the weathervanes without being seen is a mystery. Some
speculate they pose as roofers or utility
crews while the owners are away.

> Benny still can't figure out how they got
> Sid. He hasn't had any work done to the farm-
> house in years and he and his wife rarely
> leave for longer than a few hours at a time.
> All Benny knows for certain is he'll take
> Sid back, no questions asked.
>
> The police, however, have plenty of ques-
> tions. "Sid is one of the reported cases,"
> said Sergeant Jake Fears, a spokesman for the
> Vermont State police. "The question is how
> many of these thefts haven't been reported
> because the owners aren't aware of it."

Uncle Warren told the police about Audrey's suspicions. Maybe they followed up, maybe they didn't. Audrey didn't see someone removing Sid from his cupola or hear him squawking for Benny to come rescue him. She saw a guy from Greensboro looking at a barn in Brattleboro and from that she concluded he was part of a ring of thieves.

Jackson saw Cass looking up at a window below a weather-vane in Morrisville and decided Cass was the person Audrey saw so he and/or the bettor killed Audrey, framed Andrew, created the video alibi, bet on "dropped charges," and delivered the alibi to Andrew's lawyer.

Jackson decided all this less than five minutes after his eureka moment about Andrew paying the killer with odds instead of cash.

Nothing against the *Burlington Free Press*, but Jackson knew where to go for more detailed information about weathervane theft. Before he started VegasVegas, when he lived in L.A., he hung out with a guy named Alton Grimes. Like a lot of Ange-lenos, Alton went antiquing on weekends, but his version didn't involve visiting estate sales or thrift shops. It involved disabling alarms and avoiding police. Alton must have considered Jackson the live-and-let-live type because he told him all about it.

Alton answered on the first ring, like he always did. "Mr. Jackson Oliver." His voice was the audio version of a slap on the back. "If you're in town, cancel your plans, you're coming out with me tonight."

"Fortunately for my liver, head, and conscience, I'm on the other side of the country."

"About time they extradited your ass."

"You joke, but the Justice Department indicted the owner of MakeYourBet."

"You need to find a more respectable business, like mine."

"Reason I'm calling, I need a lesson on antique weathervanes. Is your phone…?"

"It's fine and I'm just a curious guy with a lot of knowledge about a lot of subjects."

"A renaissance man."

"So you heard about my recently acquired French Renaissance oak carved bookcase?"

They spent time catching up before Alton gave Jackson a quick tutorial on the world of antiques.

"Stealing's easy. Moving it's the hard part. Think of it as laundering the antique. The thief moves it to a fence who moves it to a dealer. One dealer sells it to another who sells it to another until nobody knows where it came from. Every sale, the value goes up. It keeps moving in circles until eventually it gets filtered into legitimate art markets—auctions, art fairs, gallery sales.

"Take a hypothetical slag glass Tiffany Riviere Handel table lamp, hypothetically removed from a home in Beverly Hills by a guy you may or may not know. In a few months, the lamp passed through five buyers, crossed three borders, and almost quadrupled in value. Every time it moved, it got more expensive and cleaner. It works the same way with weathervanes."

"You said 'moves from dealer to dealer.' Don't they suspect it's stolen?"

"Dude, all that time we hung out, I could have sworn you resided in the real world. Do they know in the sense of watching the weathervane get unscrewed from the cupola? No. They know by the price they're getting, the seller they're dealing with. It's like a drug transaction. The seller is a middleman and so is the buyer. Mind you, most dealers won't touch something high profile or listed on the art loss register. They need to be able to claim ignorance. 'Yeah, sure I got a good price, but that's because the seller didn't know what he had.' That kind of thing.

"Most dealers have a front room for the public and a back room for more trusted clients. I'm not saying honest antique dealers don't exist. They do. Just like cops who want to protect and serve, and strippers paying their way through college."

"If a weathervane's stolen in Vermont and ends up in an antique store in Beverly Hills, can't the police trace records back from seller to seller?"

"Records? Art's one of the biggest unregulated markets in the world. When a piece of art's bought or sold, you got the movement of the physical object from one place to another. You got the transfer of money from one account to another. But nothing linking the two. Art galleries and dealers don't ask for information because customers want to stay anonymous.

"Think about most valuable properties. You can trace them with a serial number. You can't put a serial number on a work of art. That's what makes it different from other property theft. No paper trail, business on a handshake. It's just like drugs, only more genteel. Instead of hanging drug mules from an overpass in Tijuana, the antique dealer coos over the amber-tinted milk-glass shade."

"How much of it eventually gets recovered?"

"Ten percent at best. And the rare time someone gets arrested, it's a slap on the wrist. Judges never give harsh sentences to art thieves. 'I can't put Thomas Crowne in jail.'"

Alton said his friend, Henry (code for himself), didn't have any personal experience with weathervanes. Falling off a barn and getting impaled by an arrow with a brass pig on top wasn't high on his list of acceptable ways to leave the world.

"But I can you tell you how they work. It's like anything. The ones who rise to the top are the ones who take their craft seriously. They practice climbing different kinds of buildings, removing weathervanes from cupolas, attaching replicas. If they steal at night, they practice at night. They don't leave anything to chance. They study the behavior and learn the schedules of everyone in the house. They familiarize themselves with traffic patterns at different times. They have plans and back-up plans. They do trial runs.

"Maybe they do it quick as possible at night. Or, if they know the house is unoccupied, and it's an out-of-the-way area, maybe they disguise themselves as painters or roofers and do it at their leisure in the middle of the day. They have enough people to complete the job and not one more, and they each have the appropriate skill set."

"Like an artist to make a replica?"

"That person doesn't have to be a good artist in the original-ity sense, but he has to have the skill to imitate all the details. Remember, these weathervanes can be a couple hundred years old and they don't spend that time in bubble wrap. They got dents from hailstorms. Bent tails from heavy winds. Maybe some yahoo drove by and used the weathervane for target practice. Then there's the discoloration from all those years of weather. The artist has to match all that."

Maybe this long talk made Alton's fingers itchy. He said he had to go. "Let me know if you need more background, and you better get your ass out to L.A. soon."

A squirrel ran up to a patch of dirt and started digging, consumed by the urgency of its mission. Unseen birds sang overhead. Late-afternoon sun lit up a swirl of insects above the grass. On the edge of the neighboring farm, Sisyphus the dog was running alongside a blue pickup truck.

Were Cass and the bettor from the library the thieves Audrey suspected?

After Betty the librarian had given Jackson her list of people on the computers, she slipped into gossip mode. For someone so quick to jump to the defense of local integrity when Jackson questioned the wording of the lost money clip sign, she put plenty of healthy spite into her gossip.

Blake and Tara Trotman had moved to Greensboro from Detroit around five years ago and bought a farm, where they raised buffalo.

"The beefalo on the Morning Loon menu comes from the farm. Some people say they like it, but to me it's like chewing on a dishrag. Tara was considered pretty by some people in some lighting, but she wasn't cut out for small town life, so she left Blake and moved back to Detroit. Now it's just him and the buffalo. You can ask him about the money clip in person since he makes deliveries to the Morning Loon every day."

Wally Caiden had the distinction of being the worst carpenter in Orleans County.

"Jan Lemmon made the mistake of hiring him to build a porch. It came out crooked, just like we all told her it would. She can't even serve guests a full glass of wine without worrying it'll tip over and spill. She hired someone else to install her new septic tank, and Wally stopped talking to her, which is a shame since they've known each other over twenty years."

Cass Gallaway had a tough life. His brother and mom were killed by a drunk driver. His father died of a heart attack on the job. Cass was extremely close to his father. Afterwards, he held himself responsible. Unlike Blake's wife running off and Jan's crooked porch, Cass' setbacks seemed to sadden Betty.

"He thought if he did more to bring in money, his father wouldn't have had to work two jobs. Cass does odd jobs, but unemployment's high around here. Once one of the summer lake people accused him of stealing a necklace, but we all jumped to his defense and the lake person let it drop. Best thing for everybody."

Jackson's search of "Cass Gallaway, Greensboro, antique weathervane" brought up nothing more than a page of name and address listings.

When Jackson replaced "Cass" with "Blake Trotman," he got the same useless information sites along with a Memorial Day photo Blake submitted to a contest on CaptureMyVermont. com. The caption said, "Blake Trotman and Virgil enjoy the Spring weather." Blake grinned like a dufus as he stood beside a majestic, not-long-for-this-world buffalo.

Google had nothing to say about Wally Caiden.

Tuesday, 5:02 p.m.

Tracy was alone at the front desk, writing in a cloth-bound journal.

"Where can a guy get a drink before dinner?" Jackson said.

"Be right with you. Just writing what a loser I am."

"That's ridiculous."

"Of course you say that. You got a bargain on account of me being a loser. You've done this kind of thing a million times. It's all new to me. And I got fleeced."

"The cottage?"

"Right after you checked in, someone offered three times more than you and I had to say no. Like I say, loser."

She punctuated that with two big green exclamation marks on the journal page.

"You got me to double my offer."

"Nickel to a dime."

"Who offered three times more?"

"A TV reporter."

"Which one?"

"Doesn't matter. It's too late. I'm such a loser."

"I think you're making it up," he said.

Her mouth fell open. "I am not."

"Exaggerating."

"Only because I knew you'd think that so I couldn't say the real amount or you'd assume it was less."

"How much did the TV reporter offer?"

"Two hundred more than you. And that's the truth."

He pulled out his loose wad of cash. "I'll give you two hundred more."

"Where's your money clip?"

"Don't ask."

She stuffed the money in her purse. "This is cool of you. I wasn't expecting this."

"No?"

"I hoped. I didn't expect…Enjoy your drive, Mr. and Mrs. Tompkins," she called out to the arm-in-arm couple passing through the lobby.

"Thanks, Tracy, we will. And thanks for the recommendation."

"Any time."

Tracy turned back to Jackson. "What'd you do today?"

"Kayak ride. I talked to Kerry. Warren Gunderson's niece."

Tracy laughed. "Tina and I were just talking about Warren's feud with this other guy on the lake, Burt Tager."

"Tell me."

"It's boring if you don't know Burt."

"Tell me anyway."

"Burt's not one of the rich lake people. He lives here year-round. He's got a chipmunk on his property he calls Ike, he feeds him peanuts. Ike follows him around everywhere. He's an amateur pilot."

"Ike?"

"Don't be an ass."

"Okay."

"He keeps his plane at the Rutland airport and sometimes flies it to stunt competitions. Fact he's at one right now. Burt and Warren used to be friends until last summer when Warren had a big party in his backyard, all these people up from New York, and Burt, he gets mad he wasn't invited so he dive-bombs the party in his plane. Warren's guests freak out. One of them faints.

"Then Burt leaves town for a couple weeks for one of his competitions and when he gets back, he goes storming over here to where Warren's having dinner and says, 'If you want revenge, get it like a man. Don't play mind games like a woman.'

"He accuses Warren of sneaking into his shed, taking his blue tarp, replacing it with a green one. Putting different handle bar grips on his bike. Taking the glass jars where he keeps his screws and washers and switching them. And some other weird things I can't remember. Warren totally denies it. Burt calls him a liar. Warren calls him a nutcase and says if he ever dive-bombs his house again, he'll press charges. They haven't spoken since… You're bored."

"Not bored. Thirsty."

"I've got a flask in my purse, but I doubt you like peach schnapps." She reached into her purse and brought out a deck of cards. "You know anything about gambling?"

Jackson looked but couldn't find any trickery in her wide-open eyes. If she knew who he was, she wouldn't hunt up a deck of cards as a prop for her veiled accusation. It had to be his bribe and question about drinks. She simply added one vice to make it a trifecta and assumed he gambled, too.

"I'm teaching myself to count cards so I can move to Vegas. Mom's trying to talk me out of it. She says Vegas is for lost souls."

"Maybe they make better company."

"Don't think I'll use that argument on Mom."

"Sorry, I don't know anything about gambling."

"I heard somewhere if you have an ace, seven and the dealer has a six you should double down. But that doesn't make sense. The only way you can improve a soft eighteen is with an ace, two, or three. A ten keeps your hand the same but takes away a dealer's bust card. Everything else makes the hand worse. So why would you double down?"

If he were Jackson instead of Hank, he would have explained it was true you'd make your hand worse almost fifty percent of the time, so you'd win fewer hands. But by doubling the amount of money in play on your soft eighteen, you'd end up winning about ten percent more in the long run.

But Hank didn't know this. And why did she keep pressing after he told her he knew nothing about gambling?

"All I know about black jack is they serve free drinks."

"Go to the porch. They'll take your order." She shuffled the cards.

〉〉〉

On the way past the dining room, Jackson checked a menu to make sure they had something vegan. The eggplant medallions looked good. He looked forward to a meal without Kenny saying, "You don't eat meat or dairy because you don't want animals to suffer, yet you have no problem taking money from people who can't afford to lose it? You're making up for your sins against one species by being extra kind to another."

He found a small table beside a fern in a terra cotta pot. To his right, a couple in matching purple fleece jackets sat side by side in silence, entranced by the warm, fragrant air, or using it to distract themselves from the realization that, shorn of their daily routine, they had nothing to talk about. Next to them, three middle-aged couples clustered around two tables. Two men in their sixties sat with their double scotches to Jackson's left. One was tanned and didn't wear a tie, the other wore a tie and didn't have a tan.

A waitress with an elfin smile brought him a drink menu and he ordered a glass of the Whimsey Meadow Rose, from a vineyard in Shelburne. Tan no Tie had a loud, whiskey-fueled voice he was using to explain something to Tie no Tan.

"...gained three percent market share last two months."

"Isn't that a lot?

"It's unheard of."

"Who's the big loser?"

"Bounty a little. Brawny really took it on the chin."

Tan no Tie used the Socratic method to explain the increased market share.

"Think of paper towels you've used. Are the sheets the same size?"

"Yes."

"Have all your spills been the same size?"

"No."

"Is that the most efficient use of towel?"

"No, if I spill a splash of drink, I need less than if I spill a whole glass."

"Damn right. So let people select a towel size appropriate for the size of their spill."

How was this possible? Front page murder trial taking place in your tiny town ends with a thunderbolt alibi video, and you're talking about the market share of a paper towel?

The waitress brought Jackson's wine. Maybe other people were discussing the trial. He carried his glass to the front of the porch and leaned against the railing, looking out at the pines ringing the lake.

"We had Barton Jiles over," a female voice was saying.

"What was his topic of the day?"

"He said the police set a roadblock in Hardwick to catch people not wearing seatbelts. He claims he told Officer Helton he'll go to jail before he lets the government make him wear a seatbelt."

"But Barton's always telling Fred seatbelts are the most significant safety device ever invented."

"He's told us too. But now that the government's forcing him, he says he'll never wear a seatbelt again."

"What a character."

"Why are you grinning, Jan?"

"So Officer Helton's back to manning seatbelt roadblocks? A big comedown for the man who found the bloody clothes in the lake."

"I'm sure he doesn't think of it that way."

"He did so well on the stand. People probably expected some small town deputy who had to check his blade of grass at the door."

There was a snort followed by a no-nonsense male voice. "Yeah, the police did a stellar job."

"We all thought the same thing they did."

"We thought that based on information they gathered."

"How do you expect them to know about that crazy video?"

"If Andrew didn't kill her someone else did. And that someone else wasn't a ghost. He left evidence. But the police didn't find it because they had it all wrapped up from the start."

"You think Andrew hired someone?"

"What else is there to think?"

"What about the video?"

"What about it?"

"A motel room. In his underwear. What if someone drugged him to make a blackmail video? Then Audrey's murdered and the video's useless to the blackmailer."

"Meanwhile, someone else chose the exact same night to frame him for murder? And a year later, the blackmailer, out of the goodness of her heart, decides to free Andrew?"

A family of four on bikes wobbled up the hill past the parking area. They took off their helmets, emptied their water bottles on the dirt, wheeled the bikes into the shed.

Jackson went back to his table. Tie no Tan and Tan no Tie were still at it.

"All you did was add irregularly spaced perforations?"

"The simplest ideas are the best."

Jackson didn't tune out. They'd won him over. He wondered what role Tan no Tie played in the development of these customized paper towels. He talked about them with such obvious pride. Did his company invent them? Or did he merely work for the ad agency that marketed them?

"Can't the other paper towels copy it? You can't patent something like that."

"They have copied. But we got there first. Savvy shoppers know the others are Johnnys-come-lately."

"It seems like a no-brainer. Why did it take so long?"

"Until you've worked for a packaged goods company, you don't understand inertia."

Down in the parking area, a silver-haired guy in a sport jacket was helping his wife out of a Lincoln Continental. If Kenny offered +150 odds the guy was a retired history department chairman from a leafy Massachusetts college, Jackson would put down a hundred dollars.

A green Cherokee pulled in near the Continental and two more people got out. Kerry and the kayak racer—Uncle Warren Gunderson.

They came out through the dining room and stopped beside the two tables where Jackson had done his eavesdropping. Uncle Warren shook hands with the two men while the two women made light chitchat with Kerry, who now waved at Jackson. Uncle Warren led her to the table recently vacated by the purple-fleeced couple.

The elfin waitress took their order and left. Uncle Warren said something that made Kerry laugh. She whacked him on the shoulder and laughed louder.

Now the waitress was coming to Jackson's table with a glass of wine on her tray. "Compliments of the gentleman whose bleep you kicked kayaking."

"Thank you. His word?"

"Mine. That's Warren," she said in explanation.

Jackson raised his glass, and Kerry gave him a come-over wave. So he did.

As Uncle Warren shook Jackson's hand, his shifting bicep wreaked havoc on the sleeve of his polo shirt. "Warren Gunderson."

"Hank Carruthers."

Kerry wore a Michigan sweatshirt two sizes too big. "You here by yourself?"

"Yeah."

"No one to travel with?"

Uncle Warren gave her a look. "That's rude."

"Says the guy who flipped him the bird because he beat you in a kayak race."

"He didn't see."

Jackson grinned. "I did."

Uncle Warren took a big sip of something golden surrounded by ice. "How old are you, Hank?"

"Thirty-three."

"If I were thirty-three, or you were fifty-eight, I would have kicked your butt. It wouldn't be close."

"I disagree."

Kerry slapped her hand on the table. "God, why can't you give him that?"

"Because I don't think it's true."

Uncle Warren nodded and said to Kerry, "You wouldn't understand." And to Jackson, "You think I wouldn't kick your butt or I wouldn't win at all?"

"I can't project how I'll be at your age. I'm imaging you at mine and I can't see it."

Uncle Warren took another gulp of his drink as if to say, I bet you couldn't take one this big. "Guess we'll never know."

Kerry pulled her knees up to her chest. "Thank you."

"Thanks for the wine," Jackson said.

"My pleasure. If that's what you drink. I understand my niece accused you of planning to steal my weathervane."

Kerry blew a lock of hair from her eye. "I mean, this gaudy house and he asks about the leaping deer."

"Not so gaudy you turned down the invitation to visit," Uncle Warren said.

"Beggars can't be choosers."

"You promised you wouldn't to grow up to be a snob."

"I lied."

"It's okay. Lying has its place. Done judiciously. Doesn't it, Hank?"

General observation known by all men of the world or pointed comment directed at Jackson? Uncle Warren was appraising him, this time not to project future kayaking capabilities. Tourists didn't come to a place like this alone. He probably concluded press. But he'd seen plenty of them and maybe Jackson didn't fit the mold.

"I've got five different lies going as we speak," Jackson said.

"Can't keep as many straight as I can." But Uncle Warren was smiling, poking fun at himself. "What brings you to Greensboro?"

Kerry gave an exaggerated yawn. "Like it's not obvious."

Jackson and Uncle Warren both looked at her.

"I mean, you're not a total loser, you could find someone to bring. You're not a weathervane thief. You ask lots of questions about things that aren't your business." She paused to let the drama build. "You're a private investigator. Andrew doesn't trust the police to find the truth. So he hired you."

"Is she right?" Uncle Warren said.

"That would be lie number six. One too many for me."

"Press?"

"I told Tracy at the desk I'm a photographer. I'm not. I have an interest in what happened but I can't say what. I'm surprising myself by telling you."

Uncle Warren took a sip of his drink and nodded. "No more prying from me."

"Doesn't mean I can't," Kerry said.

Uncle Warren said to Kerry, "It was a good guess. Andrew probably will hire a private investigator. Make people think he's looking for the real killer."

Kerry threw her head back. "Here we go."

"He talked to you about movies, so he can do no wrong."

"I liked Audrey more than him and you know it."

"Why are you convinced he didn't hire a killer?" Jackson said to Kerry.

"Because why would he? I know they were married and you're supposed to get bored after you're married, but he was into her. And she was into him."

Jackson turned to Warren. "A lot of money in antique weathervanes. If there was a way of accounting for that video, would you think the person Audrey saw killed her?"

"No, I wouldn't."

"You reported her suspicions to the police."

"It was my obligation so I reported it, even though I knew it had nothing to do with anything."

He held his hand up to fend off Kerry's interruption. "Suppose it wasn't just Audrey being Audrey, creating drama where there wasn't any. Suppose this guy really was planning to steal the Brattleboro weathervane. She sees him, he sees her, maybe even thinks she got his picture. Then he hears she's telling people someone in Greensboro's stealing weathervanes. Is he going to think she's saying, 'I won't reveal his name because I don't want to slander him?' No, he'll assume she told her friends who she saw, maybe told the police. The last thing he'd do is kill her and make himself a suspect."

Kerry jumped in. "Maybe he didn't see her. Besides, it's not like she was blabbing it all over town. She told you because you own a valuable weathervane."

"She told Rex."

"Of course. He's the antiques guru."

Uncle Warren explained to Jackson, "Rex Finch owns an antiques store in Craftsbury. Get the two of them talking weather-vane thefts, you'd think it's the greatest evil Satan ever dreamed up."

Then to Kerry, "What's your point?"

"The guy never heard her suspicions."

"Then he had no reason to kill her, did he? A good logic class when you get to college and you'll be fine."

"She didn't say his name because she wanted to make sure she was right first. You think all she did was check police reports? She was a woman on a mission. What did she tell you that one time? *I'm going to catch him in the act.* You thought she was just talking but I didn't."

"What did Audrey say when you asked who she saw?" Jackson said.

"She said, 'It'll surprise you. It's someone local.' I asked who but she refused to say."

Jackson said to Kerry, "You think he saw her following him?"

"And knew why. So he killed her."

"You say they had the perfect marriage," Uncle Warren said. "People with perfect marriages share things."

He leaned back in his chair and looked out over the balcony toward the lake.

"You're innocent, you were framed, and your wife told you something that might have led to her murder. Wouldn't you tell the police? Even if you didn't take her seriously, wouldn't you grasp for any possible explanation? Wouldn't your lawyer get the media talking about stolen weathervanes?"

Maybe Uncle Warren's reflective tone threw Kerry for a loop because she didn't interrupt.

"Andrew didn't say anything because he didn't want them to have other leads. He was framing himself, he had that alibi ready. I'm sure it offended his sensitive artistic soul sitting in jail all that time, but it was worth it. He's out. Home free. Too late for them to track down the one he hired. But he doesn't want people like me saying he hired someone, so now's the time for the weathervane story to come out. I can tell you this: If the police ask, he'll deny Audrey told him about the person she saw. He has to, otherwise why didn't he tell the police when they arrested him?"

"Everything doesn't make it into the news," Jackson said. "He might have told them. Maybe his lawyer wanted to make a big splash by saving it for the trial."

Uncle Warren's need to crush all rivals in whatever form the competition took had a color, purplish blue, and it was creeping up his cheeks and settling under his eyes.

"Point well taken, Hank, and now I have a question for you. You said if there's a way we can account for that video. Okay, account for it."

"They made it 'cuz they're morons," Kerry said, "A lot of people are, you know."

"Now you're being silly."

"Enough, okay, this whole subject is bumming me out and I'm hungry."

The black F-150 roared into the parking area. Blake got out and lifted a hand truck from the bed. He stacked two white coolers on it, securing them with bungee cords.

"Buffalo meat's here," Jackson said.

Kerry, who had her back to the lot, turned for a look. "You know that freak?"

"Met him at the library."

"Kerry's not a fan," Warren said.

"Are you?"

"That's not a fair comparison. I don't like most people."

"Why don't you like him?" Jackson asked Kerry.

"I told you. He's a freak."

"Concrete support for your arguments or you'll never get into law school," Uncle Warren said.

"I assert Blake is a freak. In support of my assertion, I call your attention to the fact that that freak names his buffalo. Brutus. Cyrano. Matisse. It's probably them in his coolers. He says naming them gives them a sense of dignity. He acts like they're his cherished pets, then the next day he slaughters them."

"You eat meat."

"I don't go cuddling the steer in the field before I eat it. Blake's always preaching how he's certified by some humane farming organization. Sorry, but I don't want your Brutus Burgers. And shave your head already. You look like a Brillo pad."

Blake was wheeling the coolers up the dirt pathway to the side entrance.

Uncle Warren stood. "Let's eat."

"I recommend the eggplant," Jackson lied. Well, maybe only half lied, since he had no doubt he'd recommend it if he had the chance to eat it. But he wanted to prevent the chain reaction of them feeling compelled to invite him out of sympathy for the solitary traveler, him feeling compelled to accept to avoid offending them, and Blake coming out to the porch just as he was going into the dining room.

Uncle Warren offered his hand again. He squeezed with enough pressure to make sure Jackson could never hold another kayak paddle.

"Hank, you surprised the shit out of me. I saw all that long hair and expected some whiney punk who couldn't reach the shore. But you kicked my butt fair and square."

"By a lot."

"I'm a hundred percent certain we'd have the opposite result if I were your age or you were mine. But one of the many unfortunate things about this world is we'll never know."

"Enjoy your dinner."

"If you're down at the lake, stop by any time."

"I will."

"Bye," Kerry said.

An iPhone search of "Rex Finch antiques Craftsbury" brought up the Craftsbury Antique Center. The website said summer hours, eleven to seven. If Jackson left now, he could get there in a few minutes. He wanted to talk to Rex but he wanted to talk to Blake more. But what if Blake had another delivery to make and Jackson didn't get a chance to talk to either of them? Times like this, free will sucked. He carried his wine to the far side of the porch so he could intercept Blake on his way back to his truck.

After five minutes passed, a door closed and Blake pushed his hand truck over the dirt. He stopped beside the bike shed, grabbed the top cooler, and threw it like a basketball chest pass against the wall, hissing, "Why are you even alive? You bring the wrong fucking cooler. You had them labeled and still you bring the wrong fucking cooler. Why are you even alive?"

He picked up the cooler by one handle and whipped it against the wall. Jackson moved back to the center of the porch so Blake wouldn't know he'd witnessed the scene. Blake was apparently berating himself for bringing the wrong cooler of buffalo meat. But how hard would it be to drive back to his farm and get the right one? This was not a stable individual. Jackson watched Blake place the two coolers and hand truck in the back of his F-150 and drive away.

Tuesday, 6:10 p.m.

The downtown Craftsbury shopping district was bigger than Greensboro's, which meant three shops instead of two. One was the Craftsbury Antique Center. Little bells tinkled as Jackson pushed open the glass door. The dark, woody air felt like it was discovered locked away in some great grandmother's attic and brought here alongside the furniture and tea settings and vases and gramophones. The store was a two-hundred-year-old couple's dream home, filled with everything they needed to live the good life. For her, a walnut china cabinet, yellow perfume bottle with a silver sprayer, and glass vanity table jars with gold tone lids. For him, vintage pocket watches, rooster bottle decanters, a brass deer lock.

Chandeliers hung from log ceiling beams, but Rex Finch was obviously no stickler for verisimilitude because so did wagon wheels and a fireplace bellows. Jackson made his way through an obstacle course of tables and shelves loaded down with antiques. A guy with a horseshoe of red hair and a sunny yellow big collar shirt was moving an oak wall telephone from one table to another. Like his antiques, he was of indeterminate age. He could be forty, sixty, or anywhere in between. He took a light blue handkerchief from his pocket and wiped down the telephone receiver.

"Which button downloads the apps?" Jackson said.

The guy looked him over with the most wide-open eyes Jackson had ever seen.

"Are you Rex Finch?"

"I am."

"I'm Hank Carruthers, from L.A. I was a friend of Audrey Marvel."

Rex rubbed his hand on his handkerchief and offered it to Jackson. "I'm sorry. I was her friend, too. Maybe you know that."

"Yes," Jackson said.

"You came for the trial?"

"To watch the media treat it like a sporting event? No thanks."

Rex nodded and shook his head at the same time, moving it in a counterclockwise circle. "One big reality TV show."

"I came after they dropped the charges. Because of something Audrey told me."

Rex jerked open his mouth like he was about to sneeze but he didn't, so Jackson continued. "Last summer, a week or so before she was murdered, we were on the phone and she said she thought someone in Greensboro was stealing antique weathervanes. Not from a store like this. They were climbing up barns and removing them from the roof. She said she saw someone staking out a weathervane, I can't recall the name of the town."

"Brattleboro."

"She told you, too?"

"I'm the one who got her interested in antique weathervanes."

"Did you take her seriously?"

"Very."

"I wish I had. I said, 'Yeah, yeah,' and moved on to something else. Then she was murdered and everything in the news about Andrew's clothes with her blood, well, weathervanes were the furthest thing from my mind."

"A terrible time," Rex said.

"Did she tell you who she saw?"

Instead of the headshake Jackson expected, Rex said, "She might have."

"Might have?"

"I don't remember."

"But if he knew she saw him…"

"If he stole that weathervane, the owner could get a replacement for six dollars on eBay."

"Not an antique?"

"A piece of junk. It's a free country. If people want to proclaim to the world they have no taste, that's their God-given right." Rex opened his mouth and sucked in a mouthful of air but again aborted the sneeze. He adjusted the position of the oak phone and took a step back to assess it.

"You know that how, by her description?"

"Antique theft isn't something the police take seriously. Those of us in the business do what we can. Audrey gave me the address and a few days later, I stopped to have a look. A piece of junk. When I walked up to the house, I almost tripped over a group of lawn gnomes playing poker. That's the kind of artistic standards the owners have."

"Did you tell Audrey?"

"Of course. We had a good laugh. It was the last time I saw her before…"

"No chance you got the wrong house?"

"She told me the address and I wrote it down. The weathervane was a rooster, just as she said."

"The guy was looking up from the ground. Maybe he couldn't see it clearly enough to know it was piece of junk."

"These people aren't fools. I wish they were but they're not. They know where the valuable ones are located."

"One of the people on the lake, Warren Gunderson…"

"Now that one's a prize."

Jackson couldn't tell if Rex was referring to Warren or his leaping deer. "Audrey warned him someone local was stealing weathervanes. After she was murdered, he reported it to the police."

"They spoke to me as well. I told them it was a piece of junk. They also spoke to the owners, who told them nobody stole their weathervane. Unfortunate for them, since the replica would have been vastly superior."

Alton's voice, which would be slurred with rum and cokes by now, reminded Jackson, "I'm not saying honest antique dealers don't exist. They do. Just like cops who want to protect and serve and strippers paying their way through college."

Time to set a small trap. "Thanks for the information. I wanted to compare notes before I went to the police."

The wide-open eyes opened wider. "Compare notes?"

"The person Audrey saw, she told me his name. I wanted to make sure it was the same person."

But Rex didn't seem alarmed, or even interested. He went back to shifting the position of the oak phone.

"Yes, I understand. Your friend, our friend, was murdered and you want to do something useful. I feel the same way."

"I know it was a piece of junk, but if you could remember his name."

"But I can't. If she even told me. As I said, I'm not sure she did."

"Well, thanks again. If you want to find out how it goes with the police, you can call me. I'm staying at the Morning Loon."

Rex sucked in two mouthfuls of air. "Goodbye, Mr. Carruthers."

Tuesday, 6:45 p.m.

The white lace curtains were tied open with sashes. Diners floated in warm candlelight. Each table had a glass vase with four yellow lilies. Casual elegance, the brochure said about the dining experience at the Morning Loon. There was a little more casual than elegance in the knife tear on the crocheted lace tablecloth and the smear of butter on Jackson's mahogany tall-backed chair, but it was too nice a night to quibble.

Uncle Warren and Kerry were gone. Tie no Tan was finishing up his dinner while Tan no Tie eyed the pitchers of water on a tray outside the kitchen, no doubt calculating the optimum paper towel size for an overflowing glass. The Jenkses were sitting at the table in the far corner. Tracy's fake compliment hit its mark, because Mrs. Jenks was still wearing the green scarf. Mr. Jenks wore a blue sport coat over unwrinkled tan slacks. He was closely shaven and his full head of black hair was parted at the side. All this should have come with a steely hard gaze. But failure or dissipation had softened the face and unfocused the eyes.

Eating alone had its advantages. You could think in peace. It also had its disadvantages. Your thoughts might bore you. Or confuse you.

Were weathervanes still in play as a motive? Rex claimed thieves would know where to locate the valuable ones, and Alton would surely agree. Cass, with his phantom shots and headstone monologues, didn't fit the profile of Alton's buttoned-down perfectionist. But maybe he had the job of driving around the state locating potential targets and his more knowledgeable partner would select the ones to go after later.

If weathervanes were out, Andrew Marvel moved back to the head of the line. Blake went from weathervane thief to hired killer. Or Wally or Cass. But they'd have a hard time dislodging Blake after that burst of fury Jackson witnessed.

How about the future wife of the investment banker? The stomach-revealing mesh shirt and rolled up cargo pants came straight out of the Gap's Other Woman collection. Kenny said Andrew was probably bitter that he hadn't done shit since *Shattered Worlds*. Maybe he found someone to nurse his wounded pride back to health. She could have driven him to the motel in Manchester and helped film the alibi.

But the DA's investigators spent over a year looking for motives. If she and Andrew had any relationship, they couldn't keep it hidden, could they?

After dinner, Jackson had a nightcap on the porch. He was watching mosquitoes dive into hot candle wax, trying to convince himself he was smarter than they were, when a candlelight shadow passed over his table and the future wife of the investment banker was standing beside him.

"You're a photographer."

Before he could settle on a reply, she said, "I'm a reporter. Trish Devereaux."

"Hank Carruthers."

"I said reporter. That would piss off the real ones. I have a crime blog."

She brought a chair from another table and placed it beside Jackson. "Us being colleagues and all."

Her green eyes were framed by dark crescents of sleeplessness. Her nose turned up slightly. The silver dancing figures on her earrings looked like shamans.

He guessed by the smile she was getting ready to debunk his photographer's credentials and he guessed right.

"Is your portfolio online?"

"I'm re-doing my site."

"You don't hang out with the other photographers."

"I work better alone."

"I'd love to see some of your work. How about sending me a pdf from your Hank Carruthers e-mail address?"

No point trying to protect Hank. If she was the one who logged onto Cass' account from the library, she had no reason to link him to VegasVegas. If she was only a crime blogger, she had more important concerns than figuring out the true identity of a lying fellow guest.

"You don't have to have to draw this out like a lawyer. A simple I think you're full of it will do the trick," he said.

"You didn't go the Joe Smith route. Easy to remember, but so ordinary it calls attention to itself. Sometimes people use family names. Others pick them at random."

"Hank Carruthers was a fourth grade gym teacher."

"Wouldn't you feel bad if he took the rap for you?"

"Can't. He passed away. Natural causes."

"Or made to look that way." She smiled but dropped it abruptly to make sure he hadn't mistaken it for the real thing.

"What's the name of your blog?" he said.

"*Improbable Cause.* Ever read it?"

"No."

"Five thousand page views per day."

"Don't have to convince me. I prefer blogs."

"Yeah? If some *Boston Globe* reporter asked why you're pretending to be a dead fourth grade gym teacher, you'd think, 'Why does this big shot reporter care about some small-time swindler lying about his name?' But I'm just a blogger. I've got nothing better to do."

Jackson almost laughed out his mouthful of wine.

"That's funny?"

"Sorry. I wasn't laughing at your blog. It was the part about me."

She leaned back, satisfied with his explanation. "Okay."

"It's also funny you called me a small-time swindler and I'm the one apologizing."

"Then I apologize too. A small-time swindler couldn't afford the bribes you paid. Don't get mad at Tracy. I tricked it out of her. 'Wow, who's the guy with the long hair?' That kind of thing."

He got sidetracked imagining what other than the hair "that kind of thing" included. He had a comment all lined up and ready to go about what a challenge it must have been for her to feign interest but he held back.

Tan no Tie and Tie no Tan came out of the dining room and walked down the entryway to the parking area.

"That tan guy thinks paper towels should be created with perforations that allow the user to pick the size appropriate to the size of the spill."

"That's not what he said last summer," she said.

"You were here last summer?"

"The tan one is Fred. He and Tim meet for drinks every Tuesday."

"What did he say last summer?"

"Something about consumers already having more freedom than they can handle so they want a paper towel that makes the cleaning decisions for them."

"Tim doesn't call him out for his inconsistency?"

"What's your real name?"

"Joe Smith."

"I could find out."

"Then my mission succeeded. Distract the *Improbable Cause* blogger so she doesn't get the scoop on who killed Audrey Marvel."

"Maybe I already know."

"Do you?"

She brushed a strand of hair from in front of her face. There was a rim of blue around her green eyes, eyes that were locked onto his. "Maybe."

She carried her chair back to its table. "Good night…" Her lips formed a circle like she was about to say a name. She held them a beat before pulling them up into a smile and walking away.

He mouthed the letter J and traced his finger along his lips. It felt roundish. Jackson. Joe Smith. He tried H as in Hank.

Also roundish, and so were the other five letters in the alphabet he tried. He made a much better small-time swindler than a private investigator.

He was the only one left on the porch, so he brought his half-glass of remaining wine to his cottage. The message light was blinking.

"Hank, Joe, whatever, it's Trish, turns out I'm not as tired as I thought, would you mind going back down to the kitchen and bringing up a bottle of wine and two glasses?"

That was the message that played in Jackson's imagination before he hit the play button and heard Rex say, "Hello, Mr. Carruthers, this is Rex Finch calling. If you get this message before ten, could you call me back please? Otherwise, you can call me in the morning, after nine."

He left a number, which Jackson dialed.

"Hello, Rex Finch speaking."

"Hi, it's…" He said those two words on the phone so often, always followed by Jackson, that he almost didn't catch him himself in time. "Hank."

"Hello, Mr. Carruthers. I'm sorry to disturb you but I didn't think you'd mind."

"Of course not. What's up?"

"I've been mulling over our conversation. I told you I'm certain the person Audrey saw in Brattleboro wasn't a thief. I wanted to make clear that doesn't mean I think she was wrong about the other one. Mind you, I'm not saying she's right. Just that I'm not certain she's wrong."

"I understand. Which other one?"

"She didn't mention?"

"No."

Ten seconds of slow breathing then, "I'm sorry, I'm having reservations about calling. I assumed she told you. I don't want to spread innuendo."

"I understand and it's not likely any of this is related to what happened. But if we want justice for Audrey…"

"You're right. Of course you are. Her name is Meredith Long. An artist. She has a small gallery in a converted barn on Country Club Road."

"Replicas?"

"Audrey thought so, yes."

"Why?"

"Meredith had a copper and lead horse weathervane on her barn, thirty-two inches tall, thirty-one inches wide. It would have sold for at least ninety-five hundred. One weekend when she was away, it was stolen. She never replaced it, but she didn't have the cupola removed, either. Audrey suspected her of removing it herself, keeping the empty cupola up to remind people she was a victim, so they wouldn't think of her as a thief."

"That's it?"

"There's also Meredith's skill with metal."

"Did Audrey ever see her with the person in Brattleboro?"

"No."

"You're sure?"

"She would have mentioned it. As I said, I was hesitant to call because I didn't want to spread innuendo. It also concerned me this would add credence to Audrey's suspicion of the Brattleboro person."

"Or it could have the opposite effect. I might start thinking weathervane thieves sprouted up in Audrey's mind everywhere, like bogeymen."

He hadn't spoken this way to Rex before. He was the earnestly dutiful friend. Keeping track of identities was hard enough without having to remember what type of personalities went along with them.

Rex noted the tone and chastised him. "Antique weathervanes were Audrey's passion. The thefts infuriated her."

"Just so we're clear. The person in Brattleboro, she saw him doing something that could reasonably be considered suspicious. But Meredith just happens to have a necessary skill."

"That's correct."

"You said you're not sure Audrey's right about Meredith, but you're not sure she's wrong. It can't be because she left the cupola on the barn and she's good with metal."

"No."

"Then why?"

"I think she has it in her. And that's all I want to say about this."

"Thanks for calling, Rex."

"I regret it. Goodbye."

"Bye."

Jackson got situated on the bed, wineglass on the end table, loon pillow behind his head, cow pillow on his lap, iPad on the cow pillow, and did a search on *Improbable Cause.* If it got as much traffic as Trish claimed, it would show up on the first page of results. Which it did.

Her most recent post was yesterday.

The Alibi in the Revere Motel.

The Revere Motel crouches low on Blodget Street in Manchester, New Hampshire. On the bow tie-shaped sign, "Revere" is spelled in red letters, "motel" in black. Fluorescent tubes twisted like animal balloons spell, "vacancy." A sign hanging from the bow tie promises "HBO" and "Guaranteed comfort."

The guaranteed comfort wouldn't matter to the person who filmed Andrew Marvel's alibi, but the HBO would, since the welcome screen contains a clock the viewer can't manipulate.

The motel is configured like an L, with two floors. On the longer row, the front rooms face the parking lot and the rear rooms face Lodge Street. The rear rooms along the base of the L overlook Oak Street. Room 208 is one of those rooms. The window beside the bed faces the Lilly's bar sign, where a

band called the Sea Horses was playing the night
of Audrey Marvel's murder.

Employees of the Revere Motel have been
instructed by management not to discuss the night
of June 24th, 2014. But not everyone instructed
not to do something complies. I spoke with one
of those people. He or she said immediately after
the district attorney revealed the existence of the
video, employees went through computer files and
old reservation books to see who occupied room
208 the night of Audrey Marvel's murder.

It was someone who gave the name Mike Steele.
He took it on Sunday, two days prior to the murder,
paying in advance for a full week. Not surprisingly,
he paid cash. My source tells me a lot of guests
check in without showing ID or providing a credit
card. They choose the Revere Motel because they
don't want to give their true name or leave a record
of their visit. Also, my source added, because of
the complimentary box of tissues that can be used
to smash cockroaches crawling on the wall.

The front desk clerk on duty that night was a man
named Dylan Brillo, who no longer works at the
motel. My source hasn't kept in touch with Dylan
but one of his or her friends at the motel has. Dylan
said the police came to his house yesterday. He
told them he couldn't possibly remember guests
from over a year ago. He also said he'd seen some
of Andrew Marvel's movies but had no idea what
he looked like. The police showed him a picture
of Andrew, but it didn't jog any memories.

If Andrew was framed, someone drugged him and
filmed the alibi. Why did nobody report seeing a
man carried from the parking lot to the second

floor? Maybe a comatose guest carried up a staircase isn't that unusual a sight evenings at the Revere Motel.

Why would someone make sure Andrew didn't have an alibi only to give him an unbreakable one? Why frame him only to free him? I don't have an answer. If you do, please leave it in the comments section.

Here's what I think: Andrew hired someone to murder Audrey. Did a second accomplice drive him to Manchester and film his alibi? A film director I know told me Andrew could have rigged the simple upward camera move and controlled the camera himself. In the video, a pillow conceals his left hand. It could also conceal a control box.

Did Andrew Marvel have one accomplice or two? That's the only question.

Did this blog remove Trish from the list? Women could commit murder, and so could bloggers, but Jackson couldn't imagine a scenario where a killer stuck around to blog the murder investigation. Then again, what an original cover for the Other Woman.

It looked like she started the blog in September 2013, ten months before the murder. The About tab said, "I'm a crime blogger who lives in Mt. Kisco, NY."

The first page of "Trish Devereaux" search results contained different blog posts. There was something different on the bottom of the second page. Scriptapalooza Finalist.

The link took Jackson to the list of winners on the Scriptapalooza screenwriting contest site. *Johnny Payback*, by Trish Devereaux, was one of four finalists in the 2014 spring competition. No big surprise someone interested in crime would try her hand at a screenplay, but this brought her a step closer to the world of Andrew Marvel. She might have heard he spent summers in Greensboro. If she could get a working director to read her script, it was worth a five-hour drive from Mt. Kisco.

Enough for tonight. The clock above the TV had rounded side columns of wood on either side of the brass face. Below the face was a faded painting of a house with two tall trees in the foreground. Eight o'clock. Let Kenny call him a blasphemer, but he didn't feel like watching SportsCenter. It would repeat at eleven anyway. And again at one and two, giving the illusion that time wasn't passing after all, we could rest easy, mortality was nothing but a horrifying dream.

From his bed, Jackson could see the door was bolted, but he got up and made sure. He was the only person who knew about Cass and the Morrisville weathervane. It was probably a good rule of thumb not to be the only person who knows why a killer killed, especially if the killer knows you know.

So far, Trish knew who he wasn't but not who he was. Blake knew he was a busybody who called him out for violating the library's Take One, Leave One policy. Wally and Cass didn't know he existed. Nobody knew he owned VegasVegas. But they could find out.

Before turning off the iPad, he went back to *Improbable Cause*. There was a new post.

"I met a guy tonight who may know something important. My analytics tells me someone with a Greensboro IP address is reading my blog right now. I think it's him.

His name is…"

Wednesday, 7:45 a.m.

The dining room was filled with fiftyish couples and the smell of bacon. Trish hadn't come down yet, or she'd already eaten and left. In the breakfast section of the menu, pancakes, waffles and muffins contained eggs. Scrambled eggs contained more eggs. That left oatmeal or a bowl of seasonal fruit, which was cantaloupe. Jackson didn't feel like more than coffee and fruit, but breakfast was already factored into the overpriced nightly rate, way overpriced if he counted bribes, and all things being equal, he preferred reducing the amount he was getting stiffed by opting for the more expensive menu item. So he ordered the oatmeal and shifted his attention to two people he'd eavesdropped on the night before.

He picked up their conversation at, "Oh, I almost forgot."

"Consider yourself blessed. There's no almost with me. My mind's become a sieve in my old age."

"You're a spring chicken. I read about a man in Singapore who just celebrated his hundred and eighth birthday."

"I don't believe it."

"It was in the newspaper."

"There's a simple explanation. Old age is revered in that part of the world. So telling people you just had your hundred and eighth birthday is our equivalent of telling people you just turned twenty-nine…What did you almost forget?"

"Now I did forget. How am I supposed to remember anything when I have to listen to your crazy theories?"

"By the way, Stella told me Burt Tager's coming back from his flying contest next week."

At the mention of Burt Tager, Jackson felt like he did when he walked out of his apartment positive he left something important behind but not knowing what. It had to be related to Tracy's story about Burt dive-bombing Warren's party. Burt said Warren should get payback like a man instead of playing mind games like a woman. But what did any of this have to do with Audrey Marvel or weathervanes?

After breakfast, he was finishing his second cup of coffee when Trish came in texting. Her eyes needed a machete to hack their way out from behind the forest of hair that fell in every direction. She passed two empty tables and took one on the other side of the room. He waved. She gave him a stop-and-start smile and went back to her texting.

Wednesday, 9:30 a.m.

The small square of uncut grass in front of Wally Caiden's house was burnt brown in patches. Cobwebs of old Christmas lights hung from the beam of a screened-in porch. Betty the librarian said Wally supplemented his bad carpentry by selling maple syrup and beet greens out of his garage during tourist season. Not this morning. The garage was closed. No cars or trucks were in the driveway or parked out front.

Jackson headed back to the center of town, going by Willey's and turning onto a road that wound past the Mountain View country club, where retirees in tennis whites with stork-thin legs were playing doubles. Up ahead was a red barn with a cupola but no weathervane. A carved wooden sign staked in the grass said, Green Mountain Arts. Hours: 8 – 12.

The artist Audrey Marvel suspected of making weathervane replicas was standing behind a drawing table sketching. Rex agreed she had it in her. He'd tried backtracking, but if he didn't believe it, he wouldn't have called Jackson about her.

Meredith Lane's short near-black hair was streaked with purple. She wore a gray tee shirt with either an ornately rendered eagle or simply rendered dragon. She smiled and returned to her sketching. A menagerie of animals made of twisted copper wire surrounded Jackson. Birds dangled from the ceiling. Cows grazed on the sawdust floor, ignoring a yapping terrier on his hind legs. Two loons floated on an oval table. A horse near the counter tucked his head and pawed at the floor.

"They're more life-like than a photo." Jackson wasn't just buttering her up.

"Thank you." Black purple bangs shaded her eyes as she continued to sketch.

"Humans are okay art subjects if the theme is sin or vanity or deceit, but personally I prefer honor and nobility and you need animals for that." She gave him a half smile.

Maybe he should just skip the chitchat and say, "Do you carry antique weathervanes? I can't afford the real thing, so I was looking for a knock-off. Oh, and I'll need it gift wrapped."

The indifferent gaze of the wire cat curled on a box made him miss Tomás. There were bears, a blue heron, a hawk.

He stopped in front of a deer. "I saw a deer weathervane when I was kayaking."

"I like that one."

"I noticed your barn has a cupola but no weathervane."

She looked up from her sketching. "I used to have one."

"What animal?"

"Horse."

"Thank God, not another rooster. Nothing against roosters, and I guess they're the obvious choice for a barn, but they're all over the place."

Jackson hadn't intended to take the talkative fool approach, but it felt right.

"It was stolen," she said.

"Sorry to hear that."

"I had it six years. Someone else's turn to enjoy it."

Was she serious?

She kept her eyes on the paper, pencil tapping her lips now. "The copper belonged to the Earth. Someone took it from her and sold it to the sculptor, who turned it into a weathervane and sold it to the first owner of this barn, who passed it along to me. The thieves took it and sold it to the antique store, who passed it along to a new owner."

Jackson would have to remember to tell Alton, who was

always on the lookout for good rationalizations. "You didn't steal the antique, Alton, you were participating in the circle of life."

"So if the cops recover it, they should return it to the Earth?"

She turned her head to study her sketch from a different angle. "You're thinking the ditzy artist inhaled too much incense. Tourists always ask about the empty cupola. I make up different answers and test them. The Mother Earth story results in the most sculpture sales. The truth performs the worst."

"What's the truth?"

"I got bored of the weathervane and was glad someone stole it. I prefer the insurance money."

"People don't want their artists to be mercenaries."

"That's why they eat up the Mother Earth story. They can tell their friends about the nutty artist who made their wire sculpture."

"Any other story test well?"

"I almost caught the thieves. They were disguised as Comcast Cable workers. I shot one of them in the ass, but they got away. I tried a version where they were disguised as Vermont Electric workers, but people like it better when the Comcast guy gets shot in the ass."

Jackson circled around to the front of the deer so it didn't block his view of Meredith's face. "Here's an idea."

She put down her pencil and gave him her full attention.

"Tell customers you moonlight making replicas of antique weathervanes for thieves. You took your own weathervane down to make people think you're a victim, so nobody suspects you."

She frowned, not in disapproval, but like she was imaging herself telling the story. "Not bad. A lot of customers want their artists to have a dark side."

The entrance of the arm-in-arm couple put the investigation out of its misery.

"We couldn't help wondering why you had a cupola but no weathervane."

Meredith winked at Jackson and said to the arm-in-arm couple, "I did. It was stolen."

"That's awful."

"I had it six years. Someone else's turn to enjoy it."

"But it belonged to you."

"The copper belonged to the Earth. Someone took it from her and sold it to the sculptor…"

Jackson stopped at Willey's and got stuck behind a long line of bantering photographers in the check-out lane with their tubes of sunblock, cans of bug repellant, hunting hats, and twelve packs of Bud Lite. Two more photographers got in line behind Jackson, one carrying a grill and spatula, the other with a bag of charcoal and basket of cellophaned meat.

An old-timer in line said to one of the photographers, "I remember the OJ days when there were hundreds of you guys camped outside his house. Now it's only a handful."

"Cutbacks," one of the photographers said.

The other photographer shook his bag of charcoal. "We used to expense lunch at the Palm. Now look at us."

"Haven't sold any of these in a while," the clerk said when she rang up Jackson's can of hearts of palm.

"They're my favorite," Jackson said. Which was true. With all the lies Hank Carruthers had going, it felt good to speak the truth.

As he walked out the door, the black F-150 was pulling into an empty space. Blake saw Jackson, opened his mouth in what looked like surprise, and held up his hand to say "wait."

Blake hopped out of the truck. "You accused me of taking books."

"You took the whole shelf."

Freckled hands kneaded the air. Blake took a long breath, bobbing the clown head up and down.

"In the morning I left two. I was in a hurry, no time to find two I wanted, so I came back later and that's when you saw me. I returned the cart and all the books. I even added three more of my own. You pissed me off and I was making a point, but now it's back where it belongs."

But Blake now was looking past Jackson, at the bulletin board. "Well I'll be damned. Someone found a money clip in the library."

When Blake went to the library, Betty the librarian would no doubt give him the lowdown on the out-of-towner who found it.

"It was me," Jackson said.

"Now you claim you lost a money clip?"

"I found it. Yesterday. It had forty bucks in it."

"You turned it in? But you're a punk."

"I'm multi-faceted."

Blake rubbed the reddish stubble on his chin. "I'm going to let it go. You don't know me. I can see myself making the same mistake. See someone walking off with two books from the Take One, Leave One shelf, assume he took them. I'm going to let it go. Where'd you find it?"

"Under one of the computers."

"When I saw you or another time?"

"Right after you left."

"I was at the computers. I didn't see a money clip."

"On the ground."

"Which computer?"

"Second one from the left."

Blake was thinking, or pretending to be. "Nobody at that one when I was there. Then I went back to the bookshelves. Don and Sarah Tompkins came in."

"Elderly couple?"

"Don't let them hear you say that, but yes."

"They were still there when I found it. So was a teenaged girl."

"Casey. So they're out. I can't see Don Tompkins using a money clip anyway." Blake grimaced. He snapped his fingers. "Wally Caiden was at that computer."

He shook Jackson's hand. "Good for you. Nice job."

"Sorry about the book thing," Jackson said.

"Ancient history. I'm Blake Trotman."

"Hank Carruthers."

"Visiting someone in town?"

"I'm at the Morning Loon."

"Let me a put in a plug for the blackened buffalo prime rib."

"Sounds good." Jackson wanted to keep the ceasefire going.

"It's better than good. Can't wait to hear what you think."

Wednesday, 11:45 a.m.

Jackson ate his snack on a picnic bench near the public boat launch. What kind of thief or killer would get that worked up over the accusation that he violated the library's Take One, Leave One policy, and suddenly melt when he learned Jackson returned something to the Lost and Found? Jackson could form impressions about Blake and Trish and Wally when he met him, but what could he really learn about a crime that happened over a year ago? Maybe he should go back to following Cass, see if he delivered money to anyone.

A couple in matching big-brimmed hats emerged from the lakeshore path and passed the public boat launch.

"Nice day," the woman said when they got closer.

"Sure is."

He now recognized them as the Earthlink couple, Don and Sarah Tompkins, and got ready to field questions about his search for the money clip owner, but they fell back into their private conversation as they made their way to the library.

A blue Nissan Murano with two kayaks strapped to the roof pulled onto the pavement near the boat launch. A guy in Crocodile Hunter khakis and a second in a torn blue tee-shirt got out. Fresh reinforcements.

"How's it going?" Jackson said.

The Crocodile Hunter was yanking at the strap fastening his kayak to the rack. "Not bad."

Torn Shirt said, "That won't be his answer an hour from now."

"Sure it will. Mind-numbing boredom is good for the soul."

These two were friendlier than the ones in the lake.

"Photographers?" Jackson said.

"Yup." Crocodile Hunter gave the strap two hard jerks. It didn't budge but he bore his ineptitude stoically. "They picked me for my experience standing immobile outside houses all day."

"He did the Patriots tight end, Aaron Hernandez's house," Torn Shirt chimed in.

"Got a sweet shot of the Domino's delivery guy ringing the doorbell."

"Pulitzer judges stiffed him."

Jackson had no doubt they'd refined this banter over time.

Crocodile Hunter still hadn't made any progress with the strap so Jackson loosened the buckle for him.

"Thanks, guy."

"No problem. I kayaked by the Marvel house yesterday. Didn't see you two."

"Yesterday we did farm duty," Torn Shirt said.

"Some photographers are specialists. They can only camp out in front of a house. We can camp out in front or back watching nothing happen with equal skill."

Jackson laughed and the two exchanged a look that said, "That line's a keeper."

"The police stop by his house yet?" Jackson said.

"Some are there now."

Crocodile Hunter folded his arms, maybe mimicking a cop in a movie Jackson had never seen. "'We're going to find the person who did this, Mr. Marvel. And by the way, make any big withdrawals lately?'"

"You think he hired someone?"

"Shit, yeah, I do."

Jackson genuinely wanted to know what they thought. His one additional piece of game-changing knowledge made it hard to project what he'd think without it.

"Then he'd be at the mercy of the guy he hired," Jackson said. "What if the guy didn't deliver the video?"

"Probably paid half up front, half after he got off," Torn Shirt said.

"They'll find out."

Crocodile Hunter looked serious for the first time. "Yes, they will. That doesn't stop dicks like Andrew Marvel from thinking they can get away with it."

"Okay, but why sit in jail a year? Why not have the killer deliver the video after a few months?"

"We were asking that same question last night," Torn Shirt said.

"Where I end up is he's overcautious," Crocodile Hunter said. "He figures the more time goes by, the less chance the police find evidence of his guy."

"Two months, a year, does it make a difference?"

"Maybe in his mind it does."

"We were also talking about the double jeopardy thing," Torn Shirt said. "You can't be tried twice for the same crime."

"Is it the same crime? Murder and hiring someone to murder?"

"I'm no lawyer. If he thinks it's the same thing."

"Wouldn't he do research before he decides to sit in jail a year?"

Crocodile Hunter had finally freed the kayak from its straps. "Interesting conversation, but we might be missing out on a sweet photo of a closed door."

"Take it," Torn Shirt said, "I'm going for the window with the shade pulled down."

"Need a hand carrying the kayaks?"

"Nah, we got it," Torn Shirt said.

Crocodile Hunter said, "Speak for yourself."

Jackson helped him carry the kayak to the shore, while Torn Shirt brought the camera equipment.

"There's a reporter, blogger, staying at the Morning Loon. Trish."

"*Improbable Cause*," Torn Shirt said.

"You know her?"

"She gets the good interviews and the rest of us pick up her scraps."

"She really pissed off our reporters," Crocodile Hunter said, "getting someone at that motel to show her the reservations."

Torn Shirt said, "Same as last year. She got interviews before anyone."

Crocodile Hunter changed the subject. "How'd you get a room at the Morning Loon? Already there before the video?"

"Yeah." No point getting them interested in him and his reason for coming.

"If you're interested in a swap, I can offer you a dingy room in Hardwick with a crusty green carpet that hasn't been vacuumed since the Eisenhower Administration."

Torn Shirt nodded at Jackson's laughter. Another keeper.

They placed the kayaks in the water.

"Thanks again, guy," Crocodile Hunter said.

"Yeah, thanks for contributing to my boredom," Torn Shirt nodded.

Crocodile Hunter shot him a look.

Torn Shirt's mouth dropped. "I don't mean you bored me. I meant helping me get to the place where I'll be bored."

They couldn't all be keepers.

Jackson handed them their equipment after they got into their kayaks and watched them paddle unsteadily along the shore. When they rounded the bend, he headed for the crushed reeds that marked the start of the path. A wall of pine and maples along the shoreline shielded the houses from the path, which stayed close to the shore, cutting through gaps in bushes, curving around boathouses and narrow wooden docks.

Peaceful sounds of domestic bliss floated out over one balcony. Jackson had witnessed domestic bliss. And what did it consist of? Lowest common denominator conversations about household items that needed to be purchased, bills that needed to be paid, party invitations that needed to be accepted or refused. How did this non-stop chatter qualify people as soul mates? Anybody with a mouth and voice could say things like, "Honey, did you pay the cable bill yet?" "The water's starting to boil." "How long should I cook the pasta for?"

If any couple had an interaction that wasn't taking place in a slightly different form two houses down, he'd gladly tip his hat and say, "You two have something special."

"I think Samson likes the new food with the fur ball medication." "Did you see the weather report for tomorrow?" "The lawn service guy isn't doing a very good job with the edging."

Say enough meaningless little things for enough years and you ended up with someone to grieve you when you died.

A woman wearing a golf visor was kneeling on a green Styrofoam pad gardening near the path. She smiled and he smiled back. He'd have to figure out the proper public access path etiquette. Look over and smile at the risk of appearing intrusive or walk past without acknowledgement and risk appearing rude.

One lawn contained the remains of a stone fireplace. The uncut grass made it look like ruins from a fallen civilization. Almost every house had a canoe or kayak sitting on the dock or floating beside it.

The shore jutted out, revealing a cluster of photographers aiming their cameras at the green boathouse where a police technician was bent over one of the J-hooks attached to the wall. Another crawled out from under mulberry bushes at the foot of the lawn. What did they hope to find, a year-old Diet Coke can the killer used to snuff out his cigarette butts while he waited for Audrey to come home? The police couldn't be happy about news stories they knew would accompany the photos: police conducting a search they didn't bother with last summer, looking for signs of a person they didn't believe existed.

Jackson had information pertinent to the investigation, making him a material witness. The more time he let pass before telling the police about Cass, the harder they'd make it on him. No point waiting around for one of them to get bored hunting for Diet Coke cans and start questioning bystanders.

On the way back to the public launch, he got so absorbed shifting people around in the suspect queue, he couldn't say when he became aware of light tapping behind him, a lake resident on a walk or a photographer making a beer run.

Or a cop about to ask for some identification, please. Jackson lost the footsteps when the trail softened into moist dirt but picked them up again when it crossed over fallen leaves or tufts of grass. Up ahead, the trail curved around a bend, giving him a chance to see who was following.

The footsteps stopped. Nobody was behind him. But someone had been and the only way they could have disappeared was by cutting into the property with the fireplace remains. Jackson passed through a cluster of pines and stood in the overgrown grass. The windows of the house were dark. It didn't look like anyone had been there for years.

Bricks clattered behind the fireplace. He approached slowly, circling the wall attached to the collapsed chimney. Loose bricks were scattered around the grass but there was no sign of anyone. A gunshot crack of snapped wood echoed from pines in front of the house. Jackson jumped around in time to see a flash of blue fabric moving through the trees. He stood still, listening, watching, but didn't see anything more, so he returned to the path.

Wednesday, 1:15 p.m.

Wally still wasn't home. The neighbors didn't appear to be, either. The open gate in their chain-link fence taunted Jackson. "Fool, you think Wally's going to come right out and admit he steals weathervanes? You're lucky he's not home. Come on in, have a look around. This is an opportunity for someone resourceful, which apparently you're not."

The open gate made a fair point. Weathervane thieves who replaced antiques with replicas would have parts and pieces lying around—different-sized cupolas, rods, copper globes, directionals, specialized tools.

Jackson marched nonchalantly through the open gate to a small neat lawn with strips of geraniums along both fence lines. A string hammock on a green metal frame sat in the back of the yard beneath crabapple trees.

He vaulted over the waist-high fence into Wally's yard, an obstacle course of empty plastic buckets, a car battery, a gas can, a blue tarp, dog toys. Jackson could infer with the best of them. Dog toys, ergo dog, ergo dog poop. He zigzagged his way across the yard, listening for the enraged barking of a dog who didn't have the capacity to distinguish between would-be prowlers and well-intentioned trespassers who just wanted their money back.

But the dog was out with Wally or inside sleeping. Jackson looked through the shed at the back corner of the fence. There were rakes, hoes, garden spades, shovels, tightly wound tomato cages, paper leaf bags, but nothing that looked like part of a weathervane. Affixed to the inside of one of the metal doors, incongruous among the lawn care tools like an out-of-nowhere, mystery-solving clue, was an oval Great Britain bumper sticker. Too bad this mystery had nothing to do with British cars.

Jackson closed the doors and crossed the lawn to a second shed against the rear of the house. This one was padlocked. His only experience with locks was forgetting combinations, so he hopped back over the fence and retreated to his car.

Wednesday, 1:48 p.m.

The phone message light in Jackson's cottage was blinking.

"Hank, it's Betty from the library with good news. We found the owner. Wally Caiden. He said Blake told him you found a money clip where he was sitting so I showed it to him and it was his, alright. He just left with it. Now listen to this. I told him how concerned you were. I said, 'Hank's here on holiday yet he took time to get it back to its rightful owner.' I said if it were me, I'd give Hank something for his trouble and Wally agreed. He said to tell you to stop by his house for a reward."

A white Chrysler Impala was parked inside Wally's open garage. A handwritten cardboard sign in the burnt grass said, "Maple syrup. Beet greens."

Wally must have seen Jackson pull up because he came outside as Jackson was getting out of the car. Sweat droplets covered his puffy face. His belly hung down like a half-full trash bag. Not someone built for scrambling up and down houses carrying weathervanes.

"I'm Hank Carruthers," Jackson said.

"Guy who found my money clip?"

"That's me."

Wally shook his hand. "Most people, they find forty dollars on the ground, they slip it in their pocket."

"Is that what you'd do?"

"It is. Until an hour ago when I got that call from Blake. Your act of kindness changed me." He wiped sweat from his cheek with the back of his hand. "At least I hope it did. I've never been good at turning over new leaves."

"It must have been a relief when Blake called."

"Tell the truth, I didn't notice it was missing."

"I think that is the truth," Jackson said.

Wally's mouth didn't move, but his eyes lit up like they were accompanying a grin. "Betty said you're angling for a reward, Hank."

"You have a reward for me?"

"I do."

Wally went into the garage and brought out a barn-shaped can of maple syrup.

"What an ingrate I am." He replaced it with a bigger can, which he handed to Jackson.

"Best maple syrup you've ever had. And that, my friend, is the truth."

Jackson felt absurdly grateful for the upgrade. He also felt an unexpected craving for pancakes. "I can't tell you how long it's been since I've had pancakes."

"This'll get you started up again."

"So, I've got a question."

"Uh huh."

"What happens if someone else says they lost a money clip and the librarian tells them you claimed it?"

"I'd marvel at the coincidence of two people losing a money clip one afternoon in the same small library."

Jackson held in a laugh. He felt a corner of a bill poking out his pocket. He tried shoving it back in, but it poked out again, jabbing his thumb. He'd stop and get another money clip at the Miller's Thumb.

But forget that. He liked his. "I'd like to buy your money clip from you."

Wally took a step back. "Sell you my good luck money clip? I lost it once. I can't part with it again."

"I saw one like it for forty-five dollars."

"Had to be one of those imitation knock-offs."

"I'll give you eighty."

"My grandfather on his deathbed said, 'Wally, however else you go wrong in life, don't ever let this money clip out of the family.'"

"One hundred is my take it or leave it offer."

"You're cruel."

Wally took the money clip from his pocket. Jackson counted out a hundred dollars and they completed the transaction.

"Blake seems like an honest guy," Jackson said.

"Yes, he does."

Was he being cryptic here or was his eye twitching because of the fly that landed on his cheek?

"Only seems that way?"

"He was honest enough to call me about my money clip."

"Was he on the computers the same time as you?"

"Only one I saw on the computer was an attractive young woman. You ask some strange questions, Hank."

So he claimed Trish was on the computer. Blake didn't mention her.

"I find it interesting someone from Detroit would buy a buffalo farm in Vermont."

"It wasn't a buffalo farm when he bought it."

"His wife helps raise the buffalo?"

"She might if the guy she ran off with is a buffalo farmer, too."

"That's too bad."

"Lots of things are too bad. Now before you go…"

Wally went back into the garage and came out with another large barn-shaped can of maple syrup.

Jackson tried refusing. "I don't have room in my bag."

"Leave something behind. I told you it's the best maple syrup you ever had."

The phone started ringing in the house. "Election season. Tell me how you like that syrup."

Jackson's susceptibility to jumping on the bandwagon of the most recent suspect was just like during the NBA playoffs. He'd pick the Warriors in six at the start of the series, then the Spurs would blow them out in game one and he'd switch to Spurs in six. Next game, Warriors would blow out the Spurs, and he'd jump back to the Warriors in seven.

Not this time. He was ready to scratch Wally off the list because of a combination of build, quirkiness, and generosity.

Wednesday, 2:59 p.m.

Jackson stopped under the arch for a whiff of lilac. A figure rounded the backside of his cabin. Jackson pressed himself into the lilacs and watched Trish knock on his door, wait, shift over and try lifting the window. When it didn't budge, she crouched to look under the shade. She pressed her iPhone light against the window, shook her head, clicked it off.

"Need a key?"

She hopped around. "Damn." Stomped her foot on the ground and stepped toward him. "You scared me. Sneaking up like that. Then trying to talk all cool, 'Need a key?'"

"What were you doing?"

"Looking for you."

"No you weren't."

"Yes, I was."

"Why?"

"Good question, the way you're acting."

"You knocked on the door. I didn't answer. Then you tried opening the window and using your light to look inside."

"You could have said, 'Hey, here I am.' But no, you hide in the bushes and spy on me."

"You were trying to break into my cabin. Why?"

"You tell me. Why?"

He pulled the key from his pocket. "Tell you what, I'll let you in. You can do a search."

But it didn't fluster her like it was supposed to. She smiled. "Okay."

He did a quick mental scan of the room. Was there anything that would give away his identity?

"Another time," he said.

"Now you can stop playing Mr. I've Got Nothing To Hide."

"Since we're on the subject of people with something to hide, why were you in Greensboro last summer before the murder?"

"Did you see me?"

"How could I? I wasn't here."

"You sure about that?"

"This is my first time in Greensboro."

"And your name is Hank Carruthers and you're a photographer."

She twisted a divot in the dirt with the heel of her running shoe. "Come back for the money?"

So she knew. But that didn't jive with her asking if he was in Greensboro last summer. She was watching him get thrown off, probably thinking she was on to something.

"What's your name?"

"Joe Smith."

She took his picture with her iPhone. "One of my readers will know. You're not stupid and neither is Andrew. You know the police will be watching to see who he pays."

His laughter surprised her. "I catch you trying to break into my cabin and you get bent out of shape because I snuck up on you. I ask what you were doing here before the murder and you accuse me of being the killer."

"Somebody was."

"That's true. Somebody was and somebody else helped him."

She was looking at the photo. "I predict someone gets it in under five minutes."

"Don't post it. I can give you a big story, but not yet."

"I'm on deadline."

"I'd hate to have to give it to one of those reporters hanging out with the cows."

"Give me a hint."

"We'll talk tonight."

Her lips moved Escher-like from frown to smile. "See you at dinner then."

He'd thrown away the San Jose to Houston boarding pass and the SJO airport label when he landed in Burlington. He kept his driver's license, credit cards, and iPhone with him but not his iPad. He opened the bottom dresser drawer where he'd left it and turned it on. The last site in the history was his visit to Trish's blog. He cleared the history, though it wouldn't make a difference. Anyone who opened his Mail application would see his name and a quick Google search would tell them he owned VegasVegas.

The windows facing the nearest cabin were closed. The lower panes of the double-hung windows facing the farm were half open like he left them, with the screens hooked from inside. He almost didn't see the half-inch slice in the screen above the hook fastened to the wooden frame.

He unhooked the screen and pulled it toward him until he had enough space to climb out the window. Standing outside, he had no trouble reaching in and lowering the screen then slipping his finger through the slice to connect the hook to the eye. Someone else had done the same maneuver. The question was when, while Jackson was away or some other point in the ten-plus-year history of this ratty screen?

He did another scan of the cabin. Nothing appeared to be missing or out of place. If Trish had already gotten in and she spotted him coming up the path, why act like she was trying to break in? Why not simply knock on the door?

Did someone else break in before she got here?

When he'd said she was in Vermont before the murder, she didn't admit or deny it. It wouldn't take much effort to meet Andrew. He read her script. Gave feedback. Maybe promised to help get it shown around Hollywood. Or maybe he parlayed his mentorship into something more and they were discreet enough to elude the gossips. Everything would be perfect for the two of them if they could just get rid of Audrey.

The feeling Jackson had at breakfast came back. He was missing something obvious, something having to do with the pilot, Burt Tager. This time he snagged the answer before it floated away.

The night of the murder, the first police car arrived at the Marvel house seventeen minutes after the 911 call. In the trial, the prosecutor said Audrey made the call but was too weak to speak when dispatch answered. The video alibi told a different story. Audrey didn't call 911, the killer did. He had to make sure the police discovered her body at roughly the same time Andrew, or someone, was filming the motel room alibi.

The killer knew the Hardwick police station was seven miles away, but he'd have to assume there'd be police cars closer to Greensboro, which meant he'd have to get away from the house as quickly as possible after calling 911. He couldn't park nearby while he waited for Audrey to come home because people would notice a strange car. Going by foot would take too long. The most likely scenario is he parked at the Morning Loon, where cars were always coming and going, and rode a bike along Cozy Lane to the Marvel house.

He'd conceal the bike nearby. But what if someone on a night walk saw it? They probably wouldn't, but what if they did? A cautious killer wouldn't risk someone remembering the name and color of his bike. Not if he had access to a different one.

Tracy said Burt Tager came back from a stunt-flying competition and discovered Warren's prank, but Warren denied it.

"Not bored. Thirsty," Jackson had said when Tracy described it, too fixated on his impending drink to think clearly. No, it was Ike, the chipmunk's, fault. His existence transformed Burt into a country eccentric who imagined swapped handlebar grips and screws in the washer jar while he served Ike's peanut dinner.

Why would someone put screws in the washer jar? For the same reason they replaced the blue tarp with a green one. To make it appear that replacing the handle bar grips was one of a series of oddball pranks.

Say the killer knew Burt was away for a week. He took Burt's bike from the shed and used it to get away after he made the 911 call. But when he got home, he noticed blood on his gloves. Not a problem, he could get rid of them. But if it was on the gloves, it was on the handlebars.

He could let it slide. The police were already fixated on Andrew. But the killer had a week before Burt returned home. Why not eliminate any chance of the police discovering blood on the handlebar grips? It would be so simple to replace them with new ones.

Jackson closed the window and locked the door behind him. At the bottom of the path, someone was kneeling in front of an oval of flowers. Her dark bangs swelled outward then curled in and tapered into little points that extended to the outer corners of her mouth.

"Hi, I'm Hank Carruthers, cabin six."

"Oh, hello, I'm Delilah. The manager. Tracy said you were coming. Welcome."

"Thanks."

He bent over to sniff the yellow waist-high flowers. "This is what I was smelling from the porch last night."

"Day lilies. These are from last year. The ones I'm planting now won't flower until next year."

"You only plant when it's warm?"

"Between April and October. It's hard for the roots to develop when the soil's below fifty."

She spoke with a gardener's pride, so he made a point of taking another appreciative whiff. And another because they really did smell good.

Inside the inn, Tracy was using a steel watering can to water the Boston ferns beside a mahogany table with two loons carved out of soapstone.

"I wish to register a complaint," Jackson said. "I didn't read all the fine print on the bribing policy of the Morning Loon, but most desk clerks guarantee confidentiality. You told Trish I paid you four hundred for the cottage."

Tracy swiveled her head to check if anyone was in hearing range then said, "No, I didn't."

"No?"

"I told her you paid a thousand."

"A thousand?"

"In case she talks to other reporters. I want them to think that's the going rate."

"Here's what I want you to do: I want you to open your journal and find that page where you wrote what a loser you were for getting fleeced and use it for kindling in the fireplace."

Tracy's face brightened at the praise. "Plus now Trish thinks you're a big spender. Everyone wins."

"On the subject of Trish…"

"Kind of hot isn't she?"

"How did she get a room?"

"Repeat visitor."

"How about last summer?"

Tracy closed her eyes to think. "Good question. The place filled up in like five seconds. She must have gotten here first."

"Before the murder?"

"Why would she come before? She came to cover it."

"My thousand dollars buys me more than one open ear. I need you to look something up. You guys keep accurate records. Tell me when she checked in."

"You're a freak, and you're burning through your money fast." She opened a document on the front desk computer. "Trish Devereaux. Checked in Wednesday, June twenty-fifth, 2014, at eleven-fourteen in the morning."

For Trish to drive from Mt. Kisco to Greensboro and check in around eleven she had to hear about the murder at five in the morning, but it wasn't made public until the DA's ten o'clock conference. Which meant Trish was already in Vermont, and she moved to the Morning Loon early enough to beat the rush of reporters.

Wednesday, 3:48 p.m.

The ten mountain bikes and six road bikes in the shed were lined up on a rack against the wall, helmets draped over handlebars. Jackson went with an orange Klein mountain bike.

At the start of fifth dirt road off Town Highway 1, Tager was one of four names painted on pieces of plywood nailed to a wooden stake. Loose rocks covered the packed dirt. Jackson crossed another dirt road that ran parallel to the lake. No sign but it had to be Cozy Lane. As he got closer to the lake, arching branches formed a tunnel of maple green. He checked the address on his iPhone. Number 3268 was the one-story brown house, outhouse-sized compared to Uncle Warren's and some of the other lavish places on the lake.

But he didn't stop. He rode past Burt Tager's house to the private road that branched into three separate driveways, the right one leading to the blue house with the stone chimney that led off so many news broadcasts in the last year.

He expected to see a security guard stationed outside to keep photographers away, but maybe they knew to stay off private property. The driveway ended beneath a canvas awning above a Range Rover. A rock path wound through ferns down to the house.

Jackson leaned his bike against an aluminum pole supporting the awning. He could go up to the window and call out, "100 to 1." Andrew would know or he wouldn't. If he knew, he'd open the door. Then Jackson would know.

Jackson crept closer to the window. He couldn't hear banging, walking, TV, music, or other sounds of life. Andrew might be sleeping. "100 to 1" would rouse him.

It would rouse him tomorrow, too, when Jackson knew more, enough maybe to rule out weathervanes.

Back at Burt Tager's house, a chipmunk came out from under a hedge and checked Jackson out.

"Are you by any chance Ike?"

The wooden shed, same brown as the house, was a few feet from the gravel turnaround at the end of the driveway. Jackson removed the stick securing the hasp, and opened the door. The green tarp was folded in a wheelbarrow. A silver Specialized Rockhopper mountain bike hung on a hook screwed into a ceiling beam. And there were the infamous swapped jars of screws and washers on a shelf. Jackson stepped over a box filled with ski gloves and around an old chiminea and grabbed a flashlight hanging on a nail.

The bike had ordinary black handle bar grips. The tires were fully inflated, the chain clean and oiled. The cables didn't have any rust. Other than a few flecks of caked dirt on the underside of the down tube, the frame was perfectly clean.

Jackson unlatched the seat clamp and raised the seat. There was a faint oil ring about six inches down the seat post. At some point, someone taller than Burt rode the bike. If a lot of different people had ridden it, there'd be multiple rings, but there was only that one.

He lowered the seat and returned the bike and flashlight. Ike was now outside the door, standing fully upright, striped tail twitching.

"He's at a stunt flying competition. He'll be back soon," Jackson said.

This didn't satisfy Ike, who hopped closer to Jackson.

A paper bag, bulging with peanuts, sat on a piece of two-by-four wedged between two studs.

He offered one to Ike, who grabbed it and scurried back under his bush. He must have been making allowances for Burt being out of town because he came running back before Jackson had a chance to return the bag to the shelf.

He handed Ike another one, which Ike carried back to his bush.

Ike would have kept it going all day, but Jackson drew the line at ten peanuts.

"We're talking about a guy who can spot the difference between black handle bar grips. He'll notice this bag is light ten peanuts and I'm busted."

Ike was unconvinced, but Jackson wouldn't budge. He latched the door and rode back to the Morning Loon with some *ifs* bouncing around in his head.

If the killer came and left on a bike, if he used Burt's to avoid using his own, if he had to raise the seat, then he couldn't be squat Wally but he could be gangly tall Blake.

Wednesday, 6:36 p.m.

"Hello, this is Hank?"

"I saw you going up the path." Tracy. "Hold on…Yes, Smuggler's Notch is a definite must-see, Mrs. Mackey. The name of the town is Jeffersonville…I'm back. A friend of mine, Tammy, she's got a brother in high school, Tommy. Tammy and Tommy. One of the photographers in the lake's been paying Tommy to do errands, bring him food, stuff like that. This photographer figured Andrew would wait 'til they had to leave and take his kayak out. But Tommy's a local, they don't enforce lake hours on him. So the photographer paid Tommy to hang out around the lake and call if Andrew came out. Last night, he didn't."

"Tonight?"

"A few minutes ago, but Tommy didn't call the reporter. He told Andrew, who paid Tommy more not to say anything. Tommy called me because he knows I have one ear open."

"Andrew's in the lake now?"

"You didn't hear it from me or Tommy. You're just a guest going on a night ride."

The dot on the lake became a kayak slicing through water, coming toward Jackson, turning now, its red hull like a gash on the sky, completing the turn, heading for shore. Jackson cut the distance in half. Andrew wore a yellow life preserver and a khaki hiking hat. He didn't look behind him or increase his speed.

Jackson was only about twenty feet behind him now. He could hear the light churning of Andrew's paddle.

"I don't have a camera. I'm not in the media."

No reply, no change in speed.

Jackson pulled closer. "Your wife suspected someone of stealing antique weathervanes."

Andrew looked straight ahead, as if Jackson weren't there. They reached the dock. Andrew used the paddle to pull his kayak against the tires roped to the dock and climbed out. He was wearing a retro Hawaiian swimsuit similar to the ones Jackson's adventure travel friends wore. He carried the kayak to the boathouse and hung it on the J-hooks.

Jackson was about to go the other route, call out, "VegasVegas isn't in the business of paying hit men."

But instead of going up to his house, Andrew stepped back on the dock. "Pull your kayak up on the grass, out of view."

Jackson did and followed Andrew up the sloping lawn to the porch. Andrew pulled open the sliding glass door and closed it after Jackson stepped inside. Andrew hung the khaki hat on a hook inside the door.

"Coffee?" he said.

"What? Sure. Yeah. Thank you."

Jackson sat at the round wooden kitchen table while Andrew got out cups. The knife block with one missing was on the kitchen counter next to the toaster oven.

"I'll give you Wallace and Gromit," Andrew said, "Or, if you'd prefer, I'll take it and give you the plain brown cup."

He turned to face Jackson, waiting for an answer. His eyes were the color of washed cement.

"I like Wallace and Gromit," Jackson said.

"So do I. Audrey always used a blue cup with a thick handle she made in one her ceramics classes."

He poured coffee from a stainless steel carafe. "I take milk. How about you?"

"Do you have soy milk?"

"I'm sorry, no."

"Then black is great. Thank you."

Andrew sat down across from Jackson. "What's your name?"

"Hank Carruthers."

Jackson got ready to deflect questions about his interest in things that weren't his business, but Andrew stirred his coffee and stared at it like he was waiting for his reflection to take shape.

He looked up when Jackson took another a sip and said, "Is it strong enough?"

"Perfect. I hope I didn't cut your ride short."

"I grind six scoops of beans and pour water through the filter. Four pours makes it just the right strength. I know this, but I always get greedy for an extra cup and do one more pour, even though I know it'll make the coffee too weak. And it does and I curse myself and vow I'll never do it again. But next morning I do."

What? Jackson had passed off the talk about coffee cup preferences as a delaying tactic, but he now wondered if the guy had lost his mind in prison. He'd have to steer the conversation back to weathervanes.

But first he couldn't help asking, "Why not put another scoop in the grinder?"

"It doesn't work out to one scoop per pour, but that wasn't your point. You're right, I could add enough beans for five pours. But I'm content with four when I start out. It's only later my greed takes over."

"My greed's different than yours," Jackson said.

"Explain."

"I'd want to get full value from every bean, so I'd do the maximum number of pours that still gave me great-tasting coffee. That's when my greed would kick in. I wouldn't allow myself to waste any of it, even if I knew it would keep me up half the night. Three in the morning I'd curse myself for drinking it all, then I'd remind myself how much more self-contempt I'd feel if I let perfectly good coffee go to waste just because I misjudged the amount of beans I put in the grinder."

Andrew listened carefully and nodded. "And you'd let yourself off the hook?"

"Unless I had something important the next day. Then I'd curse myself for having coffee in the first place."

Jackson took another sip. An unexpected preamble but maybe they bonded over obsessive tendencies.

The chair creaked as Andrew leaned back. "Who are you, Hank?"

"Nobody. A tourist. I met Warren Gunderson and he told me your wife suspected someone of stealing weathervanes."

"You wanted to help me?"

"It's none of my business. But then I saw you on the lake."

"What did Warren tell you?"

"She was visiting a rooster weathervane in Brattleboro and saw a guy staking it out."

"That's it?"

"She said the guy was a local. Someone Warren knew. He asked who but she wouldn't say. She didn't want to accuse the guy unfairly."

Andrew tapped his fingertips on the table like he was playing a piano melody. "Right now, I'm half thinking Audrey's on her way back from Willey's. She cut through the marsh near the boat launch and she's walking along the lakeshore path. I know it's impossible, but I'm still thinking it."

"I'm sure it's hard."

"Painful, of course, but that's not what I mean. The world where she's walking back from Willey's is more real than this other one."

Jackson was silent long enough to show he didn't callously dismiss Andrew's two worlds, then tried again. "This thief must have known she was on to him."

Sun through the screen drew a hatched pattern on the table.

"Thank you for telling me. But the police knew all this last summer. And Audrey's hobby had nothing to do with what happened."

Andrew was staring at the surface of his coffee again. Now what, a topic switch to the country of origin of the beans?

"Audrey's hobby," he said again. "She used to drive by weathervanes without a second glance. I remember pointing one out, a big centaur spinning in a rainstorm. I wanted to pull over for a closer look, but she said we'd be late for lunch. Then last summer, apropos of nothing, it became her passion. She spent hours with that antique shop owner in Craftsbury. She drove all over the state visiting weathervanes she saw in books and websites. It was good she had a new hobby, but it was so random. How can you go from not noticing them to being obsessed?"

Jackson had already decided the best way to keep Andrew talking was to participate in his digressions. Besides, he knew exactly what Andrew meant.

"I roomed with a guy in college who collected shot glasses from all over the world. It drove me crazy. There was nothing about shot glasses that overlapped any of his interests. He didn't even drink."

"Mementos?"

"Maybe if he went to the places they came from."

Andrew looked up in surprise. "He didn't get them on trips?"

"He never left the state. Whenever he heard someone was going somewhere he begged them to bring him back a shot glass. I asked him once, 'Why do you collect shot glasses, Gilbert?'"

"What did he say?"

"He said, 'What the fuck kind of question is that?'"

Andrew clapped his hands together. "We are one amusing species, aren't we?" His moist-eyed enjoyment of Gilbert the shot glass collector jolted Jackson back to his purpose for sitting there. Humans were an amusing species, true, he couldn't argue the point, but they were also a depraved and violent species that murdered people they once vowed to love. He forced out a laugh to keep the convivial mood intact.

"I made the mistake of analyzing Audrey's new hobby," Andrew said. "I told her we all need ways to fill up the hours so if we lack genuine interests we fabricate them. We're so terrified of a random existence we deceive ourselves into thinking the fabricated interest has significance."

"How'd that go over?"

"Audrey's not prone to outbursts like Gilbert apparently is. But she stopped talking about weathervanes."

This didn't bode well. "She never mentioned the thefts?"

"That's the one thing she did talk about. She thought the crime part would interest me and she was right. She said some thieves would disguise themselves as painters and steal weathervanes in broad daylight."

Jackson sipped his coffee to conceal his eagerness. Over Andrew's shoulder, retreating sun lit up the glass ornaments dangling from the window. Purple whale. Green cat. Yellow sun. Below them was a wooden loon and a row of plants in ceramic vases. He took another sip and was shocked to only now realize the flavor was hazelnut, his favorite.

"She told you about the person she saw in Brattleboro?"

"And I told her she caught a tourist red-handed in the act of viewing an antique."

"Did she tell you who she saw?"

"Same thing she told Warren. He lived in Greensboro and we knew him."

"Who?"

"She didn't say. She wanted to surprise me."

Jackson almost slammed his hand on the table in frustration. "Surprise you? What do you mean, surprise you?"

"We made a bet. She said, 'You think I'm an overreacting, paranoid fool.' I said only on this topic. She said, 'If I'm right, you owe me a week on Kauai.' I told her she had a deal."

"When was this?"

"Days, maybe a week, before she was murdered."

"She tried to catch the guy in the act and he found out. He's the one who framed you. Him and his partners."

"A few days before Audrey was murdered, we had dinner in Stowe. On the way home, I realized I botched the math and gave the waiter a seven percent tip. I felt like driving back, but decided I'd do it over the phone when I got home. But the restaurant was closed and the next day I forgot all about it. If you were to ask me who was more likely to frame me for murder, the stiffed waiter or Audrey's weathervane thief, I'd pick the waiter."

"Antique weathervanes are worth a lot of money. People who steal them study the houses beforehand. Why is it so farfetched to think she saw someone doing it?"

"Before that, she saw someone staking out a weathervane in Waterloo. And someone else staking one out in Rutland City. Anybody within a fifty-yard radius of a weathervane was a potential thief."

"Maybe she was imagining things, but wouldn't you at least tell the police?"

"It's one of the first things I told them. They thought I was grasping at straws, but Warren told them the same thing and they had to follow up. They also talked to her antique store friend. This guy told the police he visited the Brattleboro house and the weathervane was worthless. No thief would want it."

"You can't rule them out because one antique store guy said it was worthless."

Andrew went up to the window and rotated one of the vases so the single orange blossom was in what remained of the sunlight. "Want to hear something strange? I started thinking the police had it right. I did and I didn't, if that makes sense. I knew I would never harm Audrey. But the police said I did it, the news, my own lawyer didn't believe me, he couldn't hide it. My clothes in the lake, drugged with my own sleeping pills. Why would I kill the woman I love? I wouldn't. But all the facts said I did so I must have."

"You woke up a mile away."

"I blacked out, that's all I could think. I killed her and blacked out. When my lawyer told me about the video, I was almost giddy, not because it got the charges dropped. Because then I knew I didn't do it."

"I doubt the police see it that way."

"They don't. They think I hired someone and filmed my alibi."

He shifted another plant into the sun. "You see what prison's done? I'm confiding like you're a trusted friend." Then, as if he'd said something rude, "I did enjoy hearing about Gilbert the shot glass collector."

He put his cup on the counter. "I'm getting tired. Coffee doesn't keep me up the way it keeps you up. I drink too much. I'll re-phrase that. I drink a lot. Too much means it's not a good thing, and I think coffee is a good thing."

It was a dismissal. Andrew opened a drawer and took out a pad of paper and pen. He wrote down a phone number and handed it to Jackson.

"I have to get a new cell. This one's to the house. Maybe we can go on a kayak ride some night after the photographers go in."

"That would be great. I'll give you my number, too."

Andrew handed him the pad and pen. "I didn't want to presume."

Jackson wrote down his cell number. He'd freaked out enough about Trish discovering it that he'd already changed the voice mail to a message from Hank.

Out on the porch, Andrew took a long breath of lake-scented air. "My first night out I vowed never again to take things like the lake air for granted. A few more days and I won't even notice."

He was staring at the rectangle of lake framed by elms. "I'll fall asleep tonight sometime between four and five. She'll be lying next to me. This world you're asking me about will vanish and let me sleep in peace."

He wasn't fishing for commiseration, so Jackson said nothing.

"It was nice talking to you, Hank."

"Oh, hey, I almost forgot. Have you ever heard of a script called *Johnny Payback*?"

Andrew walked to the edge of the porch, so Jackson couldn't see his face when he said, "How do you know Trish?"

"We're both staying at the Morning Loon. She told me you read her script and liked it. I didn't believe her."

"Why?"

"I've been to L.A. People are always claiming some producer or director loves their script."

"It was good. Very good. I had her send it to my agent. I forgot all about it, for obvious reasons. Wonder if anything ever came of it."

He stood on the porch as Jackson carried his kayak out of the yard. He waved and went back in the house.

Was it possible to leave Andrew's house knowing less than when he entered? Audrey didn't tell him who she saw because they had a bet. Ridiculous but maybe not. She knew Andrew didn't take her seriously so she vowed to prove it.

Or did Andrew invent the bet to have fun at Jackson's expense, saying I know who you are and why you're here? But if he did use casinos to pay his killer, he wouldn't risk revealing it just so he could amuse himself with riddles and double meanings.

If Andrew was framed, why was he so dismissive of the weathervane possibility? Even if Audrey cried wolf as much as he said, he didn't have any better alternatives—at least none he shared with Jackson.

Wednesday, 8:19 p.m.

Trish sat alone at a table on the porch, wineglass on one of the white squares of checkered tablecloth, MacBook on the chair beside her. She'd watched him pass the tennis court and cross the street, so she knew he came from the lake.

"You missed our dinner."

She put her glass in front of him, and he took a sip. "Thank you."

"Let me run an idea by you. Your name is Jackson Oliver, and you live in San Jose, Costa Rica, where you get rich off the weakness of your fellow man."

The VegasVegas site wouldn't have told her anything since they took the trial odds down. If she knew about online casinos posting celebrity trials, she'd figure the rest out. Otherwise, she couldn't know why he came to Greensboro.

Unless she was the one who logged onto Cass' account.

"It's better this way," he said, "Hank Carruthers was starting to annoy me. The guy cut people way too much slack."

"Enterprise Rental clerks can be chatty."

"Maybe, but that's not how you found out."

"How'd I find out?"

"My turn to run an idea by you. You wrote a script called *Johnny Payback* that won honorable mention in a contest. You heard about a movie director staying in Greensboro for the summer so you came to show him the script. I don't know where you stayed, but it wasn't the Morning Loon. You didn't check in here until the day after Audrey's murder. Andrew's lawyer said he didn't have a motive, and he didn't. Not until he met the beautiful honorable-mention contest winner."

She turned her beaded bracelet in circles, in one direction then the other. "I almost half think you're serious."

"Why'd you switch hotels?"

"Why do you keep harping on honorable mention? Another contest that didn't come up in your search, my script won the grand prize."

"You admit you met him?"

She used the cocktail napkin to pick up a crumb of bread on the table and crumpled it into a ball. "What happens next in your idea?"

"Andrew knows he'll be the main suspect, so he comes up with a plan. He hires someone to kill Audrey and frame him. He'll get arrested, but he'll have an alibi on film. Sure, a director could rig that camera move in the motel room. But it would be easier if someone filmed it for him."

"A man checked out the room."

"He killed Audrey. You drove Andrew to the motel."

"Last person who read my script I sent a gift from wine.com. But I thanked Andrew by filming his alibi?"

"Why'd you switch hotels?"

"I have an answer to that question."

"What?"

"I wanted to."

"Yesterday after lunch, why were you were at the library?"

"I like books."

She took one more sip of wine and placed the glass in front of him. "Finish it. I've got a post to write, about an online casino owner who spent an hour in Andrew Marvel's house."

"An online casino owner who went for a walk along the lake."

"A lying online casino owner."

"Don't do the post to get back at me."

"That's not a good a reason?"

He scraped at the thick white overlapping threads on the tablecloth with his fingernail. "I can give you a bigger story."

"You keep saying that. Too late now."

Jackson took a deep breath of night air. "I love the smell of day lilies. I love how the moon casts pine tree shadows on the lake."

Trish arched her eyebrows and opened her mouth in a way that could only be described as dumbfounded.

"You think I want to suspect you? It ruins everything. I'm an open-minded guy, and I can overlook a lot of flaws. But murder accomplice is a deal-breaker for me. So I'll have to enjoy the moonlight and day lilies by myself."

"Yeah?"

"Sorry to say."

"Well, cocky, lying con man is a deal-breaker for me. Why are you a vegan, anyway?"

"How do you know?"

"The waitress Tammy."

"I don't think animals should suffer and die so I can enjoy a tasty meal."

"But you're a crook."

"We can't like animals?"

"Good night." As she stood, the moonlight sketched the outline of parted lips and pooled up in the curve of her shoulder. "I take that back. I hope your night sucks."

"Why so hostile? I don't really think you're a murder accomplice. I only half think it. Probably less than half."

She sat down again. He handed her the glass and she took a sip. "You don't trust me," she said. "That's one of your character flaws. Tell me more."

"That's the easiest question you've asked all day. I don't believe in anything. I don't do any good in the world. I can't even decide what good is."

"Then you're off the hook for not doing any."

"I'm greedy. I have more money than I need. I'm bad at forgiving when someone rips me off and makes a fool of me."

"You left out liar."

"You already knew about that one."

"Jackson Oliver. Much more musical than Joe Smith."

"So you're from Mt. Kisco?"

"Yes."

"Born there?"

"Yes."

"Family still there?"

"If I'm the Other Woman, why do my posts accuse Andrew of hiring a hit man?"

"I thought the half of me that trusts you was getting a turn to talk."

"He bores me."

"Give him a chance. You might warm up to him."

"Doubt it. I prefer the other guy. The liar who stood me up tonight."

"Doesn't happen to you much?"

"What were you doing with Andrew Marvel? What did you talk about?"

"You asked why your posts accuse Andrew? You have to admit it makes a good cover. Who would ever suspect the accusing reporter of being the Other Woman?"

"You're right. You have more insights than people would think by looking at you."

"You write blog posts every day, but on this nothing. 'I came to Greensboro to show this famous director my script and next thing you know he's accused of murdering his wife.' Where was that post?"

"Another good question. You're on a roll. Now I need to go write that post about you."

"Not fair. I told you my character flaws. You can't go without telling me yours."

"Fair enough, but I warn you it's a big one." She leaned closer to him, the way she would if they were going to kiss. "Maybe, just maybe, I'm the reason a man murdered his wife."

Her lips brushed against his earlobe. She lowered her eyes and sat there a moment before saying "Good night" and going back into the lodge.

At least this time she didn't amend it to hope his night sucked.

The wind swept across the porch, lifting a cocktail napkin off one of the wicker tables and floating it to the ground.

He stood to follow and talk her out of posting what she knew. But why? She wouldn't write the post if she helped Andrew. And if she didn't help him, what could she say anyway? She knew he owned a casino and checked in under a false name, and she suspected he talked to Andrew. But what kind of story was that? If she knew about the trial betting, she would have pressed him on it instead of pretending to walk off in a huff.

He used his iPhone to check analytics. VegasVegas had one visitor from Greensboro, who didn't go to the entertainment page. So even though she couldn't have seen the trial odds, he now knew she didn't go looking for them.

She admitted Andrew read her script, which she'd only do if she had no involvement with the murder, unless she and Andrew discussed it and decided they couldn't deny meeting last summer.

Why switch hotels? To conceal her arrival in Vermont before the murder and make it appear she came to blog about it. But that was no good. It would take the police two phone calls to trace her movement from one hotel to another. The innocent explanation made more sense: she blogged about crime and the most sensational crime in years happened in Greensboro. She'd moved closer to the action.

Jackson spent the remainder of her wine trying to come up with an innocent explanation for her presence at the library. But innocent meant coincidental.

If she'd logged onto Cass' account, that let Blake and Wally off the hook, unless she was there with one of them, the motive and the killer, logging on together.

Was it possible she was at the library because she suspected Wally or Blake?

How long was she in Vermont before the murder? Long enough to be its cause?

Jackson searched around until he found out Andrew Marvel was represented by an agent named Kathie Baker at ICM.

His phone call didn't interrupt Alton in the middle of a Beverly Hills heist, because he picked up on the first ring. "Perfect timing," he said, "my turn to ask you a question."

"Shoot."

"I'm in the car and just for old time's sake I switch on the radio, a classic rock station, and Mike from Ventura requests 'Highway Song' by the Outlaws. 'Hey, totally awesome, kick ass request. Way to make things happen, Mike,' the DJ tells him, to which Mike replies, 'Hey, thanks a lot, man.'

"Now the question I wanted to ask the DJ, which I'll ask you instead, is can Mike from Ventura calling and requesting a song really be considered an achievement worthy of such enthusiastic praise? Apparently he thinks so since he doesn't modestly disavow the praise by saying, 'Hey, man, the Outlaws are the people who deserve the credit. They're the ones who wrote and performed the song. All I did was call up and ask to hear it.'

"No, Mike from Ventura says, 'Hey, thanks a lot, man,' which seems to indicate he considers the DJ's praise legitimately earned. Jackson, do you think requesting 'Highway Song' constitutes a praise-worthy achievement?"

"I don't think the DJ was sincere. Radio stations use playlists."

"Do they still? It's been so long since I've listened to the radio. So that means they record requests for songs they already know they're going to play, then they play those requests back right before playing the song."

"I think so."

"So the DJ was toying with Mike from Ventura, making him think he'd just made his presence felt in the world when in fact his request was of absolutely no consequence. 'Highway Song' was going to be played whether Mike called or not."

"Sorry to say."

"So what's up, buddy?"

"You still have friends in the film industry?"

"One of them recently got back at a producer who cheated him by giving me a friendly tip about when said producer's house would be empty."

"Talent agencies log in scripts they read, right?"

"I'm pretty sure."

"Last summer an ICM agent named Kathy Baker read a script called *Johnny Payback* by Trish Devereaux. I need to know what date she logged it in."

Wednesday, 9:23 p.m.

The Suburban rolled to a stop beside Jackson's Corolla. Cass had a gray hoodie over his head, and he was carrying a paper bag. He looked around, saw Jackson was the only person on the porch, and sat at the next table.

"Good evening to you."

"You too."

"Staying up past nine makes you a night owl in Greensboro. You one of the reporters?"

"Photographer."

"I'm Cass."

"Hank."

Cass laughed. "You guys are everywhere. I got to wait in line at Willey's twice as long to buy my beer. But I didn't come to bitch about that. Reporters need their beer, too."

He lifted the paper bag off his lap and held it above the table. "What I got in here's gonna be in a museum someday, Hank. Unless you get it first."

Cass couldn't be trying to scam some random reporter. He had to know who Jackson was. He'd have to see how this played out. "Thanks, but I'll pass."

"If someone offered you Jack the Ripper's knife, would you pass?"

Cass reached into his bag. "When it's sitting in the display case, the museum guide's gonna tell his tour group, 'And now we get to the piece of evidence that locked up the guy Andrew Marvel hired to murder his wife.'"

He pulled out a plastic baggie containing a single twenty-five-dollar blackjack chip. It was blue and green, bearing the name Casino de Mont-Tremblant.

"A blackjack chip?"

"That's what you see. What you don't see is the fingerprints. Whose fingerprints? Could it be the person who killed Audrey Marvel?"

"Where'd you find it?"

"In the glovebox of a car parked near the Marvel house. There I was, minding my own business, breaking into an unattended vehicle. Little did I know the owner was inside killing Audrey Marvel."

"You missed the boat, Cass. Marvel's lawyer would have made you a rich man."

"He'd tell the cops I was at the scene of the crime."

Cass waved the baggie in front of Jackson like a hypnotist. "How much would you expect to pay for this chip? One thousand? Two thousand? It's yours for the incredibly low price of just four hundred ninety-nine dollars."

Jackson laughed. From the moment he limped out of the library, this guy Cass cracked him up. "What if I tell the cops about your offer?"

"Officer, I was only trying to scam one of the photographers making our beer lines longer."

"What kind of car was it?"

Cass crinkled the paper bag as he shook his head. "Hank, do you really think I'd make up a story and forget to think of a detail like that? It was a red Monte Carlo. Can't you find a better way to test my story?"

"A guy planning on committing murder isn't going to park outside the victim's house."

"He would if the car was stolen. Plus he was two houses down, in the Buddington driveway. It's concealed by trees and the Buddingtons were away. Now let me ask you this: if that guy was parked there so he could take a moonlight walk along the lake, why didn't he report the break-in?"

TV voices wisecracked from one of the second floor rooms. Cass looked up. "Wonder what they're watching."

"You're the only one who saw the Monte Carlo?"

"Go stand on Cozy Lane around ten at night and see for yourself how many people drive by. Times Square it ain't."

"You said the guy didn't report the break-in. How do you know?"

"I read the police report in the Hardwick paper every morning. I got a big ego and I like reading about myself."

Cass let out what sounded like a giggle. "You wouldn't believe the shit they put in that police report. Yesterday, item one was about someone vandalizing a pumpkin patch."

"That wasn't you?"

"Shit, no. Halloween's my favorite holiday."

"What kind of crimes do you do?"

"Nothing that would interest a big shot reporter like you. B & E. Shoplifting. Things of that nature."

Cass swung the chip in front of Jackson's face. "Going once, going twice...I'm a sucker giving it to you for four hundred ninety-nine. I put this thing on eBay and I'd get a fortune. Hey, tell you what. I'll even give you a guarantee like them TV commercials do. He's guilty or your money back."

"Sorry. I'm sure some other reporter will buy it."

Cass dropped the baggie back into the paper bag. "No harm in asking."

Another burst of canned laughter, louder than anything before, came from the room above.

Cass grinned along with the laugh track. "Must have been a pretty fucking funny joke. I wonder how much they get paid."

"The people in the laugh track?"

"Not a bad job. Get your laugh recorded, sit back and collect money every time someone says something supposed to be funny."

"Where do you think they find the laughers?"

"Look for people with no clue how the world is."

They both sat without speaking, taking in the night sky.

Jackson pictured Cass in the Hardwick cemetery, confessing his fears to the stubby headstone, pointing the phantom gun at his head, throwing his head back at the phantom bullet's impact.

He felt the urge to warn Cass about the people he was dealing with, give him a chance to unburden his secrets.

"Listen, Cass…"

Cass looked over with his guileless, laugh track smile. "I made you an offer and you turned me down. There's no bitterness in my heart. We all got to do what we think is right."

"You're the only witness to the red Monte Carlo. That's not a good thing to be."

"How long you been a photographer, Hank? Fuck it, I'm not interested. Just making conversation."

Before Jackson could weigh the pros and cons of taking Cass into his confidence, he picked up his paper bag and hopped up from his chair. "Have a good night, Hank."

"You too. Take care of yourself."

So they sent Cass to let Jackson know they knew who he was. But why invent a story about a car parked outside the house?

Or was Cass acting on his own? Did he hear about the guy with long, blond hair handing out money at the Morning Loon and invent a story to claim some for himself?

Could Cass possibly be telling the truth about a car parked outside the neighbor's house? Sure, someone might see it, but it made for a faster getaway than a bike. Cass was right to worry about placing himself at the crime scene. People like him started getting used as scapegoats the moment they left their mother's womb.

Really, Jackson had no idea what to think. Why just once couldn't a piece of information come his way that didn't have a flip side? Why couldn't something happen or get said that eliminated someone absolutely? No more "on the one hand this, on the other that," which is something he could say about the two different murder scenarios and everyone involved in both of them.

Wednesday, 10:17 p.m.

Jackson assumed the firewood in the coalscuttle was a decorative touch, but it was almost cold enough to make a fire. A brush, shovel, and log filter hung from hooks on the fireplace tool holder. But one hook was empty. Where was the poker?

The Morning Loon had enough charming imperfections that an incomplete set of fireplace tools fit right in. But why did the one missing tool have to be the one that could double as a weapon? And why did he have to make this discovery hours after finding the slice in the window screen?

He got into bed and started a solo game of Words with Friends.

Only a few hours earlier, the wind and pines were dutiful employees of the Morning Loon, giving guests a pleasant, scented backdrop, making the rustic cottage vacation complete. Now they dropped the pretense and reverted to their true dark selves. The wind hissed through pine needles, dropping pinecones and snapping branches on the cottage roof.

A pin of light through the window jerked Jackson awake. It angled toward his cottage from the farm, getting bigger, now bouncing up and down as if held by someone running. It was probably the farmer out checking his field.

This time of night?

The pine needle wind wailed a cadence to the bouncing light. Jackson jumped out of bed and grabbed the fireplace shovel, pressing himself against the wall beside the window. The light got closer and jerked upward and vanished, the person holding it no doubt thinking he was close enough and turning it off to avoid detection.

Jackson strained to hear the soft padding of feet on the grass ringing the cabin but the fucking hissing pine wind swallowed up all other sounds. The light switched back on, no there were two, side by side. They were back at the far edge of the farm again, but they were moving faster this time, approaching the cabin at full sprint until they jerked upward and shut off at the same spot as before.

He placed the looped handle of the shovel back on its hook. They weren't approaching flashlights. They were headlights on Town Highway 1 curving past the Morning Loon. The first, slower, vehicle must have had one light out.

He went back to bed. The throbbing drumbeat in his temples slowed. He had no problem laughing at himself, and it was pretty comical getting freaked out by a tractor with a missing headlight. Now he could look forward to a nice, calm sleep.

The wind shrieked. A pinecone smacked the roof. The heavy-metal drummers in his temples launched into a solo that would make John Bonham proud. He got up, put the fireplace shovel on the end table, and turned on the light.

Thursday, 5:45 a.m.

The absence of car horns and hot, fume-soaked air woke him before six. Mist clung to the field like lint. Two squirrels chased each other up and down a pine tree. The wind and pines were playing nice again. Soft, fragrant breezes made amends for the nocturnal unruliness. This was Jackson's last full day. Tomorrow VegasVegas would get blacklisted, they'd lose all their customers, and Jackson could move to that suburban street named after a tree and swap glory day stories with the former division three football star who now worked as an insurance actuary.

One more day. He knew all the players. How hard could it be to find out who did what?

Thursday, 7:03 a.m.

Jackson waited for Tracy to finish showing the arm-in-arm couple something on a map, compliment a wardrobe feature, and tell them to enjoy their breakfast.

"Oh, hey," she said when he went up to the desk.

"Morning. Have you heard of the Casino de Mont-Tremblant?"

Tracy's eyes narrowed. "I thought you didn't know anything about gambling."

"I overheard someone talking about it."

"It's in Montreal. I go maybe once a month. I've got a VIP card."

"Anyone else from around her go?"

"My friend Kaitlin. I once saw Jim Deckman. He's the manager at Willey's. Also a guy named Wally Sprenger."

Blake knew Wally was in the library when someone logged onto Cass' account. He made sure Cass waved that blackjack chip in front of Jackson's face so he could see the casino name and assumed Jackson would ask around until he learned Wally went to the Casino de Mont-Tremblant. Not a bad way of trying to shift Jackson's suspicion to Wally.

But there was another way of seeing it. Wally claimed the money clip because he knew nobody else would claim it. It was his way of putting Jackson in his place, telling him, "You and your cheap stunts don't faze me. Yeah I logged onto the account, and there's nothing you can do about it. Now go home and choke on your pancakes and maple syrup."

And now Wally was taking it a step further, saying, "Yeah, I killed Audrey, but you'll never be able to prove it."

Jackson still couldn't rule out the possibility that Cass really did break into a red Monte Carlo the night of the murder, though what were the odds he'd pick Jackson as the random media guy to sell the chip to?

He had breakfast and brought his coffee to the porch. The purple-fleeced couple came out and sat nearby. After a few silent minutes, the woman asked Jackson if he knew what flower was so fragrant and he told her day lilies.

"Day lilies," she told the purple-fleeced man.

"Day lilies." They both lapsed into silence.

The black F-150 arrived for the morning buffalo delivery. Jackson waved as Blake pushed the coolers. Blake gave the clown head a nod in response.

Jackson went up to the railing and said, "You were right."

Blake stopped. "About?"

"The money clip. It belonged to Wally."

"I told him about it. That was a good thing you did."

Jackson felt a hot tingling in his head as he got ready to catch him off guard with Burt Tager's bike.

But before he could get anything out, Blake said, "You going to make me pry it out of you?"

Jackson had no idea what he was talking about.

"The blackened buffalo prime rib. Best thing you ever tasted?"

"I had the eggplant medallions."

A thump came from under the porch. And another one. It took one more before Jackson realized Blake was kicking the bottom cooler.

"You said you were going to have the blackened buffalo prime rib."

"You recommended it."

"You said sounds good."

"I said sounds good. I didn't say I'd order it. I saw the eggplant on the menu and that's what I wanted."

"I thought we patched up that book problem."

"I didn't get the eggplant medallions to spite you. I like eggplant."

Blake gave the cooler one last, harder kick.

Ready or not, here it comes. "Do you know a guy named Burt Tager?"

Blake looked down. Jackson could only see the freckled forehead.

"Burt's lived here for years. How do you know him? He's out of town."

"I wanted to go biking and someone suggested using his."

Blake nodded at the shed. "They've got plenty of bikes here."

"I heard his is a good one. Or maybe that's gossip?"

"How would I know?"

"You wouldn't."

Blake jerked the clown head to the side, like he was trying to shake water out of his ear. "You say you didn't order the eggplant to spite me."

Jackson couldn't believe it. He was sure he'd trapped Blake, but the guy was more worked up about the eggplant dinner than about the bike.

"I told you I ate eggplant because I did."

"Wrong. You told me out of spite. It would be so easy to say you had the buffalo and it was the best you ever ate. I never would have known the difference. I would have driven away happy."

"What does it matter to you what I eat?"

"It matters because it's so simple to bring another person pleasure. Just say, 'Yes, Blake, I had the buffalo blackened prime rib and boy was it delicious.' I have to remind myself people are vicious. So easy to give others pleasure but they'd rather give pain. People aren't dignified like buffalo."

"You slaughter your buffalo."

"I don't staple numbers to their ears like the big farms. I give them names." Blake turned away. He wheeled his coolers toward the side entrance.

If Blake took Burt Tager's bike that night, he now knew Jackson knew. Flushing him out in the open and seeing what he did next, maybe that was a good thing. Maybe it wasn't.

Jackson didn't believe in fate, God, or anyone in their extended family, but as he was having a refill of coffee, and comparing it unfavorably to Andrew's, caller ID said A. Marvel was calling.

"Hi, Andrew."

"Good morning, Hank. I had a thought and I wanted to call before I talked myself out of it."

"What's up?"

"I assume you rented a car."

"Yeah. You need a ride somewhere?"

"I thought you might want to go on a hike. More of a walk, really. The Barr Hill Nature Trail."

"Sounds great. Why would you talk yourself out of it?"

"You have to admit, it's a little presumptuous to ask someone I barely know to pick me up and drive me past the photographers."

"After the coffee, I owe you."

"Then I refuse. I don't want you to do it out of obligation. I'll only go if it's something you think you'd enjoy."

"I'd love it.

"I should have asked if now's a good time. I'm a little jumpy. I've had the police here all morning."

"Pick you up in ten."

Thursday, 8:25 a.m.

As soon as Jackson pulled up, the front door opened. Andrew's hiking hat and sunglasses did a good job concealing his face.

"Thanks for joining me," he said.

"Want to get in back?"

"Yeah, probably better they don't see a reclined seat."

When they turned onto Town Highway 1, Andrew said, "How many?"

"Cows or photographers?"

"I tell myself they're only doing their job. But it doesn't work. I despise them. I can't help it."

"I'd feel the same way."

"My lawyer arranged for someone to bring groceries, but I'm going to have to go out there eventually."

Andrew was lying flat in the backseat. "You're going to want to turn left at the church."

When the pavement gave way to a dirt road, Andrew sat up. "Go left again, up the hill."

Barr Hill was steep and straight, with fenced-in fields on the right and open grass on the left.

"That's the barn up there." Andrew was obviously referring to where he spent the night of Audrey's murder.

Uncut grass around the barn extended to the pine tree line of the ridge. Jackson recalled reading that a farmer in the valley owned the land and intended to rebuild the barn when he got around to it.

"Why do you think they left you there?"

"It was a good choice. Not likely someone would come stumbling in at night."

"Whoever brought you had to go home afterwards. He wouldn't want to run into any police cars that late."

"Point being he lives nearby?"

"Why drive more than you have to?"

The trailhead parking area wasn't far past the barn. There were two others cars.

"Two one-way loops," Andrew said. "No worries about running into them. Oh, I brought sunscreen in case you don't have any."

"Thanks, I already put some on." Jackson came milliseconds from adding, "You live in the tropics like I do…"

He forced himself to repeat the thought three times: It might have been him. It might have been him. It might have been him.

"Both loops are under a mile. Not exactly Mount Everest, but there's a nice view."

After fifty feet of winding through fern glades and juniper bushes, they reached a cedar post with the letter A. They walked to post B without speaking, the steady tapping of shoes on undergrowth the only sound until Andrew broke the silence by saying, "Where do you live?"

L.A. would be easiest because Jackson had memories to draw from, but that would lead to a discussion of common experiences so he named the city his parents moved to.

"Portland."

"I love Portland. Most bike-friendly city in the country. If it weren't for the weather…"

"Yeah, you've got better weather in L.A."

Andrew didn't seem to be probing. It was polite chitchat and his heart wasn't in it.

"So, I'm sure you get annoyed by suck-up fans," Jackson said, "but I have to say *Frontier Zero* is in my top ten all-time."

"I appreciate that."

They walked on a little longer in silence before Andrew said,

"Can you believe they showed up at my house this morning at seven?"

"The police?"

"They think I made them look like fools and, to them, that's a worse crime than murder. Then you've got the DA on the news apologizing for all they put me through, and it makes them even madder. They keep hammering me with the same question. Who would free me? The person I hired would but who else? I give them the same answer. I honestly don't know. I wish I did, but I don't."

"All they can do is hope you withdraw money."

"They're watching my accounts, of course, but they seem more focused on the past. They think I planned this a long time ago. Get this. They asked about six consecutive three-hundred-dollar cash withdrawals from different ATMs over the course of an eight-month period two years ago. I said I withdraw three hundred every time I go to Costco. They said, someone like you going to Costco? I asked if they'd like to see my Costco card and they actually took me up on it."

"They'll leave you alone eventually."

They passed through a grove of spruce and came to an open space.

"This is the Woodburn Panorama," Andrew said.

A field of grass ringed by ferns and mattress-thick moss looked up at white cedars and white and red spruce and balsam firs along the summit.

Andrew peeled a piece of bark from a cedar and rubbed it between his fingers. "I appreciate what you said back there."

"What?"

"You liked *Frontier Zero*."

"I didn't say 'like.' I said top ten all-time."

"I'm going to make a comeback, Hank."

"I'm sure you will."

Andrew shook his head. "You were sincere when you praised *Frontier Zero*. Now you're being polite."

Andrew watched his piece of bark float to the ground. "A few setbacks and they act like you're contaminated. It can't be the marketing budget cut in half or the release date. It's the director's fault. Let's bury the director and give ourselves a bigger Christmas bonus."

"I'm sure it's a tough business," Jackson said for lack of a better platitude.

"Prison delayed it, but my comeback will blow people away. You'll see."

They got back on the trail and passed post G.

"You still don't think it's possible you were framed by weathervane thieves?"

"I've been thinking about it nonstop since you left. I've gone through it from every angle. Do people steal weathervanes? Yes. Do they study their targets in advance? Yes. So just because Audrey suspected half the state doesn't mean she didn't see an actual thief in Brattleboro."

"Remember your bet. She might have gone where the guy lived. Looked around for signs of weathervanes."

"That's so opposite everything about her. But, yes, for argument's sake, that's what she did. He wasn't home. She snuck into his property. She looked under the boathouse and found a stolen weathervane. She'd go straight to the police."

"Okay, she didn't find hard evidence, but she followed him and he put two and two together."

"What a risk. Wouldn't he think she told someone?"

Uncle Warren made the same point and it was a valid one.

"If weathervane thieves did kill her, framing me makes all the sense in the world. But driving me three hours, carrying me up to a motel room, making a video so they can free me?"

Jackson resisted the temptation to reveal why they might do that. If Andrew really was behind it all, he already knew. If he wasn't, he'd go to the police with the information. Jackson didn't want that to happen yet.

"Did you mention weathervanes to the police?"

"Yes, and they said the same thing they said last summer: that they went to the house where Audrey saw the person and the weathervane was worthless. Then they turned it around, asked me who it was Audrey saw. I told them what I told you. They had a good laugh over that one."

"Know what doesn't make sense?" Jackson said.

"What?"

"Last year, they couldn't find a motive so they fell back on a fight, spur of the moment, anyone can snap. But if you hired someone, that makes it premeditated, which means now you need a legitimate motive."

"Where were you when I was trying to find a good lawyer?"

They didn't talk more about the murder until the car ride from Barr Hill back to Andrew's house, Andrew flat on the backseat, his voice slow and uncertain as he said, "What do you think?"

"About what?"

"You know."

"Do I think you hired someone?"

"Do you?"

"No

"Why?"

"You're not the type."

"There's a type?"

"I can't see you doing it."

"The worst serial killers come across as the guy next door. But thank you. What about the video?"

"I don't know," Jackson said.

"Doesn't it give you doubts?"

"I didn't say I was sure. You asked what I thought."

"The police know nothing about me yet they take it as a given I'd hire someone to kill my wife."

Jackson didn't see any point saying that the rest of the world agreed with the police.

Thursday, 9:44 a.m.

Jackson never came up with ideas in the shower, possibly because he was a freak about conserving water so his showers ended before ideas had time to form. But in the shower he took after dropping Andrew off, he thought about books and movies where the killer re-visits the scene of his crime. If this obsession wasn't something dreamed up by crime writers and directors to add drama, a killer might want to attend the trial of the man he framed.

Jackson fast-forwarded through trial footage, but the video operator never cut to public seating, so there was no way to know if Wally or Blake were in attendance.

He thought about what he said to Andrew on the hike. It started out as a crime of passion. After the video, it became a meticulously choreographed murder. The prosecution had over a year to interview people who knew the Marvels. If Audrey had spoken of jealousy, people would have heard. If Andrew had been spending time with an unfamiliar woman, people would have seen.

So why was Jackson holding on to Trish as the Other Woman? Because she was one of three people who could have logged onto Cass' account from the library and because she and Andrew met at some point before the murder.

One new point in Andrew's favor was Jackson himself. If Andrew used the betting to pay his killer, he wouldn't go hiking in public with someone who could lead the police to the method of payment.

Trish had posted something new on her blog.

Where's the money?

If Andrew were pitching his plan as a movie idea, we've reached the point the studio executive would stop him. "Okay, here's the problem, Andrew. Our audience doesn't demand a good guy hero. They can admire the cold-blooded killer, provided he's good at what he does. The husband fails that test with flying colors. Maybe the police will never find evidence of the hired killer, but they don't need to. The husband has to pay him. The money trail's what leads them to the killer."

So why haven't the police found it? Why? Why? Why?

The cabin phone rang.

"Hello, this is Hank."

"Enjoying the post? A little on the short side, I know."

"How often do you check analytics?"

"I like to know my readers' tastes. If you have a solution, you can leave it in the comments section."

"It's a riddle," Jackson said.

"Is it?…Hey, want to meet on the porch? I need to show you something."

He agreed to meet her in fifteen minutes.

Alton had left a message when Jackson was driving Andrew home and Jackson forgot to listen. He did now.

"Dude, you remember my friend Scott from high school? Commercial real estate guy? He was getting bored so he took one of those career aptitude tests and he's all excited about the results. They say his true calling isn't commercial real estate, it's guitarist. I said, 'But, Scott, if guitar playing is really your true calling, wouldn't you have, I don't know, started playing guitar a long time ago?' He said, 'Alton, I wish I'd known. I wish I'd taken that test a long time ago.' I said, 'Scott, what I'm saying is, do you need a four hundred-dollar test to tell you your interest is playing guitar? Isn't it a better indicator if you buy a guitar and start playing?…' Doesn't sound as funny when I leave it on voice-mail. So, yeah, I got your information. *Johnny Payback*, by Trish Devereaux logged into ICM by Kathy Baker on June 22, 2014. *Saving Flora*, by Trish Devereaux, logged into ICM by Kathy Baker on July 17, 2013."

Thursday, 10:02 a.m.

Jackson went down to the porch a few minutes early. Trish was finishing up her post or getting last-minute instructions from Andrew on how to deal with the Costa Rican thorn in their side.

She came out from the lobby, blue backpack strapped over one shoulder. She pulled out her MacBook and placed it in front of him on the table.

"Today's post. Still in draft form. I wanted your feedback first."

> In 2003, a research chemist in Aventura, Florida, approached two homeless men in a park with an unusual offer. If they killed his wife, he'd give them a hundred dollars and two cases of Corona beer. They reported this to the police, who arrested the research chemist for solicitation of murder. Maybe he erred in not offering a more premium brand of beer, but we'll save that for another day.
>
> Point is, the research chemist wasn't as inept as he seems. He understood the police can trace the transfer of money from employer to killer, but not if the amount is small enough. He reasoned homeless people might see a hundred dollars and two cases of beer as a generous price. If the two he found didn't have qualms about committing

murder, it might have worked.

Which brings us to Andrew Marvel. Is there any conceivable reason someone would frame him and also create an alibi that freed him? I haven't come up with one. In earlier posts, I opened the question to my readers but none of them came up with one, either. We're left with the conclusion that Andrew hired someone to kill Audrey. He framed himself and created the alibi that would get him off. So it's only a matter of waiting for the police to trace his payment to the killer.

But they haven't. And hired killers don't accept IOU's.

Does that make the hired killer theory wrong? Or did Andrew find someone willing to kill for an amount too small for the police to trace? Do killers for hire in Vermont like their beer more than their counterparts in Aventura? Or maybe something else happened.

What if Andrew found a way to turn an undetectably small amount of money into one large enough to attract a skilled, efficient killer?

Casinos have always been a popular way to launder money. Buy chips. Play a few hands. Cash in the chips, presto, clean money. Do casinos have anything to offer the person who wants to turn a small sum into one large enough to hire a killer?

Yeah, casinos do. They're called odds.

Let's say Andrew Marvel gave twenty dollars to the killer and told him to make a certain bet, say the Milwaukee Bucks to win the NBA

championship at five hundred to one. He'd lose.
Odds are high because these outcomes rarely
occur. But what if the casino took the killer's
twenty dollars and paid out whatever the going
rate is for hired killers in rural Vermont, along
with a betting slip that made it appear he placed
a bet at five hundred to one odds?

No legitimate casino would do this. But what
if Andrew Marvel knows the owner of a fly-by-
night, lawless Internet casino based in Costa
Rica? What if this casino owner fabricated a bet
that never took place? Andrew would have to pay
the casino back. Maybe he'd open an account,
steadily losing money over time until he reached
the amount paid to the killer, along with whatever
fee the casino charged for providing the service.

Ridiculous. Crazy. What are the chances Andrew
Marvel knows the owner of a lawless, fly-by-night
Internet casino? Not good, I would have said,
until a guest checked into the Morning Loon Inn
the day after Andrew was freed. He was tanned,
with long hair made blond by tropical sun. He
used a false name and paid cash. My interest was
piqued. I made a call to his rental car company,
pretending I was someone I'm not, and found out
the guest's name. A few searches later, I knew he
owned an online casino in San Jose, Costa Rica.
I also learned that he used to live in L.A., where
Andrew also lives.

I didn't want to jump to unfair conclusions.
Greensboro, Vermont, might be a popular
travel destination for the online casino-owning
crowd. But I was hooked. I had to find out more.
Yesterday, I tried breaking into his cabin to see

if I could find anything linking him to Andrew. Bad luck. He caught me in the act. I pretended I suspected him of being the killer Andrew hired. He wasn't angry or aggressive. He's actually surprisingly sweet.

Last night, the guest did something none of the army of reporters have managed. He scored a one-on-one meeting with Andrew. The two of them went into Andrew's house and spent almost an hour talking. When he returned to the Morning Loon, the guest and I shared a glass of wine on the porch. I told him I knew he owned an online casino. I gave him a chance to tell his story. And how did he respond? By turning the tables and acting like he suspected me of being Andrew's accomplice, the one who helped him film the alibi.

Why did the casino owner come to Greensboro? It wasn't necessary and it gives busybodies like me the chance to create crackpot theories about how Andrew paid his killer without getting caught. Maybe he came to confer with Andrew or the killer. I don't know. I'm going to hold off on writing his name and the name of his casino. I'm not worried about him doing anything rash after he reads this post. He knows the police could find out who he is. Besides, I meant what I said earlier. He's kind of a sweetheart in his own twisted way.

"Don't publish that," Jackson said.
"Skip a day and you lose five percent of your readers."
"I'll give my story to one of the reporters."
"This is your story," she said.

"This explains how Andrew did it but doesn't say why. That's the story I'll give them…Ah, that wouldn't interest your readers. The Other Woman isn't very original as motives go."

"We're back to that?"

"She said she met Andrew for the first time when she came last summer to show him *Johnny Payback*. Only she wasn't telling the truth. She already knew him. They met the summer before, when she showed him a script called *Saving Flora*. ICM logged it in July, 2013, on a recommendation from Andrew."

"He told you this?"

"You have to admit, you make a good Other Woman. If I were the murdering type, I could see myself doing it for someone like you."

"Oops, forgot to proofread." She typed something in her post. "There. I deleted the line about the online casino owner being surprisingly sweet and replaced it with 'he's the biggest jerk I've ever met.' Much better."

She reached for the trackpad. "Time to hit publish."

"Wait."

If she was in it with Andrew, she'd never publish a post that directed the police to Jackson. And if she had nothing to do with the murder, he'd rather have her publish the truth than a post accusing him of helping Andrew pay the killer.

She waved her hand in front of his face. "Hello. We'll be in a retirement home before we get through this conversation."

"I'm sorry. You have information you want to pry out of me."

"I shouldn't have to pry."

"No, you should just have to bat your eyelashes and moisten your lips and every male within a hundred-foot radius should hand over his deepest secrets."

"You're talking about…"

"The last time we were on this porch. You touched my ear with your lips and said, 'maybe, just maybe, I'm the reason a man killed his wife.' My earlobe is still in a state of shock."

"You're not even flirting."

"I'm just relating facts."

"Well," she said with dead serious eyes, "sometimes I can be manipulative. But it's all in a good cause."

"What cause?"

"Making you like me. Oh shut up, Trish."

The night before, it was body-melting warm breath against his neck. Now it was junior high flirtatiousness. Was there any limit to her powers of manipulation? Did she want him to like her? But how could he think a frivolous thought like that, even in passing, when he should be trying to work out if she was Andrew's accomplice?

He pulled his eyes away from hers and looked down at her red Keds inching closer to his foot.

"Do you want to know what I really think?" she said.

"What?"

"That you have two seconds before I hit publish."

"Make the casino owner a fool instead of the accomplice and your post isn't far off."

She moved her hand from the trackpad.

"When you went to my site, you didn't go to the entertainment page. That's where we posted the trial."

"Andrew's trial?"

"If you think you're appalled, you should talk to my linemaker, Kenny."

He watched her frowning and blinking until the revelation appeared. "Can people bet on dropped charges?"

"Yes, they can. At 100 to 1 odds. A customer in Greensboro asked if he could bet more than our limit, which on things like this is five hundred. I let him bet a thousand. He also bet on "dropped charges" at a bunch of other casinos. Two days later, someone delivered the video to Andrew's lawyer."

"But then you know…"

"Who placed the bets. Not who supplied the money."

"That's how Andrew hired someone."

"Slow down. That's one possibility."

"Why do you say someone else supplied the money?"

"The killer wouldn't want his name on the account. But I've got a better reason. My customer's name is Cass Gallaway."

He expected feigned bewilderment, but she nodded fast as a bobblehead doll. "Trailer on The Bend Road."

"You know him?"

"Not until I saw you staking his place out."

"That was my first day here. You didn't know who I was."

"I pretended no, but yeah, I did."

"I thought lying was my character flaw."

"Doing it badly is yours."

"Thank you for the reminder you do it well. So easy to pretend you don't already know everything I'm telling you."

"How do you know someone else supplied the money?"

"I followed Cass to Morrisville, as you know, if you were following me."

"I wasn't. I got bored and went back to my room."

"We were in Morrisville when someone else logged onto Cass' account from the library."

She closed her eyes. "The buffalo farmer."

"Blake Trotman."

"Yeah."

"Why were you in the library?"

"Like I said, I got bored watching you watch Cass and I went back to my room. Then I checked The Bend Road again and you were still there. My phone ran out of juice, so I went up to the library to check something on a computer. I looked out the window and who's pulling into Willey's but the car from the trailer. I watched him come in the library and go to the computer. He was being all secretive, blocking the screen, but I saw enough to recognize your site. I worried maybe he saw me hovering behind him so I didn't follow when he left. Maybe twenty minutes later, the buffalo man came in and got on a computer."

"Did he go to my site?"

"No idea. I just remember him sitting there. Who else? Some guy I didn't recognize."

"How old?"

"Maybe forty."

"Wally Caiden. When I got back to Greensboro, the librarian told me the people there in the past hour were Cass, you, Blake, and Wally. Why'd you stick around the library after you saw Cass leave?"

"The computer…So that's why you came to Greensboro. You didn't want to pay the bet."

The "ah hah!" moment, the light switching on. It didn't seem feigned, but things were never the way they seemed with Trish. Jackson kept going. "Cass complained to the organization that can blacklist us. If I found out the bet was fraudulent…"

"That's why Andrew talked to you."

"How do you know he talked to me?"

"You just told me."

"He told you."

"You confronted him with the betting," Trish said.

"No."

"No?"

"He might know who I am but not from me," Jackson said.

"Why'd he let you in his house?"

"Two possible reasons: You told him I was on to you guys. Or stolen weathervanes."

"Stolen weathervanes?" Again, the nose-scrunched bewilderment looked legit. She turned her arm over and moved her finger from her wrist to her elbow, in little loops, as if she were writing big, cursive letters.

He ploughed ahead. "Audrey suspected a local of stealing antique weathervanes. The police looked into it last summer. You didn't know?"

"No. And if I didn't, neither did any of those useless reporters."

He told her about Cass looking up at the weathervane in Morrisville. He told her about Kerry, Warren, Rex, Meredith.

"I should have listened to myself," she muttered a bunch of times while he was talking and again when he finished. "I should have listened to myself. Andrew never had a motive. But the video. It had to be him."

Uncle Warren was so quick to dismiss weathervanes and here she was acting like it was the only possible explanation. Maybe if Warren knew about Cass, he'd react the same way.

"A Hollywood director. Of course people like you are going to post his trial. And if you didn't, the weathervane creeps could destroy the video and let him get convicted."

But it didn't take the shine long to wear off this new explanation.

"Would they kill her if she didn't have proof?" Trish said. "Why not just lay low until she went back to L.A.?"

"Two good questions."

She grabbed his wrist. "But what did Andrew say?"

"That Audrey's interest in antique weathervanes was a silly whim. He claims she never told him who she saw in Brattleboro. He doesn't think weathervanes had anything to do with what happened."

"Smart response if he hired someone. Can't seem too eager for an alternate explanation."

"He talked about imagining Audrey coming home from Willey's. How that world's more real than the one where she's dead."

"You think it's him?"

"Sometimes. Sometimes I think it isn't."

She got up from the table and walked over to the railing, came back, sat down again and scanned the text on her screen. "Sucks I have to delete this."

"It's a good one. Save a draft in case it turns out I'm lying."

He had no idea why he was engaging in silly banter when he needed all his focus to figure out what side she was on.

She leaned so close he could taste her lemon ginger tea breath. "Now what?"

"I assume you're doing a new post."

"On what?"

"On what? Everything I told you."

"We still don't know if it's Andrew or weathervane thieves. You think I'm posting half the story so one of those loser reporters can finish it?"

If she thought he was such an incompetent liar, let her spot this one. He stood up. "You can do what you want. I'm going to the police."

She grabbed his wrist again, guiding him back down to his seat. "You can't."

"I'm not a reporter doing this for fun and games. I'm a material witness. You're not the one they'll lock up for withholding evidence."

"You're so close. You can solve it. We can solve it. Lock you up? You'll be a hero."

"I found out enough. My casino won't get blacklisted. Now the police can handle it."

"You're giving up?"

She was good, playing the riled-up, ambitious journalist. She wrote that post to get him talking, to find out what he planned next. And she was hearing the one thing she and Andrew feared. He was going to the police.

"Solve it? How?" he said. "Weathervane thieves don't keep records of their transactions."

"Weathervanes have lots of parts. If we find anything in Blake or Wally's houses…"

"I already tried Wally's shed. The police can do a more thorough search."

"First we search Blake's farm."

"Ask him to go to the movies so we can have the place to ourselves?"

"Maybe he's out. He probably is. We'll check now. Let's go."

"I need a few minutes to think about it."

"You're not going to the police?"

"No."

"Promise?"

"What good's a liar's promise, even a bad liar?"

She closed her MacBook, put it in her backpack. Someone as relentless as she was didn't yield this easily. Unless she could use the time to do something important, like call Andrew and explain their predicament.

"Be back in a few."

He didn't try to stop her. He needed to follow up on something he remembered when he was telling her about the weathervanes. Andrew said Audrey drove all over the state visiting antique weathervanes she saw in books and websites. She might have checked those books out of the Greensboro Free Library.

He went to his cabin for his car keys. As he came back down the path, the black F-150 was rumbling into the parking area.

Blake wheeled his coolers up the dirt drive without looking up at the porch. Minutes later, the side door clattered and Blake called out, "See you at dinner."

A female voice that sounded like Deliliah, the manager, replied, "We're running out so quickly. Maybe even double the usual order tonight."

"You got it," Blake said, "Now I'm off to Burlington."

"Burlington?"

"Juniper Bar and Grill."

"I love that place. I didn't know they were a customer."

"As of a week ago."

"Last time I had the roast quail."

"With a side of marinated beets, Maplebrook feta."

"It was great. But next time I'll have the buffalo. Promise."

The hand truck wheels crunched over dirt. The clown head faced down as Blake navigated the driveway to his F-150.

Jackson felt like calling out, "You're overdoing it, Blake. At least look up and tell me to go fuck myself. I know you wanted me to overhear your plans. You'll be in Burlington. So I'm free to go search your farm for weathervanes."

Trish called Andrew who called Blake, who was parked nearby awaiting the outcome of her conversation with Jackson. Or maybe Trish called Blake. It didn't matter. The wife killer, his hired hand, and his Other Woman meant weathervanes were out.

But one of the few things Jackson had seen with his own eyes was Cass looking up at that weathervane in Morrisville. He wasn't ready to rule weathervanes out yet. Soon, but not yet.

Thursday, 10:57 a.m.

Betty the librarian looked up from her desk and rubbed her hands together. "Did Wally give you your reward?"

"Two containers of maple syrup."

"What size?"

"Large."

"He sells them for eleven dollars but I happen to know he gets them for seven. So he gave you fourteen. I say that's fair."

"I'm not complaining."

"If someone richer lost the money clip... Well, that's out of your control."

"He didn't seem like the kind of person who uses a money clip."

"He obviously is."

"You don't like when I accuse locals of having the capacity to lie."

She shook her head, but not to concur. "I don't count Wally. He's a con man. Nothing against con men," she added quickly to avoid offending Jackson. "But he wouldn't say it was his if it wasn't. When the rightful owner claimed it, then what?"

"Speaking of con men, someone at the Morning Loon was telling me people steal antique weathervanes..."

"It's true."

"Do you have books on weathervanes?"

She put her glasses on. The magnified eyeballs studied him. The jump from extorting money clip rewards to stealing weathervanes wasn't a big one.

She either decided he didn't have it in him or it wasn't that horrible a crime because she stood up smiling and led him past the computers to a room filled with books on Vermont and Greensboro. How could such a tiny town have inspired so many books? History, natural history, foliage, wildlife, weather patterns. She pulled out a book too big to stand upright on a shelf. *Vermont's Tradition of Weathervanes.*

"The pictures were taken by a Greensboro photographer named Robert Elwood. He and the author went all over the state cataloguing weathervanes."

She pulled out a smaller, newer looking book, *Collectible Antique Weathervanes.* "This is more of a guidebook for collectors."

"Thanks."

He started with *Vermont's Tradition of Weathervanes.* The index divided the book by county. The village of Brattleboro was located in Windham County. He thumbed through the photos. There was only one rooster, a thick preening one on top of a gray farmhouse with blackened streaks. The caption beneath it read, "Rooster on copper spire, McCarthy farmhouse, Brattleboro, Vermont."

The other book listed the same weathervane and didn't show any other roosters in Brattleboro, either.

He brought the books to the front desk.

"Did Wally ever check these out?"

"He's a con man, not a crook."

"Come on, let's have a look, just for fun."

She entered *Vermont's Tradition of Weathervanes* and moved aside so he could see the screen.

He didn't expect to see Wally. He expected to see Audrey. And did. She'd checked it out twice.

"I told you," Betty said.

"You were right."

Audrey saw the picture of the McCarthys' rooster and drove to Brattleboro to see for herself. That's when she spotted Cass.

She told Rex, who passed the information along to Cass and the other thieves. Then Rex found another rooster weathervane in Brattleboro, a worthless one, and claimed that was the one Audrey saw, making weathervanes a dead end as a motive. Rex was protecting his suppliers of stolen merchandise. He was the one who warned them about Audrey's suspicions.

Jackson went to one of the computers and searched, "Rooster weathervane stolen Brattleboro McCarthy."

Nothing about any theft, but if Audrey saw Cass there, they'd leave that one alone.

Did this mean Trish wasn't playacting, that Andrew was nothing more to her than a conduit to Hollywood? Did Blake have a legitimate new customer in Burlington?

Thursday, 11:33 a.m.

Jackson parked two stores down from the antique store. Bad luck that Rex was helping a customer. That gave him time to anticipate Jackson's questions and come up with answers.

Jackson edged his way through overflowing shelves and tables, inhaling the grandmother's basement scent of hooked rugs and musty wood, ducking under brass pots hanging by chains from the ceiling, dodging a pewter pitcher and almost kicking over a tin milk can in the process. Bright sunlight through the single window looked aged and dust-filled by the time it reached the back of the store where Rex was ringing up a sale.

The customer left and Rex assembled his features into something that looked like curiosity. "Hello, Mr. Carruthers."

"I want to check out that rooster weathervane in Brattleboro."

Rex blinked his eyes. "I can't leave the store now."

"I can find it."

He was all set for a helpless shrug and Rex saying it was a year ago, how could he possibly remember where it was? But he said, "I'll give you the address."

"You still have it?"

Rex pulled out a sketchbook. He flipped through the pages, placed the book open on the counter in front of Jackson. "Here."

An address was written beside a rough sketch of a rooster. It wasn't the address of the McCarthy farmhouse.

This guy was no slouch. He must have written it down and sketched the rooster around the time Audrey confided what she saw, adding credence to his claim that was the address she told him.

Jackson copied it down on his iPhone.

"Does this help in any way?" Rex said.

"By help, you mean…?"

"Finding the person responsible."

"It just might, Rex. It just might."

Back in his car, he searched "McCarthy farmhouse," "Brattleboro," and "weathervane" and came up with Arthur and Kendra McCarthy. Their phone number was listed.

He switched the iPhone settings to No Caller ID and dialed the number. Voice-mail picked up after four rings, one of those doddering old codger electronic voices, not the crisp authoritative female message voice he was used to.

His phone was ringing. The McCarthys calling back.

"I'm sorry I didn't get to the phone in time." It was a woman's voice, out of breath.

"Mrs. McCarthy?"

"Yes?" Now her voice was out of breath and suspicious.

Jackson did a quick pivot. Instead of Sergeant Jake Fears of the Vermont State police he'd be Robert Elwood, photographer from *Vermont's Tradition of Weathervanes*.

"This is Robert Elwood, the photographer. Do you remember me?"

"Of course. How are you, Mr. Elwood?"

"Robert, please."

"It's so nice to hear from you, Robert."

"Thank you again for letting me include your marvelous rooster in the book."

"Oh, no, we're so thankful you wanted it."

"The reason I'm calling…an odd reason, actually. I don't suppose you remember my assistant, Kaitlin."

"No."

"She didn't come to all the shoots. Get to the point, Robert. I have a bad habit of rambling. Kaitlin stopped working for me shortly after the book came out. I've recently learned that last summer in June she visited a lot of the homes featured in the book and warned owners that thieves were targeting their weathervanes. I only learned of this recently, and I'm calling to reassure you she had no basis for getting people alarmed unnecessarily."

Robert Elwood had to learn when to shut up.

"She left a note under our mat. It said she spotted someone suspicious studying our weathervane but she didn't know for certain."

"Did she identify herself as my assistant?"

"No, the note was anonymous."

"Did you report it to the police?"

"Art thought it was a prank. Someone who read the book."

"And this was a year ago, mid June?"

"That sounds about right."

"Well, like I say, I'm not sure what prompted her to do this, but I wanted to reassure you that you don't have to worry."

"Oh, but we do keep a close watch. Not because of that note. It's terrible all these thefts."

"I know. Well, it was nice speaking to you again, Mrs. McCarthy."

"You too, Robert. I can't tell you how many people have praised that book of yours."

"Of mine? Of ours. It wouldn't exist without people like you."

A few pleasantries later they hung up. Sergeant Fears never could have gotten her to open up like that.

Jackson pictured the scene last summer: Rex in the back of the store, dusting off an antique typewriter, counting the money he was making off stolen weathervanes, when the door tinkles and breathless Audrey rushes in with a story about a Greensboro guy casing out the rooster on the McCarthy farmhouse. The danger bells in Rex's head tinkle. Did she recognize this person? Yes, Cass Gallaway. Rex puts down the blue handkerchief and shifts to damage control. He's the authority on stolen weathervanes. He'll take charge. Make sure you don't tell a soul, he says to Audrey. If he's an innocent admirer, like you, we don't want to accuse him unfairly. But if you're right, if he's planning to steal it, we don't want him having any inkling people are on to him. Audrey agrees, but she warns her friend, Warren, without mentioning Cass by name.

〉〉〉

Rex was standing on a small stepladder placing a walnut-colored music box on a shelf when Jackson came back in the store.

"Just had an interesting phone call with a Mrs. McCarthy in Brattleboro. Owner of the antique rooster weathervane."

Rex came down from the stepladder. "I know it, of course."

"Not from the Walmart discount bin, is it?"

"It's a valuable antique."

"Know what she told me? Rex is a liar. She didn't use those exact words. She said Audrey warned her to watch out for thieves last summer, and I filled in the blanks. That's where Audrey saw the guy, not the address you gave me."

"I wrote it down," Rex said.

"Yeah, you told the truth about that part. You did write it down. You found a worthless rooster weathervane in Brattleboro. And you wrote down the address."

Rex turned away and fussed with a silver letter opener with a Charles Dickens head. "Please leave my store."

He put the letter opener back in its cup and sucked in two big mouthfuls of air. Jackson used a hanging fireplace bellows to shield himself from the sneeze that never came.

"When the police followed up on what Warren told them, you gave them that bogus address. What thief would stake out a worthless weathervane? It couldn't have anything to do with her murder."

"Audrey did like the McCarthy rooster. If she warned Mrs. McCarthy, I'm sure it was to tell her there was a thief looking at weathervanes in Brattleboro."

"Way to think on your feet. They value you for more than fencing their merchandise. But that's not what Mrs. McCarthy said. She said Audrey told her she saw someone staking out *her* weathervane. Not that there was a thief in town with a fondness for roosters and he might be stopping by."

"If you ask other people in Brattleboro with antique weathervanes, you'll probably find Audrey also warned them."

It was Jackson's turn to pick up the Dickens letter opener. Rex watched with anxious eyes. "You'll smudge it," he finally said.

Jackson put it back in the cup.

"Nobody cares about a shady antique dealer. But you warned this guy Audrey spotted him. Then he killed her. That makes you a murder accomplice."

"You're wrong, Mr. Carruthers."

"Who did you purchase weathervanes from last summer?"

"If you know anything about the antique business, you know we protect the anonymity of our customers."

"Especially the ones that would come in here and club you with an antique wagon wheel if you gave them up. What about Meredith? Why'd you tell me about her?"

"Audrey suspected her of making replicas for the reasons I told you."

"You gave me her name so I wouldn't find the real thieves."

Rex trailed along as Jackson walked to the door.

"Mr. Carruthers, Andrew Marvel hired someone to kill Audrey. The police know that and so does everyone else. You need to ask yourself why you're not seeing it."

Thursday, 12:36 p.m.

On the drive back to Greensboro, Jackson imagined a now-alarmed Rex calling his partner, the two of them talking it over, a conversation extended by Rex's near-sneezes and his partner pointing out for the umpteenth time if Rex insisted on dusting all the antiques with that handkerchief of his, no wonder he was always on the verge of sneezing. Then they'd get back to the gist of the conversation: Hank Carruthers now having proof Rex gave the police the wrong information, something only a fence would do. What now? Maybe nothing, if they didn't have weathervanes lying around and the police couldn't trace non-existent transaction records. Rex breathed in two large mouthfuls of air and his partner hung up out of fear that this time the eardrum-punishing sneeze would be for real.

Not long after this imaginary call ended, Jackson got a real one in his cabin from a blocked number.

"Hello?"

"You want to talk?"

"Who's this?"

"Come on, man, don't be like that." The smile in Cass' voice had vanished.

"I told you I'm not interested in that poker chip."

"If you want to talk, get on Route 15. There's a small graveyard as you're entering Hardwick."

"On a hill."

"I'll be waiting."

"I need to tell you something first."

"Tell me later."

"People I work with know why I'm here, who I came to see. So if anything happens to me..."

Cass' voice shot up an octave. "What kind of a...Jesus... You talk like that on the phone? You'll get us all...Jesus...I'll be where I said. You don't show up in an hour, I'll figure you're not coming."

"I'm not coming unless you listen. People at my place know everything I know."

"I listened, I heard. Now I'm leaving. You want to talk, see you there."

Cass hung up.

Did Blake really expect Jackson to believe he was making a delivery in Burlington? But ambushing him in a public cemetery made no sense. It wouldn't be the first time a human being did something that made no sense.

Thursday, 1:07 p.m.

Cass was crouched in front of the squat headstone. If Jackson hadn't witnessed him conversing with it before, he would have assumed Cass was reviewing the plan with someone out of view.

Jackson walked along an uneven row of headstones until he reached one next to Cass' squat confidante.

"Hello, Cass."

He had small abrasions on his pale arms. He took a deep breath. "Everything's fucked up."

"You say it like it's my fault."

"I've got a proposal. I call the Offshore Gaming place and tell them you paid. You get on a flight home tomorrow."

"Changing your tune."

"Yeah, I am," Cass said.

"Don't you want to know what I've found out?"

Sweat beaded up on his pale forehead like hot oil on a pan. "No, man, I don't care. I really don't."

"The person you made the bets for does, so here it is. Audrey Marvel saw you checking out a rooster weathervane in Brattleboro. She guessed you were stealing them. So your partner killed her."

"Oh, man, you know nothing about anything."

Cass circled the squat headstone, faster and faster, kicking dirt, dislodging rocks. Jackson could make out the name on the headstone: Tommy Gallaway.

"Then it was murder for hire. Trish filmed Andrew's alibi. Blake killed Audrey and used you to place his bets. He made up that poker chip-in-the-car story so I'd think it was Wally."

"This isn't a game, man."

"It's Blake, isn't it?"

Cass stopped pacing. He looked down at the ground while he caught his breath.

"You could have killed her too, Cass, but you didn't. You've got a good heart. You try to hide it but you can't."

Cass looked at Jackson with a drowning man's eyes. "We're done talking. You'll leave tomorrow or you won't."

"I'll have to confirm with Ed Trumane you reported we paid."

Cass looked from the squat headstone to Jackson, mouth open like he couldn't believe his good fortune. "Of course."

"When will you call?"

"From my car."

"Then I'll call Ed when I get back to my cabin. If you told him we paid, I'll get a flight tomorrow."

And in the interim, he'd stop by the Hardwick Police Station. He didn't care about stolen weathervanes. A better person would, but he didn't. They'd crossed the line when they killed an innocent person.

Jackson stepped toward the gate.

"Hey?"

Jackson turned.

"Sorry, man," Cass said.

"About what?"

"Being an asshole on the phone."

Thursday, 1:45 p.m.

Jackson was wrong. It turned out he could fit both cans of maple syrup in his duffel bag if he strapped his Tevas to the handle. But one can was putting too much stress on the zipper. Maybe instead of wrapping the cans in T-shirts, he should flatten the shirts on the bottom of the bag.

In reality, the zipper was fine. He was distracting himself with different packing options to put off calling Ed Trumane which, in turn, delayed his visit to the police. That wouldn't be fun. They'd despise him for withholding evidence and turning a murder into amusement for bettors and profit for himself. If the egg they'd been wearing on their faces since the video surfaced put them in an ornery enough mood, they might transfer him from his Morning Loon cottage to a Hardwick jail cell.

He re-packed the bag one more time and made the call.

Loud house music was turned down and Ed said, "Yeah?"

"Ed, it's Jackson Oliver."

"Hey, good to hear from you, buddy. Pay that bet?"

"Has Cass Gallaway called you?"

"No complaints since I told him I was giving you three days."

"Just trying to stay on top of things."

"I appreciate that, buddy. Hey, listen, I got someone from the Chamber of Commerce here."

i.e. I can't hold the bong she's passing me without putting down the phone.

Did Cass maybe reach someone else at the Offshore Gaming Association who didn't give Ed the message? Not likely. Ed handled non-payment issues.

The vague forebodings Jackson felt meant nothing because he had them all the time and nothing ever came of them. But they didn't want to be accused of crying wolf, so they ratcheted up the warnings, pumping hot blood through his head, churning things up in his stomach.

The door of another cottage opened and closed.

"My God, how could that happen in a cemetery when he's paying his respects to his father? My God, how could someone do that?"

It was the manager, Delilah, on the phone. "I'm going to call you back, okay?" she said.

Jackson intercepted her before she reached the path. "What happened?"

Her don't-alarm-the-guests reflex silenced her for a beat before she said, "Someone was murdered in Hardwick."

She grabbed Jackson's hands and squeezed. "He was in a cemetery paying his respects to his father, and someone smashed his head open. Oh, my God, my God. They found him lying on his father's grave."

Jackson put his arm around her.

"I'm sorry," she said, shivering.

"Shhh."

"This doesn't happen here."

"The police found him?"

"Someone walking by. The police are there now. Someone hit him so many times part of his brain was dripping out his eye socket. This doesn't happen here. It doesn't happen here."

She shoved her face into his chest. He stroked her hair as she hugged him tighter.

Jackson could have prevented it. He could have convinced Cass to talk, but he let him walk away.

Delilah lifted her head. "They found him on his father's grave. This doesn't happen here." She ran down to the lodge.

The police were in the Hardwick cemetery, but soon they'd be in Jackson's cottage. "Did you pay Cass Gallaway the hundred thousand you owed him? Why did you come to Greensboro? Did the Offshore Gaming Association threaten to put your casino out of business if you didn't pay? Did you beg for more time? Did you meet Cass in the cemetery? By the way, what happened to the fire poker in your cabin?"

Cass could finger the killer so he had to go and Jackson was just the man to pin it on. He had a motive that put to shame some crazy story about phantom bettors and weathervane thieves. All he needed was the opportunity. So someone arranged the meeting in the graveyard.

Jackson lay on his bed, listening to the scratching of pine branches on the roof mimic walkie-talkie static rising up the hill. He kept his iPhone beside him, voice memos open, ready to record the phone call the killer would never be foolish enough to make.

Jackson was going to take the fall. He was doomed. He was fucked. The police would find his prints in the cemetery. They'd find his fireplace poker. Maria had warned him against taking the bet, and he brushed her off with a quip. "We should have a two-for-one special on dumb-ass bets," he'd said, and he laughed, just like he laughed at deep truths like pride goeth before the fall.

He came here passing judgment as if he were an avenging fury when really he just wanted to hold on to his money. He didn't swing the fireplace poker, but what difference did it make? Thieves stole weathervanes. Crooked dealers took their cut. Husbands killed wives. Jackson took the last dollars from the pockets of the weak and desperate. Different shades of darkness, all deserving punishment. Now it was time to man up and take his.

His phone rang. Ed Trumane. "Way to come through, buddy."

"Cass called?"

"Guy was feeling good. Said you even gave him a five hundred-dollar bonus for his troubles. Now that's how you do business. Get this. Guy made me promise your casino wouldn't get in trouble. Oh, and he asked me to tell you he'll be recommending you to his friends. Go figure." Ed snorted out one of his horselaughs. "Two days ago, he wanted to come to Costa Rica and burn down your casino."

"When did he call?"

"We just hung up."

So it was the killer calling, pretending to be Cass.

"Strange question," Jackson said, "did his voice sound the same as before?"

"What?…of course…wait…Oh, wow, are you a member of the psychic friends network? I remember him saying, 'Sorry if you're having trouble hearing me. I lost my voice. Out celebrating my winnings.'"

So it could be Jackson himself, pretending to be Cass, calling after he killed him, making sure VegasVegas didn't get blacklisted.

The message to Jackson was clear. You got what you came for. You don't have to pay. Now go back to Costa Rica and take your half-assed theories with you.

The killer framed Jackson for self-protection, not to get him arrested. He didn't want Jackson locked up in the station, talking. He'd make sure the police wouldn't find anything linking Cass to VegasVegas.

Cass funded his account with two separate Money Gram wires to the VegasVegas agent in Malaga, Spain. If Cass got rid of the transaction receipts, which he would, since setting up the account violated the law, the police wouldn't have any reason to visit Money Gram stores in Vermont.

The branches scraping the roof went back to only being branches scraping the roof. The police wouldn't learn Jackson's reason for killing Cass unless he went to them with the killer's reason.

Thursday, 2:33 p.m.

Jackson was off the clock. His casino was no longer in danger of getting blacklisted. He could pack up his cans of maple syrup and book a flight out of Burlington.

Or he could build a case against the real killer stronger than the case against him. First there was the minor detail of finding out who that killer was. Blake might have killed Audrey but not Cass. He made a point of letting Jackson overhear he'd be in Burlington, unable to commit the murder he had to know was on the schedule. He named the restaurant, making it easy to check.

Jackson drew a blank until he saw the search results on his iPad. Juniper Bar and Grill.

He called and asked for the manager.

"Hi, I work with Blake Trotman from Greensboro."

"He left," the manager said.

Jackson discarded the lost sunglasses ruse he had ready and said, "Already? What time did he get there?"

"Around two o'clock."

"Okay, thanks."

Jackson had left Cass at around one-thirty.

According to Google maps it was 60.1 miles—one hour, twenty minutes—from Hardwick to Burlington. Even if Google mapmakers took speed limits and stoplights more seriously than a murderer on his way to his alibi, Blake couldn't kill Cass at one-thirty and get to the restaurant by two.

Trish didn't answer her phone.

〉〉〉

Jackson found Wally, screwdriver in hand, bent over a lawn fountain. He wobbled across the grass. "Well?"

"The syrup? Haven't tried it yet. I plan to. I'm looking forward to it."

Wally watched with unblinking eyes.

"Can I describe a hypothetical situation?" Jackson said.

"Please do. I like them better than real ones."

"Suppose that money clip never belonged to you."

"That'll take a lot of supposing. All those years pulling it out of my pocket, beaming with pride at the impression it made on the people around me. Okay. It never belonged to me."

"Blake told you someone found a money clip in the library with forty dollars. Would you claim it and risk having the real owner claim it afterwards?"

"Under the hypothetical situation you laid out, it would depend."

"On what?"

"How much resale value I thought it had. How likely was it the real owner would believe my story that coincidentally I, too, had lost a money clip."

Wally walked over to the table with the cans of syrup, placed the screwdriver on it, came back.

"Have you ever driven a red Monte Carlo?" Jackson said.

"No."

"Did I see you in Hardwick a few hours ago?"

"No."

"Did you see me?"

"You're an unusual individual."

"Do you steal weathervanes?"

"Are we still being hypothetical?"

"Real now."

"No, I don't. I can't see any situation where I'd do it either, except maybe if you guaranteed me I wouldn't get caught, wouldn't have to climb on a roof, and the person I took it from wouldn't be too broken up about it."

Jackson considered throwing out the name "Cass Gallaway" to see how Wally reacted. But when Wally heard about the murder, if he hadn't already, he might decide the police should talk to a guy named Hank Carruthers in the Morning Loon.

"From now on, all questions are real."

"Okay."

"Did Blake tell you the person who lost the money clip would never claim it?"

"I wouldn't have believed him if he did."

"Why?"

"I don't believe much of anything he says."

"You think he's a liar?"

"I think everyone is."

"I'll prove your point. That was my money clip. I pretended to lose it to get the librarian to tell me who was in the library."

"Why not go to the library and see for yourself?"

"I wanted to find out who was there before I got there. Someone sent me an e-mail from one of the computers and I wanted to find out who."

"Why not look at the name of the sender?"

"He didn't use his real name. You had to know the owner wouldn't claim the money clip. I think it was Blake's way of laughing at me. I think he told you."

"You're wrong."

"Why say it's yours?"

"I have an answer to that question, but I don't have the proper motivation to give it to you."

"Could that proper motivation be purchased?"

"I got my fair share of money out of you already. It would cause embarrassment to another party. If you were to give me your word of honor it doesn't get back to that party."

"Okay."

"Betty told me to claim it."

"Betty the librarian?"

"She talked to Blake and it wasn't his. It wasn't mine. The young lady wouldn't carry a money clip. That meant someone lost it earlier in the day. Most of them were out-of-towners, who wouldn't have the decency to give you a reward for your effort, which Betty believed you deserved. If I claim it, I get a handsome money clip, she gets the money, you get a reward, and the out-of-towner learns the valuable lesson about the importance of being careful with their money. That was Betty's reasoning."

"Can't argue with any of it," Jackson said.

"Betty likes you. I was going to give you one small can. She insisted on two big ones."

"I like her, too. I won't tell her I know."

"She'll sense it. That's okay. She won't mind me telling you. She was thinking about doing it herself."

Jackson tied his kayak to the dock and nodded to Apollo. A course of croquet wickets had been set up on the yard. Half a croquet mallet that looked like it had been snapped in two was lying on the ground. It had blue rings. Two good bets: the other half was floating in the lake somewhere, and Uncle Warren had recently been playing the blue ball.

The groomed white stone driveway was surrounded by more sculptures. Neptune stood with his trident watching Jackson go up to the door. The doorbell sounded like a Bach fugue.

Warren opened it, nodded at Jackson, and looked back down at his phone. "Close it, will you?"

"You don't get any extra time," Kerry called out from an unseen room.

"Don't need any."

Jackson followed Warren to a sunny room that felt like it belonged on a listing of luxury vacation home rentals. "The living room is tastefully decorated with cherry wood furnishings to create an easygoing waterfront feel. Floor-to-ceiling windows beneath vaulted ceilings fill the space with natural light. Colorful indoor plants enhance the feeling of tranquility. The porch offers a striking water view as you recline on cushioned wicker sun loungers. It faces west, giving you a front row seat as the setting sun paints the sky orange."

Kerry was sitting on a sectional sofa facing a wall-mounted big screen TV. Jackson caught a glimpse of Words with Friends on Warren's phone.

Warren made a play. "You resign?" he said to Kerry.

"Wait a sec." Kerry answered her ringing phone. "Dad, you know you shouldn't talk while you drive. That's forty minutes away. Take your time. Put Mom on. Hi. No, tell him to take his time. We have company anyway. See you soon. Love you."

"Twenty seconds left in your turn," Warren said.

"It was my parents."

"You know the rules. If I'm not mistaken you were just enforcing them when I answered the door."

"I resign." She hit the button ending the game and went out to the porch.

Warren turned to Jackson. "You play Words with Friends?"

"I'm okay. Hanabuddha would beg to differ."

"Who's Hanabuddha?" Kerry said.

"Sixty seconds per move. Kerry will time us with her phone."

"Kerry has better things to do," Kerry said.

Jackson gave Warren a bow. "You win. I concede."

"Doesn't work that way. You don't come over here and deprive me the pleasure of payback."

Warren went into a kitchen with pendant lights hanging over a half-filled blender on a marble countertop.

"Anything to drink? How could I forget? Wine."

"Nothing now, thanks," Jackson said.

Warren poured the remainder of the blended drink into his glass and came back to the sofa.

"When Audrey told you about the person she saw in Brattleboro…"

Warren cut him off. "I'm done talking about that. The scumbag hired someone to kill her and everything else is fantasyland."

Kerry flopped onto the sofa. "You learn something, Detective Hank?"

"Not interested," Warren said. "But you're more than welcome to get your butt kicked in Words with Friends."

Jackson took out his iPhone. "One game. I win and you answer my questions about weathervanes."

"I said not interested."

"So you think I'm going to win?"

"I'm sure I'll win. Even if you get all the big letters."

Kerry tossed a sofa cushion at Warren. "We don't want to hear your boasts. Bet the man."

"Let's play," Warren said.

The subset of fate that governs Words with Friends outcomes sided with Jackson. He drew the z, j and x. He scored over 550 points for only the second time in his brief playing career. Warren didn't even break 400.

When the bell ended the game, Warren elbowed the sofa cushion and shouted, "What the fuck just happened?" He gave a sheepish grin and said, "Ask your questions."

"You said when Audrey told you about the Brattleboro guy, she said, 'It'll surprise you. It's someone local.'"

"That's right."

"How did you interpret that?"

"I took her to mean, it'll surprise me, it's someone local."

"Why would it surprise you?"

"She thought it would surprise me a Greensboro person had it in them to steal. Which of course is ludicrous. It wouldn't surprise me in the slightest. Why would Greensboro people be immune to human nature?"

Kerry jumped in. "Oh, so stealing is human nature?"

"Most of us repress that part of our nature because we fear the consequences. You haven't learned yet because everything's been handed to you. You'll learn once you're out in the real world."

"He's just baiting me," she said to Jackson. Then to Warren, "You shouldn't act like an idiot in front of people who might think you believe this stuff."

Warren had a whisky grin.

"That's how Audrey said it? 'It'll surprise you. It's someone local?'"

"I didn't have a transcriptionist with me at the time but yes."

"See, I was thinking, it could be the other way around. It's someone local. Pause. It'll surprise you. I think she meant the person would surprise you."

Warren sat quietly nodding his head and said, "Yes, I think you're right."

"What local would surprise you?"

"Anyone on this lake would surprise me."

"Snob." Kerry threw another pillow at him, which he deflected with his non-drink-holding arm.

"The waitresses at the Morning Loon. The owner of Miller's Thumb. I don't know." He cut himself off, thought a moment. "No. I'm recalling the exact words Audrey used. 'It's someone local. It will surprise you. Oh, yes, it will surprise you.' She wouldn't have said it that way if it was some random local."

Jackson's question was now locked and loaded. Do you know a guy named Cass Gallaway? He held back. He trusted these two but he couldn't reveal his connection to someone just murdered.

Why would Cass surprise Warren anyway? Did they know each other? Betty the librarian said someone on the lake once accused Cass of stealing something. Was it possibly Warren? Or was Warren one of the people who jumped to his defense?

"Think of someone," Jackson said.

"I won't. I'm going to forget all about it. This weathervane thing is a complete waste of time. It's an injustice to Audrey to give that scumbag husband of hers the slightest benefit of the doubt."

"I'll wring it out of him," Kerry said to Jackson. "Leave us your phone number."

Warren extracted the promise of next-day rematches in both kayak racing and Words for Friends before he let Jackson leave.

The tinkling of the door brought Rex from the back. He was carrying a desk globe.

"Hello, Rex."

Rex nodded twice. "Mr. Carruthers."

"That's not necessary. Unless you want to stay in character. You heard about what happened to Cass?"

"I don't know anyone named Cass."

"That's true. It wasn't true yesterday but it's true today."

"Excuse me, Mr. Carruthers."

Jackson was blocking his path to a small space on one of the shelves between a silver teapot and a tortoise-shell card case. He backed up so Rex could place the globe on the shelf.

"Cass can't tell the police who killed Audrey. Who does that leave?"

Rex pulled the blue handkerchief from his pocket and dusted the globe.

"I know your habits by now, Rex. You dusted the globe in back. You're doing it again to hide your nervousness. I'm sure you've thought about it. You probably never stop thinking about it. A guy willing to kill two people to keep them from talking. Is he really going to think twice about getting rid of a corrupt antique dealer?"

The handkerchief fell to the ground. Rex picked it up, shook it out, and continued dusting.

"Cass was the weak link. Now that honor goes to you."

"Mr. Carruthers?"

"Yes, Rex."

"You look around this store and what do you see?"

"A lot of cool things. I won't deny it."

"A life's work."

"Point being what? You'd never give it up by admitting you're a crook?"

Rex sucked in two mouthfuls of air and Jackson hopped back out of range, but instead of sneezing, Rex passed through the narrow aisle, dodging a protruding butter churner, and went to the front door. He locked the door and turned the sign to say Closed.

"Mr. Carruthers, I'm going to ask you to imagine something."

"On the condition you stop calling me that."

Rex dabbed at a dome lunchbox with the handkerchief.

"Condition two, stop dusting the antiques. Condition three, you suck in a mouthful of air like you're about to sneeze, you go through with it. Now what is it you want me to imagine?"

"I'm going to ask you to imagine part of what you say isn't wrong."

"Where I'm from we call that right."

"As you wish. Imagine Audrey saw someone she thought was stealing weathervanes and confided it to me. Imagine I knew she was right because I did as you suggested."

"Fenced stolen goods."

"I don't expect you to grasp nuance so, yes, imagine that, and imagine I told my client that Audrey saw him outside the McCarthy farmhouse and suspected him. Shortly thereafter, Audrey was murdered. Warren Gunderson told the police about Audrey's suspicions, and the police came to me. Imagine I was confronted with a choice. Tell the truth and make myself and my client suspects in Audrey's murder or find a different house, with a different rooster weathervane."

"Just the victim of bad timing. You happen to develop a motive the very week before she's murdered?"

"You put it well. Bad timing."

"That sounds nice, Rex, and I'm sure you spent a lot of time working it out. Problem is I happen to know Cass was a weathervane thief."

"Can I ask how you know this?"

"I saw him checking out a hummingbird weathervane in Morrisville."

"Maybe you're also a victim of bad timing. You saw him looking at a weathervane at the very same time you heard about Audrey's suspicions."

"Let's clear up the confusion. Tell me who she saw in Brattle-boro."

"My client prefers anonymity. But I will tell you his name isn't Cass."

Jackson wanted to stay on the attack but his thoughts had gotten snagged on what Rex said. He too was a victim of bad timing, basing everything on seeing Cass look up at a window beneath a weathervane. He didn't want it to be Trish and he didn't want it to be Andrew, so he kept up his dogged pursuit of the weathervane gang.

Rex took a step closer and said, "Mr. Carruthers, if my client had anything to do with Audrey's murder, I wouldn't ask you to imagine I had a motive. I'd continue to say you were wrong about the weathervanes, knowing the police could never prove anything."

Jackson looked helplessly for a flaw in the reasoning. "Why tell me now?"

"You say this Cass person was murdered, and the police are investigating. I'm hoping you don't tell them about me."

"I'll think it over."

"That's all I ask, Mr...If you're not Mr. Carruthers, what should I call you?"

"Blind fool. I also answer to sucker."

Rex cocked his head sideways and looked Jackson over with those wide-open eyes. "Before you go, could I ask a favor?"

"What?"

"You're taller than I am. Would you mind lifting that music box to the top shelf?"

Rex carried the stepladder over to a spot with a space on the highest shelf and Jackson climbed up with the music box.

Rex handed him the handkerchief. "If you don't mind. The brass fastening."

Jackson wiped the fastening and climbed down. Rex unlocked the door and turned the sign back around. He was open for business again.

As Jackson headed back to the Morning Loon, he played the messages left on his phone while he was with Rex.

"Hey, fuck up, it's Kenny. Should I call my Uncle Franz and ask if he needs a counter boy for his deli or you paying that bet? Hey, can you believe the Red Sox got swept by the Brewers at home? Later."

"Hank, it's Kerry. It's important. Call me."

When he called back, she said, "Someone got murdered in the Hardwick cemetery. Cass Gallaway."

"I heard the manager talking about it."

"Uncle Warren hired Cass for handyman type work. He liked Cass. One of the nosey busybody neighbors accused him of stealing a necklace from her house, and Uncle Warren defended him. He's the one Audrey saw. It has to be him."

"I'm sure he's not the only person who would surprise your uncle."

"Are you being dense on purpose? It means the weathervane thing's for real. One of his partners murdered him because Andrew's innocent and the police will find out about the weathervanes."

"But if weathervane thieves framed Andrew, why would they free him?"

"Now you're sounding like my uncle."

"He's right. They wouldn't free him and make themselves the new suspects."

"I need to think about it. There has to be a reason. And you'd better think about it, too. You're the one who got me started on this."

He gripped the steering wheel harder to keep his shaking hands from jerking him off the road.

〉〉〉

Jackson sat in front of his cottage trying to figure out what next. Why would it surprise Warren if Audrey had suspected someone accused of theft once before? It wouldn't. Why would Rex admit fencing stolen merchandise if he could be connected in any way with Audrey's murder? He wouldn't.

Look who was coming up the path with her trusty blue backpack. Trish had the gall to glare at him like she'd been wronged. "You promised you weren't going to the police."

"I didn't."

"Where have you been?"

"Didn't I tell you? I went over to the Hardwick cemetery to split Cass' head open with my fire poker."

She took a step back and stared.

"That's why you're here, isn't it? To ask me to do to a guest post on your blog. How to kill someone you owe lots of money to."

"Why are you saying this? What's wrong with you?"

"Finally a question that doesn't stump me. What's wrong with me? I didn't get in my car and drive straight to the airport when I first saw you in the lobby. That's what's wrong with me. Part of me can't blame Andrew. It only took you two days to make a sucker out of me. You had two summers to work on him."

"Tread carefully," she said. "You can't take everything back later."

"I just got back from seeing Rex. He admitted he's a fence. He said the person Audrey saw in Brattelboro wasn't Cass."

"Of course he's going to say that."

"No, not of course. He wouldn't admit he was a fence if he was tied up in the murder. He didn't want the police thinking he had a motive. That's why he found a house with a worthless weathervane and said Audrey saw the thief there. I said 'bad timing, you get a motive the same week Audrey's killed,' and he said something interesting."

"What?"

"'Bad timing for you too, Mr. Carruthers. You see Cass looking up at a weathervane the same time you hear Audrey suspected someone of stealing them.' He's right. I've been chasing weathervane phantoms when the whole time the obvious solution's been sleeping a few hundred feet away in a feather soft bed in the inn."

She didn't bother protesting and why should she? She and Andrew won.

"What do you mean bashing Cass' head in?"

"I made you think I was going to the police. You and Andrew didn't want that so you had Cass call me to set up a meeting in the Hardwick cemetery. He said he'd tell the Offshore Gaming Association I paid the bet if I promised to leave Greensboro tomorrow. I agreed. When I got back, the manager said someone cracked his head open in the cemetery."

"This really happened?"

"Even the cows and reporters in the field must know by now."

He watched her give in to her reporter's twitches, pulling out her iPhone, going to her Twitter timeline. "Nothing from the Hardwick police."

"Want to hear more of what you already know or should I stop?"

She put the iPhone in the backpack pouch, zipped it hard.

"I know Blake didn't kill him since he was making a delivery in Burlington. That leaves Andrew. It's easy enough to sneak him past the photographers. But I'm tired of talking. Tired of thinking. You win."

He picked up a rock and threw it against one of the pine trees.

"Want to hear something pathetic?" he asked. "Part of me's still hoping you'll toss me some crumbs. 'If things were different, if I hadn't helped my boyfriend kill his wife, who knows, maybe the two of us…'"

"There's a line, Jackson. You're running toward it at full speed. Cross it and we both lose."

"You didn't betray me. I barely know you. Played me for a fool. That doesn't cross the line. Facts don't cross the line. Three people could have logged onto Cass' account. You, Blake, Wally. You met Andrew two years ago, but you pretended not to know him."

"There's a difference between pretending not to know him and ignoring your annoying questions. Two years ago, I came here to get him to read a script. He only liked it okay, but he was nice enough to have me send it to his agent. Last summer, I showed him one he liked much better. I sent that to his agent, too. And that's the extent of my relationship with Andrew Marvel."

"A couple months after you met, you started to establish your cover with that blog of yours. You had fun with your little private jokes. You said 'a director friend told me Andrew could film the alibi on his own.' Wonder who that director friend was? Bet you two had a good laugh over that one.

"Everything worked out like you guys planned. Then I show up. No worries. You can keep an eye on me, find out what I'm thinking, what I'm planning. You even act like you suspect me so you have a reason to stick close. It all came clear when you read me that post about my casino. I acted like I was going to the police to see what you'd do. Two hours later, Cass sets up a meeting in the cemetery. And here we are."

Trish turned away from him. "You're wrong. You have no idea how wrong."

She played the part well, all the way down to the fake tear she wiped from her cheek when she turned back to face him.

Her well of phony tears ran dry and she slammed her heel to the ground.

"Now I'm addressing the small part of your brain that wasn't baked dry by the Costa Rican sun. Andrew won. I won. You have a motive. You met Cass at the cemetery. The police will think it's you. It's done. So why am I here?"

"To make sure I leave."

"I filmed the alibi. Who killed Audrey?"

"Wally or Blake."

"You found the bike with the raised seat."

"Probably Blake."

"Andrew paid him with 'dropped charges' odds."

"Right."

"You were sure it was weathervanes, now you're sure it's not. You were wrong. Maybe you're wrong again. Let's say you are. Let's say I'm not the Other Woman, I'm nothing but a blogger. Let's say Rex was lying and it really was Cass Audrey saw outside that farmhouse. What does that make Blake?"

"One of the thieves."

"He killed Audrey because she was on to them."

"Right."

"Then it's possible Blake has weathervane stuff in his barn."

"Trespass in the home of a killer? Brilliant idea."

"Would I set you up like that? If you say yes, I'll walk down the hill and you can do whatever it is you do."

The feeling he was missing something was stronger than ever. It was something at the heart of the crime, much bigger than swapped-out handle bar holders. The best bettors hedged their bets. They didn't bet on one outcome or the other. They bet on both. How did this apply here? He had no idea, but he sensed this piece of gambler's wisdom would help him discover the truth.

He knew Trish wouldn't set him up. She didn't have it in her. She might even be conflicted about her role in playing him for the fool. The last thing Andrew wanted was Jackson dead in Blake's barn. And Blake couldn't know when the police would discover Cass so he'd stay away from Greensboro as long as possible.

Trish repeated her question. "Would I set you up like that? Would I, Jackson?"

Jackson stood up. "Let's find out."

〉〉〉

Eight buffalo watched Jackson and Trish ride Morning Loon bikes along the fence line. A black metal sign welcomed them to Bent Tree Farm. Jackson unlatched the gate and they wheeled their bikes along a dirt road that passed between two sections of crumbling stone wall and through another gate with a disconnected lower hinge. They laid the bikes in the uncut grass and walked the rest of the way. The road separated into a Y, leading to the main house on the right, and a barn on the left. The black F-150 wasn't there.

The house was a gray two-story A-frame with a brick chimney going up the middle. What looked like a woodshed was attached to the corner of the house. Pieces of trellis leaned against the porch. Wind had twisted off half the corrugated metal roof of the woodshed. Jackson pressed his foot against the moisture-softened wood of the landing and put his ear against the door. No sounds inside. He tried the door. Locked.

"Let's start with the barn," Trish said.

He now counted a total of twelve buffalo grazing in different parts of the field. The walls and door of the barn were made of unpainted vertical planks with streaks of gray and black that looked like fire charring. He moved the cinder block keeping the doors closed and they went inside.

Empty stalls lined both walls. The barn must have originally been built for horses. A faded red tracker was parked against

one wall. A pickaxe, shovels, saws, and other tools hung from
nails on studs. They spent half an hour opening every cabinet,
looking under clutter on every shelf. Two levels hung on nails
above one shelf. The night the headlights woke him, Jackson
visited websites on weathervane installation. For the most part it
required simple tools like a level, caulk, Philips screwdriver, drill,
a hacksaw if you had to adjust the height of the installation rod.

He opened the wooden drawers below the shelf and pulled
out a canvas bag with a caulk gun and grease and five Philips
screwdrivers of different sizes. A green Makita drill case sat
upright beside the bag.

He tried sounding nonplused as he said, "Tools you need to
install weathervanes. All in one place."

Trish looked over the haul. "Every barn in the county has
tools like this. But nice job."

He circled the barn feeling for loose floor planks. Trish
climbed the wooden ladder through the square hole to the
hayloft. Neither of them found any weathervanes.

"How about the building at the edge of the field," she said.

"You know what that is, don't you?"

"What?"

"You don't want to know."

They crossed over tamped down grass, passing a truck tire
about eight feet in diameter on a cement pad. Blake had converted it into a feeder filled with grain. The buffalo standing in
groups of two or three took no interest in them. Another fifty
yards brought them to a rectangular holding pen with grated
catwalks on either side. They opened the gate and entered the
pen. Grass and hay covered the mud. There were two gates on
the opposite end. One opened to a narrow chute that didn't look
wide enough to contain a buffalo.

They went through the second gate. This longer chute curved
like a pool slide to make the buffalo think they were walking in
a circle. When the curve straightened, the chute narrowed until
there was only space for a single buffalo. Rubber matting was
laid over the dirt as they reached the stun pen with a built-in

head restrainer and catwalks above, from where Blake could place his gun against the buffalo's immobilized head. The skull of a buffalo was too thick for the stun bolt guns used on cattle. You needed a .357 rifle. The floor and walls of the stun pen were covered with dried blood and hardened clumps of brain matter. Shards of skull crunched like seashells as they passed through the discharge door to the windowless slaughter floor.

A buffalo carcass hung from a hook on a hoist trolley mounted to an I-beam. Blood had dripped out into the steel bucket on the floor. Jackson switched on the overhead lights. A single fluorescent bulb in the three chain-mounted ceiling fixtures cast a dull glow. The other bulbs flickered and went dark, like life expiring. Trish reached for Jackson's arm, wrapping her fingers around his wrist. Another switch on the wall turned on a ventilation fan. It was too loud, so Jackson switched it off again. The smell of hot rotting garbage floated out from vats and buckets along the wall. Trish was looking up at the matted red fur and smile-shaped gouge on the neck of the buffalo.

Congealing stench clogged their throats. Jackson coughed and sucked in air before he could speak. "Blake bleeds the carcass. Then it gets skinned, eviscerated, and split open with an electric saw. Next stop, Morning Loon dinner menu, with a side order of home fried potatoes and a garden salad."

"How do you know this stuff?"

"I watched videos. It's why I stopped eating meat."

"How long do buffalos take to bleed out?"

"Cattle take less than a minute. It's probably similar."

"Then why is it still hanging here?"

"I'm sure the Cass thing was last-minute. Blake didn't have time to finish."

Her fingers around his wrist tightened. "Or he's back."

"He's not back. He has to stay away for his alibi."

"You don't know that. You talk about him like he's a rational person."

"His truck's not here."

"That's what he wants us to think."

She gasped like blowing out a candle and jumped to face the chute. "Did you hear that?"

His stomach did a backwards somersault. "What?"

"What?" he said again when she didn't answer.

"Like someone tapping a drumstick on metal."

"I didn't hear anything."

"He's not going to leave this fucking thing hanging here. He's out there."

They stood still, listening, her hand rubbing up and down his arm, her face against his neck. She moved her hands to his shoulders, turning him to face the opposite corner of the room. Outside the semi-circle of overhead light, against the wall, was a bathtub with a blue shower curtain.

She spoke in a whisper. "The freak showers here?"

"After a long day pulling out entrails…"

She aimed her iPhone light at the wall opposite the bathtub where a bunch-up tarp was wedged between two industrial sized hold coolers.

Jackson stepped toward it. She yanked him back.

"It's nothing. A tarp. I can see it from here."

"You can't see what's behind it."

He kicked it, trying not to imagine a thick freckled hand shooting out and grabbing his foot.

"Nothing." He shook the tarp to show her.

She pulled him against her, the sweat of her hands soaking through the front of his tee-shirt. "What was I thinking? I never should have suggested this. You never should have suspected me. If we ha…"

She broke off mid-word and spoke in slow breaths. "Act normal. Be calm. I'm going to tell you something. It'll freak you out, so be calm, be ready."

Fever-thick sweat dripped from his forehead into his eyes.

"There's someone standing in the bathtub."

He rotated slowly and now he saw it too. A fuzzy outline of a tall man against the unlit shower curtain. If he had a gun, they

were helpless. If he didn't, they could get out before he had a
chance to jump them.

Jackson's attempt at a casual voice came out like scraping
metal. "Nothing in here."

He put his arm around her shoulder, keeping himself between
her and the man in the bathtub as they edged toward the chute.

When they passed out of the semi-circle of light, the outline
of the man became more distinct. He didn't move, didn't turn
to track them as they passed. Something wasn't right. His head
was double the size of a normal head. It was flattened on top,
like a partially inflated beach ball. Trish noticed, too, because
she slowed along with Jackson.

He guided her toward the carcass and reached under the dehiding machine for what he thought was a piece of wood but
turned out to be a hind leg. The man in the bathtub still hadn't
moved. Jackson stepped toward the shower slowly, then lunged
forward and jabbed the shower curtain with the leg, knocking
the man backward. His body leaned rigid against the wall.

Trish yanked open the shower curtain. "What the fuck is this?"

The life-sized human figure wore heavy boots and blue overalls.
His oversized forehead and face were covered with sesame seeds.

"You've never seen him before?" Jackson said.

"Of course not."

"He's a character in a horror movie. His name is Burger
Head."

Trish kept her eyes locked on Burger Head like she expected
him to come to life and jump out of the bathtub. "Hit him."

"He's not real."

"Fucking hit him."

Jackson jabbed the chest with the buffalo leg. Trish gasped
at the thud of Burger Head hitting the metal wall.

She grabbed the leg from Jackson, unfazed by the red, still-
moist flesh, and poked at Burger Head, the give of the rubbery
body finally convincing her it was nothing but a lifeless man-
nequin. She looked down at blood squeezing through gaps in
her fingers and dropped the buffalo leg on the ground.

Jackson's relief that it wasn't Blake behind the shower curtain made him almost giddy. He rubbed his arms, feeling the cool tingle of a fever breaking, and described the movie like they were chatting over dinner instead of standing in dark clouds of slaughterhouse stench.

"Burger Head was created by an ad agency to be spokesman for a fast food company, and they cast a voice actor who's a vegetarian but takes the part for money. Burger Head gradually takes over the mind of the actor and comes to life. He can't stand being the cause of so many animals getting slaughtered so he tries to get the ad agency to kill him. But sales are good and they refuse. So Burger Head kills the fast food marketing executives one by one in his slaughterhouse."

"You saw this movie?"

"On Netflix."

"Burger Head wouldn't like a buffalo killer like Blake."

"Unless he made an exception for people in the slaughterhouse brotherhood."

"Uhm, so here we are discussing a homicidal maniac who idolizes a character that operates a slaughterhouse. Isn't this the kind of conversation horror movie victims have right before the maniac catches them?"

"We'd hear the chute gate creak."

Trish wrapped her arms around his chest as they stood listening for the creaking gate. She pressed her lips against his ear. "Enough weathervane hunting for today."

But instead of leaving she took out her iPhone and did a search. "It says *Burger Head* was filmed in 2005 at Stage 3 Productions, Warren, Michigan."

"Blake used to live in Detroit. He must have seen the production and got himself a memento."

"Yeah, well the interesting part is I remember Andrew telling me Michigan had a big incentive program to attract film production. He said that's why he shot part of *Golden Lancehead* in Detroit.

"When?"

"I know that was his last film." She did another search. "Also 2005. It doesn't say where. Let me try the Michigan Film Office. Here we go. Filmed in Boulevard Properties in Detroit."

"The librarian said Blake and his wife moved here around five years ago."

"Big coincidence he comes here too unless Andrew told him about it.

"So Blake lives in Detroit. He's a movie fan. He goes to the productions and somehow meets the director of one of them, who sells him on the charms of a tiny town in Vermont."

Trish rubbed her fingers over the sesame seeds on Burger Head's forehead. "It's weird they meet in 2005, and Blake moves here five years later."

And there it was.

"Always hedge your bets," Jackson said. "Don't bet on one outcome. Bet on both."

"Time to leave. The dead buffalo fumes have gone to your head."

"*Golden Lancehead* was Andrew's last film. Then it was five years of rejections."

"What does that have to do with Blake moving to Greensboro?"

Jackson unbuttoned Burger Head's overalls. "There's a scene in the movie where one of the fast food executives fights back and pushes Burger Head into the dehiding machine. It takes out a chunk of his stomach."

He pulled down the overalls. A triangular gouge was missing from above Burger Head's hip.

"Blake wasn't just a movie fan. This is one of the original props."

"There's sites where you can buy props like this."

"There's also prop makers who take their work home with them."

"Blake moved here to make weathervane replicas?" Trish re-buttoned Burger Head's overalls. "Let's stop tempting the horror movie gods and get out of here."

Searches of "Blake Trotman, prop maker, and Michigan" came up empty. Jackson took a screenshot of the photo of Blake and the buffalo, Virgil, from CaptureMyVermont.com, and he and Trish sat outside his cabin making calls and e-mailing the screen-shot to production companies and prop houses in Michigan. It didn't take long to get a hit.

"That's Billy Blake," the woman from D-Town Productions said. "We hired him on a lot of jobs and so did other studios. Is that a real buffalo or a prop?"

"Real. Do you know if he worked on the film *Golden Lancehead*?"

"We weren't involved in that. Billy just up and vanished one day. Where is he working now, L.A.?"

"He got out of the business," Jackson said. "He and his wife moved to Greensboro, Vermont."

"He had that girlfriend, Tanya. She vanished, too. I guess they got married and moved away."

Next they tried Boulevard Properties, but nobody remembered if Billy Blake worked on *Golden Lancehead*. They tried the L.A. production company that financed the movie, but nobody would give out information.

"I know a shortcut," Jackson said.

Alton picked up on the first ring, as always. "Need more on that screenwriter girl, Trish Devereaux?"

Trish gave Jackson's chest a backhanded swat.

"Yeah, I do," Jackson said. "Can I trust her?"

"I wouldn't."

"Why?"

"Trusting people leads to trouble. Trusting women leads to double trouble. Hey, so I'm driving down Alta Boulevard in Santa Monica and I get cut off by this Lexus LX with a Free Tibet bumper sticker. I'm thinking, this is a cosmopolitan area, I guess it's possible a carload of Chinese policy-makers will pull up behind the Lexus and say to themselves, 'Fellows, that Lexus SUV driver is right. We should free Tibet.'

"Then I get to wondering, how do luxury SUV drivers decide which faraway people living under an oppressive regime to put on their bumper stickers? Free North Korea? Free Bahrain?

Plenty of oppression to object to there, but I guess none of those bumper stickers have quite the same magic. Put a Free Tibet bumper sticker on your Lexus LX and in one fell swoop you're compassionate, worldly, politically engaged, you hang Buddhist prayer flags on your back porch, and there's a very good chance you've climbed Mount Everest…So what's up, another favor to add to the ledger?"

"More movie stuff. Andrew Marvel filmed part of *Golden Lancehead* in Detroit in 2005. I need to know if a freelance prop maker named Billy Blake worked on it."

"A prop maker? After we just got through talking about weathervane replicas. And now Andrew Marvel's in the mix? I assume you know he's yesterday's news in Hollywood? He'd be lucky if someone hired him to direct a YouTube video."

"I promise to tell you everything over drinks."

"And I promise you're buying."

After they hung up, Trish said, "Who is that guy?"

"Antique thief friend from L.A."

"You do get around."

"Let's assume Alton calls back and says Blake worked on *Golden Lancehead*, because that's what he's going to do."

"Even if he didn't, they met. They had to," she said.

"Andrew told me he had a big comeback planned. The studios won't hire him to direct a YouTube video? Fine, he'll finance his comeback on his own with money from stolen antiques. Blake makes the replicas. Cass helps remove the weathervanes, Rex was the fence. Then Audrey finds out and confronts Andrew. The motive we've been looking for."

"The motive I've been looking for. You thought I was the motive."

"I'm thinking how Audrey told Warren Gunderson about the weathervane thief she saw in Brattleboro. She said, 'It's someone local. It'll surprise you. Oh, yes, it'll surprise you.' She wasn't talking about Cass. She was hinting at the person behind it all—Andrew."

"She didn't want to tell on her husband."

"Maybe she thought she could get him to stop. Maybe she threatened to call the cops. Who knows? But she did something that got her killed."

"And there's no proof of any of it."

"What if I go the police?" Jackson said.

"And say what?"

"Everything I know."

"You know Cass bet on dropped charges. What else?"

"Someone else logged onto the account. We have a record of that."

"Cass logged on twice."

"He was in Morrisville." But he saw her point. "They'll say I invented that."

"They'll also say you invented the bit about him looking at a weathervane."

"Someone warned the McCarthys."

"The McCarthys don't know who and the warning never mentioned Cass. What else do you know? Blake has a skill that might be useful in making replicas, and maybe he worked with Andrew."

Jackson stared at his iPhone screen out of habit, because it solved most of his other problems.

She stared at it, too. "That's it."

"What's it?"

"You're going to record Andrew's confession."

"Okay. Sure. Yeah. Problem solved. Let's go celebrate."

"When you were in his house, what room?"

"Kitchen."

"What's the first thing you see?"

"See?"

"In the kitchen."

"The stainless steel carafe."

"Keep going."

"What's the point?"

"Keep going."

"A Wallace and Gromit coffee cup. My cup. A black ceramic container where he keeps coffee beans. Three glass ornaments dangling from the window. Plants in ceramic vases on the windowsill. A wooden loon."

"Andrew taught us the value of a good replica. The ceramic vases would be too hard to match. It has to be the loon."

She typed something in her MacBook and handed it to him. It was an image search for wooden loons. "I get a lot of commenters on my blog. I get to know some of them. Niles owns one of those online spy stores. Hacker, freak, nerd, anarchist. Totally cool guy. He's made every kind of covert listening device. He's built them into cigarette packs, wristwatches, once he even made a tiki drink with a cherry transmitter and cocktail umbrella antenna. It would be a cinch for him to fit a microphone into a wooden loon."

She held the screen in front of Jackson. "Which one?"

Only then did he realize she was serious. "Record him with a loon microphone?"

"He leaves the house and we replace his loon with ours. You tell him you need to talk."

"He doesn't leave the house. Someone shops for him."

"He went kayaking. He'll go again." She nodded at the images. "Which one?"

The black loons had solid white breasts with rings on their necks made of white vertical lines. Some had black eyes, but most had red eyes with black pupils. The plumage was composed of different patterns of white squares, dots, and lines. Some loons looked skyward. Others twisted their heads like they were plucking an insect from their plumage. Most looked straight in a floating position.

Trish reconsidered. "This won't work. Too many different patterns. Andrew might spot the difference. Maybe we could put the transmitter somewhere in the kitchen. Under the table or in the cupboard. It's not like we have to hide it permanently. Just for one short conversation."

"I can tell you exactly which loon he has," Jackson said. "It's identical to the two on the front desk in the inn. They probably got them from the same place."

"Perfect," Trish sent a text and got one back. "Niles will call me in five."

Jackson's whole life he'd been looking gift horses in the mouth and that wasn't about to change now. He couldn't get past how Trish led him straight to the pivotal clue. If he hadn't recognized Burger Head, she would have, and she'd do her Googling and make the Detroit connection between Andrew and Blake.

When her phone rang, she jumped up from her chair and speed-walked toward the adjacent cottage, letting it ring three times before answering. Jackson strained to hear Andrew's slow, staccato voice, but Trish was too far away.

Why would she lead Jackson to the connection between Andrew and weathervanes? Was there any possible reason? There was. So he'd give up his Other Woman fixation. Andrew's motive was weathervanes. It was also Trish. If Jackson was going to stay in town and give the police one of the motives, Andrew wanted him to forget about Trish and give them one they could never prove. And now Trish had to play along and act like they were setting a trap for Andrew. It must take a lot of self-discipline for her not to break into hysterical laughter as she recounted to Andrew how Jackson fell for the Loon Swallowed the Microphone plan.

She came back with a moist-lipped smile, tapping her iPhone against her forehead. She couldn't stand still. She bent over and brushed her hand over Jackson's hair and just as quickly hopped back a step.

"Niles is hooking us up with a supplier of listening devices in Burlington. He says the transmitter's the size of a lighter. We just have to drill a hole in the bottom of the loon. He'll walk me through everything."

❭❭❭

While Tracy was in the kitchen helping prep dinner, Jackson and Trish looked over the two loons on the front desk. They were identical except for the eyes. One had red, the other black.

"Well?" Trish said.

"I was kind of preoccupied at the time, you know, trying to guess if he killed his wife."

"Close your eyes. Andrew's making coffee. You're looking around."

"Red."

"You're sure?"

"Positive."

Trish slipped the red-eyed loon into her backpack.

Jackson wanted to go with her to Burlington, but they decided he should stay in Greensboro in case Blake was keeping tabs on him.

After a dinner of eggplant medallions, Jackson stopped to say hello to Tracy at the front desk.

"You want to hear something totally freaky?" she said. "Someone took one of the wooden loons."

"I thought there was something suspicious about Mr. and Mrs. Jenks."

He watched part of the Red Sox game in his cottage. Trish texted to say Niles' friend had already installed the transmitter and was now showing her how to use her iPhone to record the radio signals it transmitted.

A few innings later, Jackson's phone rang. The caller ID said *A Marvel.*

"Hi, Andrew."

"Hope I'm not calling too late."

"Not at all."

"I never asked how long you're in town. I'm glad you're still here."

"I've only been here three days."

"Greensboro's too sleepy for some people."

"Not me. I love it."

"Hey, I was going on a kayak ride tomorrow and I thought you might want to join me."

"Sounds great."

"The photographers show up at eight."

"Oh, you mean the morning?"

"Is morning inconvenient?"

"No. I'm always up early."

"Want to meet by my dock at around six-thirty?"

"Perfect. See you then."

Jackson texted Trish to make sure the loon would be ready. She said she was already on her way back to Greensboro.

The plan might work if he could get Andrew talking about something other than coffee. But whose plan was it—Jackson and Trish's? Or Andrew and Trish's?

Over the next hour, all but one of the lights in the inn went off. A pinecone clattered across the roof. Wind through the pines sounded like ripping screens.

He woke to a bright light pressed against the window that turned off before he knew if he saw it in a dream or for real. He rolled out of bed and lay on the floor, the wind and his own quick breaths preventing him from hearing any other sounds. The light didn't switch back on, but now he could hear footsteps over grass outside his door followed by what sounded like rocks scraping together. He crawled across the floor to the fireplace tools and grabbed the shovel. He crouched in front of the door. One, two, three...he yanked it open, and jumped out holding the shovel like a baseball bat. Nobody was out there. He circled the cottage, ending up by the table and Adirondack chairs. Something dark was on the table. His iPhone light illuminated a plate with steak, potatoes, and salad greens. The menu's blackened buffalo prime rib dinner. A paper napkin beneath the fork and knife had a message scrawled in black pen. "The buffalo's name was Hank."

Jackson was an introspective guy who'd always given himself high marks in the self-knowledge department. The Jackson he thought he knew would never have picked up the napkin and laughed, and when he finished laughing, shouted, "Thank you for the room service, Blake."

Friday, 6:30 a.m.

Jackson crossed Town Highway 1, passed the tennis court, and followed the path to the Morning Loon section of the shore. Every tree concealed Blake. He was crouched behind every bush. Every wind-blown branch resembled an arm bent at optimum knife-plunging angle.

When Jackson paddled up to the dock, Andrew was already in his kayak, paddle resting on the cockpit, khaki hat shadowing his face.

"You handle a kayak well," he said.

They paddled away from shore.

"I hate to slander such a beautiful lake, but ocean kayaking's my favorite. Audrey and I used to take trips to the Channel Islands. We camped on Santa Cruz Island."

"Yup," Jackson said.

"You've been there?"

"Day trip. I wanted to stay longer, but I couldn't get a permit. The ferry ride over we were surrounded by a school of dolphins."

"Sounds amazing."

"It was."

"I think the two most beautiful places to kayak—well, you hate to rank things like that—but the Channel Islands and, this is going to surprise you unless you've been there, the Upper Peninsula in Michigan. Lake Superior side."

"I've heard about it."

"I filmed a couple projects in Detroit. I always made sure to work in a trip to the UP."

Jackson imagined the smirk on Andrew's face at the way he revealed that Trish gave him a play-by-play of the Burger Head investigation and how they found out Blake and Andrew worked together in Detroit.

Andrew increased his pace. He wasn't trying to challenge Jackson, like Warren. His paddling had a steady trance-like feel, like he was retreating into that other world he pretended to prefer over this one.

Jackson was happy to follow. He wouldn't have to imagine a paddle blade to the temple. The day's first sunlight sparkled on the green water. The headwind nicked off tips of waves, spraying his face. A solitary maple leaf floated down from the sky. Jackson shortened his stroke to avoid pulling it under water. He was now struggling to keep up with Andrew. The steady pace shouldn't be burning his shoulders and making it hard to breathe. It wasn't the exertion. It was fear.

They reached the public boat launch, then did a lap around the seven-mile circumference and slowly crossed the lake back to Andrew's dock. Trish had more than enough to swap out the loons so long as Andrew left the sliding glass door open like he did the last time he went kayaking.

"How'd it feel?" Andrew said.

"Beats working out in a gym."

"I mentioned the UP. Something strange happened there."

"What?"

"It was glassy, no wind, and I made the mistake of not wearing a life preserver. I didn't notice the cork had gotten dislodged. I wasn't far from shore, maybe a hundred yards, when I felt the kayak taking on water. I had to make a snap decision. I could stay with the kayak, but the water was cold. Nobody else was around. Or I could swim for shore, even though I knew there was a current. I took off my shirt, kicked off my Tevas and went for it. After a few minutes, I realized I wasn't making progress. I was getting tired.

"I imagined a rescue helicopter swooping up from behind the cliff. I wasn't hoping, I was actually expecting to see it. I had to convince myself it was impossible. I dove down to the bottom to calm myself and when I came up I switched to backstroke. When I started running out of strength, I kicked down, and felt a rock. I made it. Then I was walking back along the shore toward my campground, and I saw my Tevas in a little crevice. Walked a little further and there was my shirt. Further on, my kayak. I kept imaging the next thing I'd see washed into shore was my body, that I'd really drowned, and thinking I was walking along shore was the last gasp of my conscious mind, struggling to stay alive."

The calming dive to the bottom, the backstroke, the human will, the fine line. Andrew didn't drown that day and because of that Audrey was dead.

They'd reached the dock. Jackson followed Andrew up the lawn. If he'd locked the sliding glass door, they'd go around to the front, but he led Jackson up the red wooden stairs to the porch.

"Good thing you didn't hire Wally to build the deck," Jackson said.

Andrew threw his head back and laughed. "You've heard about his carpentry?"

"He built one so crooked the owner couldn't serve a glass of wine without it spilling."

"That would be Jan."

"She hired someone else to install her septic tank and they haven't spoken since."

Andrew laughed some more. "Let's have some coffee," he said as he pulled open the sliding glass door.

Jackson placed his backpack on the chair next to his. The loon sat on its windowsill perch between two plants, staring at Jackson with black eyes that should have been red. Seeing it now in its natural setting, Jackson was sure of it. How had he fucked up the eye color? He watched Andrew fill the kettle with water and scoop coffee beans into the grinder. While the water was boiling, he used a measuring cup to water the plants.

"Audrey made these vases for desert succulents, but she had so many she brought some to Vermont."

"They look good."

"The succulents look better. I could bring the vases back to L.A., but I'll probably leave them here, even it means I have to give visitors the caveat she created them for smaller plants."

"It's your call, but I don't think the caveat's necessary."

Andrew got out the Wallace and Gromit cup and the brown one. He hesitated before reaching for the kettle and pouring more water into the filter.

"Got something for you." He took a carton of Silk soymilk from the fridge. "I can't claim credit. My lawyer's grocery shopper got it. You like it frothy?"

"Please."

He shook the carton, pulled open the seal, and poured a splash in Jackson's cup. He put milk into his own cup and carried them to the table.

"I'm going to drink it slowly," Jackson said. "You might not offer me a second cup after you hear what I have to say."

"You lied. You're really a reporter. No, it can't be that bad." Andrew's unblinking eyes didn't go with his bantering words.

"You got the lie part right. I'm not Hank Carruthers. My name is Jackson Oliver. I own an online casino in Costa Rica called VegasVegas."

"Paris Paris. New York, New York. VegasVegas."

"You're the first person to get the joke."

"Impossible."

"I have to explain the name must be five times a week."

They both laughed. Andrew sipped his coffee and so did Jackson.

The laughter turned to silence. "An online casino owner visiting Greensboro?"

"We have unlimited space on our site so we post all kind of things. Entertainment props like *The Bachelorette*, political elections, celebrity murder trials…Your trial."

"If I deprived you of a refill for that, I'd be the worst hypo-crite. Do you know how many films I've based on the tragedies of others?"

"One of my customers is a local guy. Cass Gallaway."

"Don't know him."

"You never will. He was murdered yesterday in the Hardwick cemetery."

Andrew kept the washed cement eyes on Jackson, shaking his head and saying, "My God."

"Cass placed a thousand-dollar bet on dropped charges at 100 to 1. This was two days before the video was delivered to your lawyer. I came to Greensboro to find out what he knew before I paid. I followed him to Morrisville where I saw him ringing the doorbell of a house and looking up at the upstairs window. That's what I thought at the time. I later found out about Audrey seeing someone casing out a weathervane in Brattleboro and realized that's what Cass was doing at the house in Morrisville. Looking up at their weathervane. He's the one Audrey suspected."

Andrew picked up his coffee as if to take a sip and slammed it hard on the table, shattering the cup. The words squeezed out in a whisper. "You should have said so."

He went to the sink for a rag. "All your phony questions— 'What did Audrey tell you? Who did she suspect?' You were toying with me."

He wiped splashes of coffee from the floor. Jackson ripped a handful of towels from the roll beneath the cupboard, and wiped the table. "I didn't want you telling the police. That's part of it. I wanted to believe you were framed, but I couldn't be sure."

"Let's stop talking while we wipe up the spill."

Andrew picked up shards of cup and carried them to the trashcan beneath the sink. He took another cup from the cabinet, a white one with the green outline of Vermont.

With his back still to Jackson, he said, "You're thinking it's a good thing I got greedy and did that extra pour."

"Yes, but I didn't think it was time to joke."

"You can be yourself. Please do. I thought it over, and I under-stand why you didn't want the police to know about your bettor."

"Not until I knew more. Which I now do. Shall I go on?"

Andrew returned to the table with his new cup. "Please."

"When I followed Cass to Morrisville, someone logged onto our site from the Greensboro Library. I was able to narrow it down to three people: Blake Trotman, Wally Caiden, and Trish."

"That's why you asked about her script."

"She told me you two met last summer. I found out that wasn't true. You met the summer before Audrey's murder."

"She had a different script, about an elephant. You didn't ask when we'd met."

"She misled me about that, not you. A hidden relationship. There's your missing motive."

Andrew waited for Jackson to say more, but Jackson out-waited him. He wanted to hear what Andrew had to say about Trish now. Andrew got up and shifted one of the plants near the loon. "Something's different."

He stepped back and surveyed the row of plants.

Jackson kept his eyes locked on a purple flower. "A new blos-som. The purple one."

"The trillium? No, that's not new."

Andrew studied the plants a few more seconds and returned to his seat. "I am, I was, happily married. Trish was just an attrac-tive young woman with a script and a lot of initiative. I won't flatter myself by saying she had the slightest interest in me as anything more than a connection to Hollywood. I admired her for not pretending otherwise."

"That's a shock. She's good at pretending."

Andrew raised his eyebrows, maybe surprised at the resent-ment Jackson couldn't keep out of his voice.

"I saw two possibilities," Jackson said. "One: You wanted Trish, so you hired Blake or Wally to kill Audrey and leave evi-dence framing you. Trish filmed the alibi and Blake or Wally bet on dropped charges. That way no money changed hands. Two: Blake or Wally were stealing weathervanes with Cass. Audrey found out so they killed her and framed you. The "dropped charges" bets made them money on the side."

Andrew nodded in a deliberate way that made it look like he was processing new information.

"You asked me after the hike if I thought you hired someone, and I told you no. I was convinced it was related to weathervanes. But then the antique dealer, Rex, told me the rooster weathervane in Brattleboro was worthless. No thief would want it."

"Back to me again."

"Back to you but not completely. Something about Rex's story bugged me. I went to the library and found a book on local weathervanes. There was a picture of an antique rooster on a farmhouse in Brattleboro. Audrey checked the book out twice. I talked to the owner of the farmhouse. Audrey warned her to watch out for thieves."

Andrew straightened in his chair. "But Rex said…"

"He found a worthless rooster weathervane and claimed it was the one Audrey told him about. He was covering for the thieves."

"You can't be serious. He sold their stuff?"

"Right. So there's Cass, Rex, and either Blake or Wally. Then someone to make the replicas. The artist at Green Mountain Arts has that skill.

Andrew held his hand up, stopping Jackson. "Meredith?"

"Have you seen her wire sculptures? She could copy a weathervane no problem."

"There's not a person in Greensboro less likely to steal antiques."

"You're sure of that?"

"I'd bet everything I own."

"You've got good instincts. It was someone else."

Andrew got up and poured more milk into his cup. "Someone else."

"I snuck into Blake's barn because I was looking for weathervanes. I didn't know what else to do. No luck. But there was something strange in the slaughterhouse. A life-sized model of a horror movie character named Burger Head. It didn't take long to find out Blake used to be a prop maker in Detroit. You can see how that changed my thinking."

Andrew stared at his reflection in his coffee. "I knew it couldn't be Meredith."

"You filmed part of *Golden Lancehead* in Detroit in 2005. You and Blake met. Five years later, he moved to Greensboro. He had a skill and you knew how he could put it to better use."

Jackson held his cup tight, poised to throw it at any sudden movement. But Andrew only shifted in his chair.

Jackson went on. "You're washed up. Hollywood doesn't want you. Nobody takes your calls. Fuck the studios. You'll finance your new movie on your own. Blake made the replicas. Cass helped remove the weathervanes. Rex got rid of them. Everything was going great until Audrey had the audacity to get interested in antique weathervanes. You refused to let her get in the way of your comeback. Blake killed her and left evidence implicating you.

"The police and DA were more than happy to arrest the husband and put you on trial. After the alibi freed you, the police would suspect you of hiring someone but they'd never find any payment. Since Blake killed Audrey, he had to stay as far as possible from things, so you used Cass to register for the accounts and when it came time to kill Cass, you had to do it when Blake was in Burlington. You probably thought you had no choice. I'd go to the police about the bet and they'd get Cass to talk."

Jackson felt out of breath, like he'd run a sprint. "Pin Cass' murder on me and you accomplish two things: shut him up forever and force me to leave you alone."

Jackson put his iPhone on the table. "I'm not secretly recording your confession. It's just the two of us. When did you find out I was here? Probably when Rex told you about someone claiming to be Audrey's friend from L.A."

Andrew flicked his finger against his neck, steady like a metronome. "I didn't find out you were here until a few moments ago. Please don't be offended when I say I prefer the company of Hank Carruthers."

He stared out past Jackson toward the lake. His voice got so soft Jackson had to strain to hear. "Am I imagining this conversation? I must be because it can't be real."

He pressed his thumbs against his closed eyes, opened them again and nodded at Jackson. "Audrey always told me I trust people too easily. She wasn't here to warn me about you."

Jackson held his cup in the air, watching his shaking hand spill coffee over the rim. "You fucking murdered your wife. You murdered a harmless nobody who helped you steal weathervanes. You framed me for murder."

"If you honestly believe that, you have no choice. You have to go to the police."

Jackson made a move to stand, but checked himself. The loon was his only hope.

"They'll want to believe you," Andrew said. "But then they'll start asking questions, like how did I get to the Hardwick cemetery and back?"

"Blake picked you up. You used his car."

"I think you said Blake was in Burlington. Does he have a second car?"

"I don't know."

"I don't think he does."

"He stole it."

"Did anyone report a stolen car? I'm just saying these are questions the police will ask." Andrew sounded like someone trying to help a friend sort out a predicament.

His voice got soft again. "And what did you say my reason was? I killed Audrey because she suspected this Cass person of stealing weathervanes? It was the end of June. Audrey would be returning to L.A. in August. Yet I'd kill her instead of waiting for her to go home?"

"She confronted you. She threatened to spill your secret."

"She suspected me of committing a felony but didn't leave? Didn't confide in any of her friends? And do you think—?"

He cut himself off and blew out a long breath. "I'm done defending myself. You'll do whatever you want."

Jackson grabbed his backpack. "I'll do it now. Pour yourself another cup. The cops will be here in five minutes."

The plan never had a chance. Andrew wouldn't admit anything. Jackson felt an irrational hatred for the taunting black eyes of the loon. He crossed the wooden floor toward the porch. Andrew didn't try to stop him and why should he? The arrogant prick no doubt thought he had Jackson figured out enough to know he'd never hand himself over to the police. But big picture Andrew was about to get tripped up by something so insignificant Jackson hadn't considered it until this moment.

He turned back to the table. "I'm not a fool. I owed Cass money. He could blacklist my casino. I met him at the cemetery. I know the police will take me over you. But I have no choice. Cass called me at the Morning Loon. They'll figure out the call was forwarded to my cottage. It's only a matter of time."

Andrew stopped him as he was sliding open the door. "Sure you won't have another cup? There's more here than I can finish myself, and I know something that might interest you."

When Jackson sat down, Andrew nodded at his backpack. "Mind if I have a look?"

"Go ahead."

Andrew unzipped it, took out the shirt and shook it in the air. He flattened the pack on the table and squeezed the compartments.

"Your phone?"

Andrew made sure video and Voice Memos weren't recording. He placed the iPhone softly on the table. "You should know I'm not that careless. Cass didn't use his phone to call the Morning Loon. He called from the pay phone outside the post office."

"I was right. You fucking framed me." Jackson said it with the bitterness Andrew would expect from someone he framed for murder.

He watched Andrew fill both their cups and add a splash of soymilk to Jackson's and milk to his own.

"No need to worry," Andrew said. "I don't want the police finding out about you."

"Maybe you haven't noticed, but your plans have a way of falling apart."

"Cass used the pay phone every time he called your casino and the Offshore Gaming Association. Did you mention him to anyone?"

"Only Rex."

"You're in the clear. Rex is a wily little creature. He's the only one of them I could rely on."

Jackson swallowed. Andrew had admitted involvement in Cass' murder. Jackson swallowed again and cursed himself. He'd visualized himself cool and nonchalant as he took in the confession but here he was losing control at the very first admission.

"Cass used Money Gram to open the account," Jackson said. "He wired money to my agent in Malaga."

"Cass destroyed the receipts, so the police have no reason to visit Money Gram stores."

"If the guy from the Offshore Gaming Association hears about Cass…"

"How would he?"

"He wouldn't."

Jackson pretended to gather himself and took a big breath of what he hoped sounded like relief. "I can stop worrying about the cops."

"Cass was in the Hardwick paper today. Tomorrow he'll be gone. He comes from a rough background. This kind of thing happens to people like Cass."

Jackson sipped his coffee. "What was the point? I said I'd leave town if Cass told the Offshore Gaming Association I paid the bet."

Andrew stretched his neck from one shoulder to the other. "I'll tell you, if you're interested."

"I am."

"Today is August 7th. Six years ago, August 9th, I had a meeting with Beakin Productions, the company that produced *Frontier Zero* for Sony. It didn't go well. They had no interest in any of my projects. I left but forgot my sunglasses. As I was returning to the conference room, I heard one of the junior marketing executives say, 'The guy's not totally washed up. If we need someone to film our Christmas party, maybe he can bid the job.' And they all laughed. *Frontier Zero* grossed three-hundred-seventy million, but now I was the butt of a junior marketing executive's joke.

"That's the day I said fuck the studios. I found the perfect script, got commitments from actors. My producer said we could do it for 3.5 million. I got hooked up with a retired German banker who agreed to finance it. Two months before we start shooting, he says he wants me to put his girlfriend in the movie. Not as some extra in a deli buying a sandwich. He wants the script rewritten to feature her. Her acting experience? She once played the part of a woman suspended from a giant swing above the audience in a Wild Tortoises rock video. That's the day I said, 'Fuck the studios, fuck retired German bankers. I'll do it myself.' I won't bore you with different ways I tried raising money. Nothing worked until I stole a horse weathervane that netted me six thousand. Not much, but it was a start, and I learned there were plenty more valuable weathervanes all over the Northeast."

"Meredith's horse?"

Andrew nodded. "I ordered the replica from a prop house I used to work with in Culver City. Cass had spent the week helping me re-do the boathouse. It took the two of us less than an hour to swap the weathervanes.

"I'd met Blake while I was shooting *Golden Lancehead* in Detroit. I got back in touch with him and pitched him on my new business, and he moved here the following summer. I'd always taken a lot of scouting trips to different parts of the country, so Audrey didn't think twice when I left town. Three years, fifty-six weathervanes in Vermont, Maine, Massachusetts, New York, New Hampshire. Average sale price sixty-two thousand. My comeback was within reach.

"Which brings us to last summer. When Audrey turned into the weathervane vigilante, it was the closest I ever came to believing in God. Who else would spite me like that? But then

I saw the humor in it and she had no way of finding out. In a way, her fixation gave me a good cover."

"Like Rex."

"Rex was genuinely infuriated by the thefts until I gave him a chance to join in. He became Audrey's antique guru. At the beginning of June, he told me Audrey had spotted Cass outside the McCarthy farmhouse and guessed why. Now we had a problem."

Andrew's fingernail tapping against his cup sounded like a ticking clock. "Audrey was a better detective than I thought. She saw me talking to Cass in town and got suspicious. There's a crawl space under the boathouse I used to hide weathervanes. I had one there when she decided to search the property. She confronted me and I told her everything. In a way I was relieved. I wanted her to share in my comeback. I read her the script, explained how I could get the movie done for less than five million. I told her it was my ticket back. Our ticket back. She loved the parties more than I did. People didn't treat her special because she has a degree in nineteenth-century French literature. It was because of me."

Andrew walked up to the sliding glass door, looked out at the lake. "All these years you think you know someone."

He picked up the carafe, realized his cup was still full, and came back to the table. "I honestly thought my plan would make her proud. I mean what a cool way of financing my comeback. Scaling roofs in the dead of night. Taking what you need to get ahead. A nice little 'fuck you' to polite society. Who was I hurting? These hicks in their barns don't know the difference between their weathervanes and Blake's props. They should be honored they're helping me make a movie that will change the world.

"I told Audrey I'd stop as soon as I got the movie financed. Her response? 'I'm giving you one month to buy back everything you stole and return it to the owners or I go to the police.'"

Andrew seemed to be watching for Jackson's response, so he shook his head and said, "I'm sure she didn't mean it.

"But she did. She did mean it. The year before she had no interest in antique weathervanes, but now she'd become the weathervane vigilante. Do you know how much Rex could have gotten for that Brattleboro rooster?"

"Half a million?"

"Seven hundred fifty thousand. It would have pushed me over the top. I would have been filming by Christmas. But Audrey slipped a note under the mat warning the owners, so we couldn't touch it."

Andrew sipped his coffee, closed his eyes. "I couldn't understand why Audrey was siding with the junior marketing executive and the retired German banker and the hicks in their barns. Why was she betraying me? I'd come so far. No way was she stopping my comeback. When I realized she wouldn't change her mind, I pretended to break down in remorse. I said I didn't know what came over me. I promised to get counseling and pleaded with her not to tell a soul, even her closest friends. It would ruin us. I've always been an anal person. I consider every possible solution to a problem so I don't have to hold myself accountable later."

Andrew opened Jackson's backpack and again felt the contents inside as he continued talking. "I went through all the possibilities. Get rid of evidence and let her go to the police. Scare her with anonymous threats. Kill her."

He unzipped the front pouch even though it obviously didn't contain anything. "I almost didn't include that one. A man can't get away with killing his wife. But, like I said, I'm anal. I imagined different scenarios. Fake an accident. Stage a phony robbery. Convince her to go for a night swim."

He moved his hands up and down the foam straps, squeezing. "None of them worked, but I didn't expect them to. I scratched 'kill her' off my list."

He placed the backpack on the table. "I'm a Lakers fan. I sometimes go to Bovada.com to look at NBA futures and one day I clicked on the entertainment page for no reason and saw the Chester Simmons murder trial, that TV newscaster guy."

Jackson felt a wave of exhaustion, but he didn't want to miss a word of this part.

"I never heard of something like that. I found articles about betting on the OJ trial, Phil Spector, Robert Blake. I once fooled around with a script idea where someone frames himself and gets himself off so he can't be tried for the same crime twice. When I read those articles, the two ideas came together. Here was a way I could prevent Audrey from destroying my comeback, and at the same time I could make up the money I lost when she deprived me of the Brattleboro rooster."

"Some of the betting money was for you?"

"I'm the one who'd have to spend a year in jail, the one who'd lose his wife. Of course I wanted my share of the money. But I didn't want to kill Audrey. I tried again. I showed her my storyboard with sketches of sequences I had planned. Amazing scenes people will always remember the way they remember the crop duster in *North by Northwest*, Major Kong riding the nuclear bomb. I read the e-mails from actors saying how eager they were to be part of it all. I explained how the constraints of a low budget movie would be a blessing, how it would force me to rely on my craft and ingenuity instead of easy special effects. All she said is, 'I told you you've got one month to return everything you stole.'"

Jackson had enough. More than enough. But Andrew still hadn't admitted to killing Cass.

"Can I have a refill?"

"What? Oh, of course. I've been hogging it all, haven't I?"

Andrew poured him another cup and stirred in a splash of soymilk. "If you stick around town, I'll show you those storyboarded scenes I was talking about. You'll see what I mean."

"That would be great."

Maybe Andrew sensed Jackson's forced calm because he said, "I hate to be like this, but would you mind standing?"

Andrew patted the sides of his swimsuit.

"Now spread your legs apart."

He tapped his open hand against the inside of Jackson's thighs and his anus. "I said a lot of things."

"I understand."

"Talking Blake into it wasn't hard. I think in his heart of hearts he's always wanted to know what it's like to graduate from killing buffalo to killing people."

"You put a lot of trust in him."

"You have to work with the tools at hand. I intended to use him only for replicas. But when it came time for Audrey, he was my best option. He took the job seriously. Every day, he practiced with a kayak so he could dump the clothes in the lake. He planted all the evidence implicating me without leaving any traces of himself. He found a bike that couldn't be linked to him and used it to get away from the house. He's a Looney Toon, but he nailed it."

"What if he got nervous and destroyed the video?"

"I had faith in his greed. I also kept a copy. It worried me I'd be in jail when they were placing the bets. I told Blake we shouldn't win more than a few thousand from any one casino. With the long odds and the number of casinos that posted celebrity trials in the past, I said we'd all come away with more than enough money, even with small bets. It never occurred to me Cass would increase the bets to keep more for himself. Would you have come here if he only won a few thousand?"

"I would have thought something weird was going on."

"Would you have come here?"

"Not for a few thousand."

"Cass learned the hard way I was right."

"What's done is done," Jackson said. "I still think killing Cass was an unnecessary risk. Why would he talk and ruin his weathervane gig?"

"Blake was getting antsy. He accused me of being scared to get my hands dirty. I could have pushed back. Maybe I should have. Like you say, what's done is done."

"You used the fireplace poker Blake took from my cabin."

Andrew's eyes blinked rapid-fire. "Nobody took anything from your cabin."

"It's missing."

"The police could trace it back to you. I didn't want that."

"Probably just an incomplete set. You had Cass tell me that story about a black jack chip in a red Monte Carlos so I'd think it was Wally instead of Blake who logged onto Cass' account."

"That was Blake's idea. I told him it was waste of time."

Andrew pulled the corners of his mouth up into a boyish grin. "I assume you know this, but I do enjoy hanging out with you. If circumstances were different…"

"But they're not."

"No, they're not."

Jackson sipped his coffee like he wasn't in a rush to go anywhere. He'd never felt so tired. He had to get back to the cabin and take a nap.

Andrew was flicking his finger against the cup again. "When I first started out and I got special treatment from people because I was a director, it nauseated me. But I got used to it and learned I needed it. You don't know what it's like to have an entire country quoting lines from your movies. Every female eye making offers. At every restaurant, the host saying, 'I love your work, Mr. Marvel.'"

He rubbed his hand back and forth over hair growing back thick. "It's sad, Jackson, sad. If Audrey hadn't become the weathervane vigilante, she'd be picking out a dress for the Oscars soon. Because that's the kind of film I was going to make. I am going to make. You'll be watching from some Costa Rican bar. When I go up to receive my award, I'll wink at the camera and you'll know it's for you."

"I look forward to seeing it."

"I'm glad you forced me into this. I knew you wouldn't judge me the way Audrey did. You see the world with clear eyes. You're angry I framed you and I can't blame you. But you understand why I did what I did."

"Yes." It was Jackson's most difficult lie yet.

"There's one last thing I want to ask you. When I told you about the kayak in the UP, did you think I made it up?"

"Almost drowning?"

"The part at the end, that I thought I'd really drowned."

"Oh, that."

"You thought I invented it?"

"Just that part. Thinking you were about to see your body wash in to shore."

"I'd think the same thing. It seems like a flourish someone would invent afterwards. But the truth is I was more scared about seeing my body wash in than I was when I thought I was drowning. The wind got colder all at once and I felt like I was only half there. I'm telling you this because I felt the same way in the motel room after Blake texted me Audrey was dead."

Jackson let a few silent minutes go by before saying he'd better get going to make it back while they were still serving breakfast. He stood up but fell back on the front of the chair and rolled off. He tried pushing himself off the wooden floor, the pillow-cool floor.

> > >

Consciousness didn't do a slow fade from black. Jackson opened his eyes and knew everything. Andrew had drugged his coffee. They were in Blake's barn, and Jackson's legs were fastened to the chair legs with nylon tie-down straps from a bike rack. Another strap fastened his wrists to the chair back. Trish was tied to a chair a few feet away. Andrew sat on a stepladder facing them. Blake stood against a bale of hay, holding a rifle. It was now night, and it smelled of manure and dust.

Andrew eyed him. "He's back among the living. I'm sorry, Jackson, but you had no intention of leaving town."

"The soymilk."

"It's lucky for me you don't take your coffee black."

"More of your chloral hydrate?"

"It took longer than I thought. Didn't you wonder about such a long-winded confession?"

"I thought you were proud."

"Did you really? I'm not. I'm filled with regrets and I'm about to add more."

Blake jabbed the barrel of the rifle into the hay. "Chitchat. More fucking chitchat. Fuck the chitchat."

Andrew followed Jackson's gaze to Trish, who had her head down, staring at the floorboards.

"Blake found her outside my house."

Why didn't Andrew mention Trish recording his confession? Did she see Blake coming in time to hide her iPhone?

Jackson tried pulling his wrists apart, but the strap didn't loosen.

"You're losing it," he said. "First Cass, now this. Don't you think I told people at my casino everything before I went kayaking with you?"

"No, I don't."

"I'm a fool?"

"I don't think that, either. You needed a confidante. So you told Trish."

"I don't trust Trish. You tie her up so I think she's not in it with you?"

"I'm not sure how to say this, but at this point it doesn't matter what you think."

Blake shouted, "I heard you."

"Heard me?" Andrew said.

"Not you. Him." Blake jerked the clown head at Jackson. "'Thank you for the room service, Blake.' Like you were on top of the world, nobody could take you down."

Jackson strained his legs against the straps, tried shifting his hands again. The pickaxe hung on two nails on a stud above him. Could he reach it before Blake had time to react? He had to free his hands.

"He's looking at the pickaxe."

Andrew gave Blake a slow headshake. "You would too in his position. He's tied to the chair and you're holding a rifle, but if it'll make you feel safer I'll move the pickaxe."

"The guy pisses me off. I can promise you this, he's going to feel pain."

"No, he's not. Don't listen to him, Jackson, you won't feel pain and neither will Trish. I promise."

Blake nodded the clown head at Trish. "Why isn't she saying anything?"

"Ask her, not me," Andrew said.

Blake walked up to her, put the rifle barrel under her chin, raising her head. "Why aren't you saying anything?"

Trish smiled at him. "You're going to die tonight."

Andrew stood to check any violent response, but Blake mimicked her smile and moved back to his position against the bales of hay.

Andrew looked from Trish to Jackson. "I'm sorry Blake and I have to discuss this in front of you." He turned to Blake. "How do you dispose of the buffalo offal?"

"A guy comes and hauls it away three times a week."

"If it contained something other than buffalo remains...How closely do they examine it?"

"Are you fucking serious?"

"No need to get worked up. I go through all the possibilities. It's my nature."

"It's my nature not to listen to this shit. Hide two bodies in the offal? The punk's right, you're losing it."

Andrew let ten seconds pass before saying, "I'm all ears. Tell me your solution."

"Intruders on my property and I shot them."

"Maybe. Maybe that's our only play. It's not ideal."

Andrew strolled around the barn. He picked up a fertilizer spreader, turned the handle, put it back on the table. He flicked his fingernail against a strapped bundle of garden bags.

"Buffalo can be ornery, can't they?"

Blake's mouth softened. He shook his head and grinned. "You can get a buffalo to go anywhere it wants to go."

"A friend of a friend tried taking a selfie with a buffalo in Yellowstone. It gored him. He almost died."

"Serves him right."

"Some farmers dehorn their herds."

"Some farmers staple plastic numbers to their ears. I hope they all rot in hell."

"When does the guy come to haul away the offal?"

"Tomorrow."

"Can I tell you an idea?"

"Tell me."

"We take one of the buffalo heads from the offal bin and saw off the horn."

Blake slammed the rifle butt against the hay. "It's fucking Rodin and Luther in there. You're not dehorning them."

"Blake, hear me out. We saw off the horn and use it on Jackson. He came here to sabotage your slaughter equipment and he got too close to the buffalo. It gored him."

Jackson pulled at the straps. He felt the one around his wrist loosening. When he tried again, he realized he'd just imagined it. It was tight as before.

"Why would he disable the equipment?" Blake said.

"To prevent them from getting killed. He's a vegan."

"No, he's not." Blake turned the clown head to Jackson. "Are you?"

"Yes."

Blake ran at him and planted his boot in Jackson's chest, knocking the chair over. "You promised to eat the blackened buffalo prime rib dinner but the whole time you were fucking with me. I'm nothing to you. An insect under your shoe. Soon this insect will be buzzing around your dead body."

Clattering to the ground, the chair felt less sturdy than it looked. Jackson couldn't break the straps, but if he had a chance maybe he could snap the chair legs.

Andrew lifted Jackson's chair from behind and returned to his stepladder. He didn't hurry Blake, who finally said, "We're not dehorning Rodin or Luther. Titan will do it. He's in the holding pen now. He'll do it. He'd consider it an honor."

Jackson tried to get a goodbye glance from the last pair of friendly eyes in his world, but Trish didn't look up from the floorboards. Blake strapped his rifle over his shoulder. He and Andrew carried Jackson's chair out of the barn.

"Set him down," Blake said. "I don't want him grabbing the rifle."

"His hand are strapped."

"I'm bringing the rifle to the holding pen."

Andrew exhaled a long breath as Blake walked away. Jackson expected some of Andrew's friendly banter, but he sat on a flattened tree stump with his back to Jackson, looking up at the sky. Jackson forced his legs inward and jerked them apart. The chair legs moved more each time he repeated the motion. He needed more time.

"You're making a mistake," he said.

"You're probably right."

"It's not too late."

"But it is."

"Trish didn't do anything. She was standing outside your house."

Andrew rotated on the stump to face Jackson. "What was she doing there?"

"She a reporter. You're the big story."

Jackson's words misfired. If Trish managed to hide the iPhone from Blake, Andrew would find it.

Jackson hadn't heard Blake's approach, but he was back beside the chair. Andrew hopped down from the stump and the two of them lifted the chair and carried it to the holding pen. Blake's rifle leaned against the gate. A solitary buffalo stood inside the pen. They set Jackson down.

"I thought the herd hangs out together," Andrew said.

"Luther was Titan's best friend. He's upset Luther's gone and he's been acting aggressive to the others, so I put him in here."

"Do we put Jackson inside?"

"Titan gets jittery around too many people. Go back to the barn. I'll carry the punk inside."

If Titan didn't do his bidding, Blake would probably shoot Jackson and he didn't want Andrew interfering. Andrew didn't move. Maybe he didn't like Blake telling him what to do. Finally he said, "Shout if you need me," and went back toward the barn.

Blake pushed the gate open a few feet. Titan looked over, but didn't seem interested in what he saw. Blake lifted the chair from behind and hauled Jackson inside. He brought the rifle in and latched the gate. Cool morning air softened the manure scent. Jackson looked up at the bright sun that would go on being bright when he was no longer around to see it. A plank leaning against the fence, soft mud beneath his feet, thick clumps of grass—they offered him one last chance to crack the riddle of existence.

"Hey, buddy, how you doing?" Blake said in a falsetto voice.

Titan swung his head, this time keeping the moist eyes on Blake.

"This man wants to harm Papa. He accused Papa of stealing books, and he lied to Papa and now he wants to send Papa to jail. I know how you feel about people who want to harm Papa."

"Papa killed Luther," Jackson said.

Blake slammed his cupped hands over Jackson's ears. "You don't talk to him."

Titan took slow steps toward them.

"Don't let him talk bad about Papa."

Titan's snout was inches from Jackson's face. Wet breath swirled upward. His two horns curved around the thick brown Mohawk of fur. A reflected cloud was a tiny dot on the wet, black eyes.

"You want Papa to show you?"

Blake backhanded Jackson across the face. "That's what we do to people who want to harm Papa."

Jackson coughed out blood. "Papa's a nutcase. You know that, don't you, Titan?"

Blake pulled back his arm and punched Jackson flush in the temple. The pain took his breath.

Titan turned and walked away. He lowered himself into a sitting position, facing them. Blake went for the rifle. He'd given up on Titan. He was going to take care of it himself. Jackson couldn't stop him. He pulled his legs apart, felt the chair legs give. They wouldn't snap.

But Blake stepped in front of Jackson's chair and faced Titan. "Buddy, you're going to let him talk that way about Papa?"

He stomped his boot on the ground. "Titan." He stomped again, closer to Titan's face. "Titan."

Titan lowered his head to sniff a patch of grass in the mud. Blake placed the muzzle between Titan's horns. "Papa lets you graze in the open field. He gave you a name. Don't betray Papa."

Titan flicked his tail and turned his head to face Jackson. Blake removed the rifle, leaving a dent in the thick brown fur. Titan looked at Jackson with eyelids lowered over night-black pupils, and Jackson saw sadness to rival any human sadness. With two soft grunts, Titan lowered his head, placing it on the mud in front of Jackson's shoes.

"Titan." Blake jabbed the barrel against Titan's nose. Titan didn't move. Blake pulled the rifle back and gave two hard jabs, the second one splitting Titan's nose apart.

It was a single upward motion, standing and swinging his head forward in unison. Titan's left horn pierced Blake beneath the ribs. He raised his head and jerked it down again, tossing Blake to the ground. Jackson tipped his chair on top of Blake to stop him reaching for the rifle, which lay in the mud beside Titan. But Blake didn't move.

"Everything okay up there?" Andrew's voice came from outside the barn.

Jackson rolled himself and his chair over mud to the fence, rotating on his back so one of the horizontal bars slid between the front and back chair legs. He rocked forward and back, wedging the front legs between two bars. There was too much space between the bars to snap the legs.

"What's going on up there, Blake?" Andrew's voice was louder, closer.

Jackson rolled toward the two chute gates. He came so close to Titan he felt tail hair brush against his cheek. The bars of the chute gates were vertical and closely spaced. As he rotated on his back, he heard a creak and saw Andrew step inside the holding pen. Jackson rocked the chair so one of the bars slid between the chair legs and his ankles. He threw his body forward, snapping the two front legs from the seat. He shook his legs until both chair legs fell to the ground and used his feet to slide the looped straps from around his legs.

Andrew was taking small steps toward the rifle beside Titan. He took one more step, and Titan stood. Andrew hopped back and ducked outside the pen. Jackson could see him motionless outside the fence.

Jackson wedged the top of the chair back under a horizontal fence bar. Now that he had use of his legs, a single upward lunge snapped the chair back from the seat. He slid his wrists from the loosened straps. He was free. He looked across the pen at Andrew, but he was gone, most likely to the barn for a weapon. Titan was sitting again. Jackson approached slowly from behind, scanning the mud for the rifle. It had to be under Titan.

"You got to move, Titan."

Titan twitched his tail. He had his fill of humans telling him what to do tonight. What would Andrew find in the barn? Would he go in the house where Blake kept another gun? Jackson crossed the pen to the section of gate where he'd snapped the chair and climbed out.

As he landed on the grass, he managed to roll forward in time to avoid the hunk of wood arcing at his head. Andrew's second swing connected. Protruding nails dug into his shoulder. Jackson kicked upward and Andrew hopped out of range, giving Jackson time to jump up and pull the nails from his shoulder. Andrew moved back and forth in a semi-circle, crouched like a wrestler, out of range of the wood, making feints toward Jackson, trying to draw him into swinging the wood.

The semi-circle expanded. Now Andrew hopped into a dark shadow patch of elms. Jackson lost sight of Andrew's feet, so he rotated his trunk, anticipated Andrew's forward thrust and swung with all his strength. The nails hit Andrew on the flesh above his left hip. He hissed as he twisted backward, the hip rotation pulling the wood from Jackson's hands.

Jackson dived at his legs, tackling him, and hit him with three rapid-fire punches to the face before Andrew stunned him with an elbow to the neck. Andrew scrambled up and ran toward the open field, Jackson in pursuit. Andrew angled back to the barn. He was running by the truck tire feeder when Jackson got close enough to tackle him from behind. The hard ground felt like live electrical wires against his ripped-up shoulder. He twisted to the left, hoisting Andrew over the tire. Jackson got one hand behind Andrew's neck and the other wrapped his head in a vice grip and shoved his face into the ground-up grain.

Andrew writhed, but Jackson braced him against the tire, using both hands to grind Andrew's head deeper into the grain. Andrew's movements slowed. His backward kicks weakened. Jackson didn't want to suffocate him. He counted the time to himself. Forty seconds, fifty. At a minute twenty, Andrew's body went limp. Jackson didn't dare remove his grip. Andrew could be feigning unconsciousness. Jackson counted out another twenty seconds and slid his hand from the back of Andrew's neck to the front to feel for a pulse. He was still alive.

Jackson pressed his head under the grain another twenty seconds before releasing his grip. Andrew's face remained buried in the grain. Keeping his full weight on Andrew's body, Jackson scooped away grain in front of Andrew's face. He now wished he'd hung on to the bike rack straps. In one quick motion, Jackson pushed himself off Andrew and the tire.

He backed away, feeling his pocket for his phone, but it was gone. He walked backwards until he reached an elm tree, where he stood watching another five minutes. He edged backward toward the barn, turning every few steps to make sure Andrew was still unconscious. He'd free Trish. They'd get away from the farm and call the police.

When he looked back at the tire, Andrew was gone. A burst of white light crumpled Jackson to the ground. He blinked away blood and saw Andrew holding a piece of busted brick, the grain stuck to his forehead and face making him look like Burger Head. Jackson pushed up but fell back onto the ground.

He shook his head, trying to stop the sky from spinning in circles. Burger Head grinned. He walked up to Jackson, raising the brick to the sky with both hands, bringing it down in slow motion, but falling forward instead, upended by Jackson's lunge.

The spinning sky slowed. Jackson vomited. Burger Head picked up his brick for another try. Jackson staggered to the holding pen, where Titan sat sniffing the grass. Jackson crossed to the other side of the pen. Andrew didn't hesitate. He stepped around Blake and Titan, sticking close to the fence, holding the brick at his side, circling to where Jackson stood inside the chute gate.

Jackson moved through the curving chute, following the path of the buffalo death march, sliding his hand along the cool smooth metal for balance. He crunched over skull shells of the stun room and looked up through the opening, where white clouds were suddenly blotted out by Andrew leaping from the catwalk, knocking Jackson to the ground. Both his hands clamped onto Jackson's neck.

Jackson flipped forward, landing on top of Andrew on the slaughter room floor, but a sideways roll put Andrew on top again, and he pounded sharp elbows to Jackson's neck and eyes. They rolled across the cold metal floor. A fist to Jackson's temple spun the walls behind him.

As Andrew hopped out of view, Jackson struggled to stand. A high-pitched wail came from behind a stainless steel compacting machine to Jackson's right, and Andrew stepped into the light swinging a carcass-splitting saw back and forth. Jackson pushed himself backward over the floor and into the bathtub. He used the Burger Head prop to fend off the downward arcing blade. Andrew lunged forward a second time, arms outstretched, slicing open Burger Head's chest. Jackson lay on the bottom of the tub with half of Burger Head as a shield. It was all about to end. Andrew raised the saw in the air and let out a scream like a blade ripping through metal.

The saw clattered to the floor. Jackson scrambled up to see Trish standing above Andrew. He was lying face-first on the floor, the pickaxe embedded in the back of his thigh. Andrew didn't resist as Jackson and Trish dragged him across the floor.

Jackson wrapped the rope around Andrew's waist and under his arms and fastened it to the hook. The electric hoist pulled Andrew up to the ceiling where Luther had hung the day before.

Jackson bent over until his breathing slowed and he looked up at Andrew. "I never told you why Trish was outside your house. We replaced your wooden loon with one that had a microphone inside."

Trish put her arm around Jackson. "We recorded everything you said."

Andrew dropped his chin to his chest to look down at them.

"Comeback's over," Jackson said.

Andrew closed his eyes. "All because a nobody named Cass got greedy."

❯❯❯

The parade of sirens started minutes after Trish made her anonymous call from the pay phone outside the post office. She and Jackson were now sitting on the bed in his cottage with the iPhone they retrieved from under a mulberry bush outside Andrew's house.

"Moment of truth." She hit the play icon.

> "Audrey made these vases for desert succulents, but she had so many she brought some to Vermont."
>
> "They look good."
>
> "The succulents look better. I could bring the vases back to L.A., but I'll probably leave them here, even it means I have to give visitors the caveat she created them for smaller plants."
>
> "It's your call, but I don't think the caveat's necessary."
>
> "Got something for you. I can't claim credit. My

lawyer's grocery shopper got it. You like it frothy?"

"Please."

The microphone had worked. They got the confession.

Trish created a new post titled, "Andrew Marvel's Confession" and uploaded the mp3 file. She nodded at Jackson, who nodded back, and hit the publish button.

Next she called the Hardwick police station and asked to be connected to Detective Grimes' voice-mail.

"Hi, this is Trish Devereaux from the crime blog *Improbable Cause*. I just published a post with an audio file of Andrew Marvel's confession. The guy who got him to confess is named Jackson Oliver. He's sitting with me now. I'm also the one who made the anonymous call earlier about Andrew Marvel and Blake Trotman. We'll be waiting for you in Hank Carruthers' cottage at the Morning Loon. Bye."

She reached toward the patch of blood on Jackson's shoulder. "Does it hurt?"

"It's mostly numb."

"You need to get it looked at."

"Thanks."

Neither of them could force back tears that turned into body-shaking sobs.

When he got himself under control, he said, "You didn't tell me how you freed yourself."

"They tied me with pieces of torn cloth. A nail in the wall was all it took."

Judging by the approaching sirens, Detective Grimes had just checked his voice-mail messages.

"Think they'll arrest us?" Jackson said.

"Not with that confession out there. They'll give us some serious shit, though."

"I'm the material witness who withheld evidence."

"They'll save their most serious shit for you."

"Then I'd better invite you to Costa Rica now. Not a lot of crime to report on, but you're resourceful. You'll find some."

"I already know a guy who's violating the Internet Gambling Act and stole the identity of his dead fourth grade gym teacher."

"So you'll come?"

"Doubt it. I hold grudges."

"How long?"

"It doesn't feel good hearing yourself accused of murder."

"It's a compliment in a roundabout way. The Other Woman, by definition, is irresistibly attractive."

The sirens came to a stop outside the Morning Loon.

"They'll go inside and ask which cabin Hank Carruthers is staying in," she said. "That leaves you about a minute to convince me to change my mind about Costa Rica."

Acknowledgments

Thanks to Annette and Barbara for their editorial guidance. And thanks to Margaret and to all the hard-working people at Poisoned Pen Press.

To receive a free catalog of Poisoned Pen Press titles, please provide your name, address, and e-mail address in one of the following ways:

Phone: 1-800-421-3976
Facsimile: 1-480-949-1707
Email: info@poisonedpenpress.com
Website: www.poisonedpenpress.com

Poisoned Pen Press
6962 E. First Ave. Ste 103
Scottsdale, AZ 85251

NUV 1 8 2016

CPSIA information can be obtained at www.ICGtesting.com
Printed in the USA
LVOW08s1513051016

507533LV00004B/852/P

9 781464 206290